THE
OUTER
BUOY

ALSO BY JAN DE HARTOG

BOOKS:

The Peculiar People
The Centurion
The Commodore
Star of Peace
The Trail of the Serpent
The Lamb's War
The Peaceable Kingdom
The Children
The Captain
The Call of the Sea
(*including* The Lost Sea, The Distant Shore, A Sailor's Life)
The Hospital
The Artist
Waters of the New World
The Inspector
The Spiral Road
A Sailor's Life
The Little Ark
The Distant Shore
The Lost Sea

PLAYS:

William and Mary
The Fourposter
Skipper Next to God
This Time Tomorrow

JAN DE HARTOG

THE
OUTER
BUOY

A Story of the Ultimate Voyage

A Cornelia & Michael Bessie Book

Pantheon Books   New York

Grateful acknowledgement is made to Doubleday for permission to reprint an excerpt from *Far Journeys* by Robert Monroe, copyright © 1985 by Robert A. Monroe. Reprinted by permission of Doubleday, a division of Bantam Doubleday Dell Publishing Group, Inc.

Library of Congress Cataloging-in-Publication Data

De Hartog, Jan, 1914–
    The outer buoy : a story of the ultimate voyage /
Jan de Hartog.
        p.   cm.
    "A Cornelia & Michael Bessie book."
    ISBN 0-679-43604-9
    1. Space flight—Fiction.   I. Title.
PR6015.A674098   1994
823'.914—dc20   94-9780

Book design by M. Kristen Bearse

Manufactured in the United States of America

First Edition

9 8 7 6 5 4 3 2 1

To the memory of
ETHEL FINCH MEIN,
indomitable woman,
gallant soul. Godspeed and
happy sailing!

I AM INDEBTED to Dr. and Mrs. Robert E. Rakel of Houston, Texas, who took me in, a cantankerous old tomcat not given to leaping into laps, and enabled me to complete this book in their guest quarters during the chaos of an intercontinental move. Also to Roger Billica, M.D., and Colonel Charles LaPinta, M.D., who, although in no way accountable for the results, opened the doors of the inner sanctum of the Lyndon B. Johnson Space Center in Houston for me. And, last but not least, to Dale Johnson, designer and manufacturer of the Lunar Rovers, who introduced me to the true art of our generation.

My largest debt, however, is to my friend and publisher of forty-five years' standing, Simon Michael Bessie, whom I followed from Harper and Row to Atheneum, then to HarperCollins, and finally to Pantheon. There is a particular savor to literary marital loyalty: after the first question "Who is writing this book, you or I?" the writer becomes happily accustomed to the fact that the answer is "Both of us." In this instance, the answer manifests itself once again in the subtitle to *The Outer Buoy*. My suggestion was "In Praise of Fat Old Men"; Mike substituted "A Story of the Ultimate Voyage." The solution might have been "The Ultimate Voyage of a Fat Old Man," but there comes a moment when it is decided who is writing this book.

So, as always, with love and admiration, the fat old man knuckles under to the ultimate authority: his dashing, worldly, irreplaceable, and insufferable publisher: Mike.

THE
OUTER
BUOY

I

OLD WIDOWERS in their eighties are of little interest, even to other widowers in their eighties. Thinking back, that must have been the reason why they chose me. The fancy stuff about my "navigational expertise," "experience as a leader of men," and "knowledge of human nature" was hogwash; the moving finger ultimately pointed at me because, after Sylvia's death, nobody gave a damn any longer whether I had a soul or flew to the moon.

Except those interested in flying old men's souls to the moon. I had no idea such people existed until, one April morning earlier this year, I was wakened by the roar of an engine and the squeal of tires braking outside my bungalow. Our sleepy, not to say snoring, village of retirees in the South of France was not accustomed to cars playing chicken on its streets, so, pulling myself out of bed, I ambled, yawning, over to the window, peeped through the curtains, and saw, parked in front of my house, a red sports car, a monstrosity with the grin of a shark. For a moment I thought that, wonder of wonders, my youngest son, Martinus, the Air Canada pilot, had decided to pay me a visit, the first one since the death of his mother a year ago. But then the car door opened and a pair of shapely legs swung out. This could not be for me, she must be the liberated granddaughter of my next-door neighbor who had overshot the mark.

The driver stood up, a red-haired woman in a pale green dress with the fashionable stevedore shoulders, and strode straight to my front door. She must have mistaken the address, or hoped to find a dotty old lady inside to whom she could flog some discontinued perfume, or budget fashions for dignified maturity. As she was about to knock she looked toward the window and I recognized her.

Miss Bastiaans? What the devil was *she* doing here? I could not possibly receive her like this—in pajamas, my robe blotched with yesterday's eggs, the living room a mess, dirty dishes stacked on the breakfast counter, the floor around my recliner strewn with peanut shells and cracker crumbs like the bottom of a parrot's cage . . .

She banged the knocker. What could I do? Pretend I was not at home? Hide in the bathroom? Well, hell! It wasn't old Kwel himself! Just his—

Bang! Bang! There she went again, damn woman. I wrapped my robe tighter, knotted the belt, and opened the door. "Miss Bastiaans!"

There she stood, seemingly no older than when I had last set eyes on her more than a decade ago. "Good morning, Commodore, may I come in?"

I had had time to regroup. "Sorry, Miss Bastiaans, it's nice to see you, but right now my house is a mess and, as you can see, so am I. What can I do for you?"

"Let me in—and hear me out." Her smile never wavered; her eyes were exactly as I remembered them: blue, loveless, knowing. "I have some urgent business to discuss with you that cannot wait."

"Fancy that," I said—my nickname for half a century. "I'll tell you what: give me twenty minutes to dress and clean up while you get yourself a cup of coffee in the square opposite the station."

"Oh, but I'll be happy to clean up for you!" she cried, actually making a move as if to force her way past me.

I half-closed the door. "Miss Bastiaans," I said, "you heard me. Come back in twenty minutes." I closed the door; it took a while before I heard the engine start, followed by the same squeal of tires that had first alerted me.

Well, what do you know? It still worked. Even so, she had conned me into receiving her in twenty minutes' time, so I'd better get cracking. Shave, dress, clear the counter and the parrot's cage—better dress first, rather than have her catch Father Christmas in the bathroom with his pants down.

I was in control of the situation until I cut myself shaving. Damn! God damn! That did it. I was bleeding like a stuck pig, so I put a dab of cotton on it, then proceeded to pour the glass with my daytime teeth into the toilet and my overnight urinal into the washbasin. Old age! One of my neighbors, barely able to walk, blind as a bat, deaf as a post, had a decorative tile on his wall, donated by a jolly daughter, with the motto: *Old Age Is Not for Sissies*. Indeed! I was now virtually a gorilla, could not remember my own daughter's married name, poured my dentures into the toilet and urine into the washbasin. And why? Because a woman in her fifties—which she must be by now—had arrived on my doorstep at nine in the morning to discuss "urgent business" that could not wait. Like death?

I had reason to be wary; I had been there before. Ten years ago Miss Bastiaans had been secretary-cum-dollybird of the ninety-year-old owner of Kwel's International Towing Company, for whom I had sailed the better part of my life. She was in her early forties then, elegant, witty, and ruthless. She, along with her decrepit old boss, had seduced me at the age of seventy to take one of their newest and biggest boats, the *Isabel Kwel*, to Taiwan for scrap, towing a dry dock too big for the Panama Canal. The *Isabel* had turned out to be a lemon, and the old slyboots sold her to a Chinese financier at a discount, brushing over her ailments. I, "our oldest and most experienced master," was invited to sail the damn thing to Kao-hsiung, Taiwan, not as the captain of record, of course—my license had expired even before that lemon was born—but as adviser to the Chinese master and his crew. No captain in his senses would have taken it on; don't ask me why I did it. Maybe because it was Christmas. Our little bungalow was full of inflatable gnomes dangling from the ceiling, grandchildren playing tag in my rose garden, sullen teenagers sprawled on the floor in front of the television, and two visiting dogs, both trying to mount Sylvia's poodle underneath the dinner table, with assorted daughters and daughters-in-law lifting the tablecloth and yelling, "Fifi! Crosseyes! Naughty!" I was an easy prey for Miss Bastiaans, who helped seduce me into towing the lemon halfway around the globe with a Chinese Pinocchio for a captain and the chorus from *The Pirates of Penzance* for a crew.

In mid-Pacific the lemon was hit by typhoon seas, took off, danced the tarantella, and nearly capsized, drowning the lot of us. Against all odds, I docked her in Kao-hsiung at the break-up yard, only to discover that I was in the doghouse as far as the Chinese owner was concerned. It turned out he had insured her at replacement value, convinced that if the Roaring Forties didn't do it, with that bunch of dilettantes and a superannuated old salt on the bridge, the South Pacific in the typhoon season surely would take care of her and end his financial troubles. So it was not as a conquering hero but as a nasty old spoilsport that I was put on a plane with my tame rat and my canary and sent back to where I came from. That had been my last voyage. The final chord to a sailor's life, like that of a Tchaikovsky symphony. And why? If I were to believe Captain Fransen, our head of operations who met me on arrival, it was not because of the old man, who was by then no more than a ventriloquist's dummy, but because of a witty, charming blue-eyed woman with an irresistible smile. I had become the victim of the world's greatest expert in manipulating old men.

She came on board herself in Kao-hsiung a few hours after I had brought in my piece of junk. I had pulled the engine-room telegraph on *Finished with engines* for the last time in my life and was lying, flaked out, on the bunk in my bedroom, when a woman's voice intruded.

"Commodore?"

I opened my eyes. In the doorway stood Miss Bastiaans, with the sunlight behind her. In my half-sleep I thought: Death will not be an old monk with a scythe and an hourglass but a beautiful young woman in a doorway with the sunlight behind her. I got arthritically to my feet, slipped in my lowers, which I had put in my breast pocket, and asked her what I could do for her. Well, with her that's always more than just a polite question. Arnold Kwel had died two months before, while I was at sea, and left her half his fleet and half his shares. Now she was about to start her own salvage and towing company in the Dutch Antilles, a gold-mine, and she wanted me for her head of operations. When I told her I would not dream of it, she backed off and pouted. Still, she had the kindness to send a tailor and a barber, since all I had to fly back home in was the top half of my number-one uniform and a pair of Bermuda shorts that reached below my knees. The barber may have been the more necessary of the two. The cook had taken care of cutting my hair over the past six months and had changed me into a mad old keeper of the Great Wall of China. Within twenty-four hours of her visit, I was transformed into a dignified bank manager carrying a cage with a fluttering canary through security to board a plane for Amsterdam. Twelve years later, here she stood in a doorway again, with the sunlight behind her. No wonder I was wary.

I wolfed down my breakfast banana, plus four cookies, the painkillers for my arthritic shoulder with a gulp of orange juice, and more cookies. I wished Sylvia were here. I—

Back came the sports car, as unobtrusive as the fire brigade. Tires squealed, a door thumped.

"Ha! Miss Bastiaans!" As if she were not expected. "Did you have coffee, as I suggested?"

"No, Commodore."

"All right, then, let's turn on the whatsis." I hurried to the kitchenette, the eager host, and hit my shin on the sharp edge of the coffee table. Dutch curses, hopping on one leg, holding the other—she saw her chance. "Commodore, did you hurt yourself?" She put her arm around my shoulder with a dose of Chanel No. 5 strong enough to anesthetize a rat.

It took an effort to slip out of her half nelson, then I headed for the counter again. She cried, "Oh, let me do it!"

"Miss Bastiaans," I commanded, *"sit down!"*

She said, "Yessir," and did so.

Now I had to make the damn coffee myself. All I had available in the way of mugs was the one I'd just used, the rest having been stacked out of sight as unfit for human consumption until the maid had had her way with them.

"How about a simple snort?" she asked, now standing right behind me.

I turned around. "Don't tell me you're ready to booze it up this early in the morning?"

"It depends on the occasion," she said with that ravishing smile.

So I poured a glass of sherry and took it to her. She just looked at it. "Oh, sorry," I said. "I forgot. How could I?"

Indeed, Miss Bastiaans drinking a Russian customs inspector under the table with Dutch gin had been a memorable episode in our shared nautical history.

I fetched the crock of Dutch gin from the icebox and poured us both a shot. "Peanuts? Crackers?"

"No thank you, Commodore. Now stop fussing and sit down beside me." She patted the seat of the sofa. "How's the leg?"

"Oh, that was nothing." I took our little glasses to the coffee table and went to put them down, but hers never made it; she snatched it from my hand and, pinky in the air, knocked it back like a deckhand.

"Seconds?" I asked.

"Why not? But don't you bother, I'll get it myself." She rose and headed for the icebox.

"Bring the crock," I suggested.

She came back with it, topped me up, and poured herself another depth charge. I must say I was beginning to enjoy her company. What the devil had got into me earlier? She was a charming woman, really. "Sorry I sent you away," I said brightly. "As you can see, I needed a moment to clean up and cut my throat. Ha-ha! Here's looking at you."

Down the hatch. Well, time to talk sense before our little barque with its two passengers capsized in a gale of giggles.

"What are you laughing at?" she asked, frowning.

"Oh, nothing," I said. "Private joke. At my age there is no greater delight than laughing at your own jokes."

"Share this one with me.'

I shared the little barque in the gale of giggles with her; she thought it was a riot. "I never knew you had such a sense of humor, Commodore! You always seemed so stern, so—no, no, no more, please!"

"Come on, Miss B. You can't walk on two legs." I poured us a third.

"How many legs does it take, Commodore?"

"Four, unless you are a centipede. Ha-ha. Come on, woman! Have a bit of cheese, some nuts . . . Crackers, by the way, are in the tall cupboard in the kitchen, top shelf. The cheese is in the icebox."

She came back with a plate of crackers, bite-size slices of cheese, a bowl of peanuts, just as she had always—

Oh God, Jesus—here it comes, one of those heart-wrenching bouts of sorrow, inarticulate, pointless, just a tearjerker that trips you up when you least expect it. Hearing someone call "Sylvia!" in the street. Finding a little box with one earring that Helen must have overlooked when she helped clear out Sylvia's stuff. A tune on the radio, the station with the Golden Oldies. Reaching out in half-sleep in the middle of the night and finding nothing.

"Okay," I said, "let's have it. Why are you here?"

"To start with, Commodore, when I heard that your wife—"

"Come, Miss Bastiaans. She has been gone for over a year. What is the urgent business that cannot wait?"

She looked at me for the first time with what might be honesty. "I have a job for you," she said.

I took a moment to restrain myself, then I said, "Don't be silly."

"Why not?"

"For God's sake, woman, I am eighty-two years old! I need double spectacles to read the paper! I need a hearing aid! Diapers are next—"

"I have not come to offer you a ship, Commodore. It is something different this time."

"A position as caretaker in a kindergarten?"

She sighed. "If this is going to be the form this morning, I might as well pack up." She made as if about to leave: gathering of purse, touching of hair, looking around to see if she had forgotten something.

"Miss Bastiaans," I said, "stop playacting, start from the beginning." I wanted to refill our glasses but she covered hers with her hand.

"As you wish." I took a sip of mine and leaned back, ready to listen.

"When it became obvious," she started, "that the straight-line oceangoing tow business was going into decline, I sold my ships and my interests and started to look for a sensible use of the money. At first I did some dabbling in real estate but it didn't really interest me. Then, as it happened, I was offered an exclusive placement agency for top executives in London. Very discreet, no—"

"You mean, headhunting? Is that what you do now?"

"You make it sound as if I collect trophies on safari, Commodore! What you have to offer is a lifetime of navigational expertise, a vast experience of handling men, a youthful sense of curiosity—"

"What about my knowledge of old tomcats?"

She was not to be distracted. "We want you to head a group of men your age, all unattached, experienced navigators, men mentally and physically prepared to go to America to take part in an experiment of the space age, the like of which has never been considered before."

"To do *what*—?"

She ignored me. "We are not talking about silly old men who, when they hear that one of them is having an affair, ask 'Who's catering?' We are looking for World War II veterans, men like yourself, men who have led commando raids into enemy territory, pilots who blew up dams single-handed and made it back alive, couriers who were parachuted into France, only half of whom ultimately returned—"

"Miss Bastiaans," I said, "the men you are looking for are Douglas Fairbanks and Errol Flynn."

"Please, Commodore."

"Sorry, too old? Then Pete Schwarzenacker, or whatever his name is. This is B-movie stuff."

She gave me a level look, then picked up her purse again. "You were right. I did arrive here too early. What does the rest of your day look like?"

I pretended to think. "Well," I said, "let me see—whatever is left of this morning I'll spend writing . . ."

"Letters?"

"Oh, no, little sketches. Memories of life at sea between the wars, personal reminiscences, that kind of thing."

"But that's wonderful," she said, staring at me. "I didn't

know you wrote. Could I read some of them by any chance? I'd love that."

"I write them strictly for my own use, Miss Bastiaans."

"I know. But we have shared quite a lot of sea days, haven't we? I truly would be fascinated! Ships and the men that sail them were my life too. Couldn't I read just one?"

I have since come to the conclusion that this was the moment the noose was slipped around my neck. Having no experience as a writer, I was unaware of the lure of vanity mixed with uncertainty that compels authors to read their works aloud. "Well, I wouldn't mind your reading one, but my handwriting is like a physician's. A Chinese physician's."

"Why not read one to me? Just one! Please?"

"Well, I don't know . . ." I stood up and wandered over to the cupboard to get the stack of dog-eared exercise books, the harvest of nine months of daily sea-babble, and started to leaf through them. "First I made a list of subjects, then cut the list into strips and rolled each strip into a little ball and put them all in a cookie tin. Every morning I shake the tin and—well, here, maybe this one. You are of the profession. It's called 'Tugboats.' "

"Oh, lovely!" She settled down to listen.

"To tow huge inanimate objects across the ocean at a snail's pace is what oceangoing tugboats are about, or to slam full speed into the teeth of a gale going to the aid of a ship in distress. I personally found the long, slow trips towing a dry dock from the Clyde to Australia around the Cape, or a whole floating sugar refinery in sections to the mouth of the Orinoco, more exhilarating than the salvage business. During those long trips, the officer of the watch develops a tendency to gaze astern at the tow instead of ahead, which is a habit difficult to shake. Later in his career, when he transfers to the merchant marine and is a mate of a freighter whisking along at twenty knots, he will occasionally, on the bridge, experience a sinking feeling at the sight of the empty wake.

Worse, he may forget how fast his ship is and find himself on
top of yonder trawler before he knows it.

"Tugboat crews, numbering from thirteen to forty-
five, depending on the size of the vessel, are like families
presided over by a father who, for me in my young years,
embodied in his breasted chest all the best qualities of life on
earth from armadillo to man. A tugboat master's opinion on
anything under the sun was so simple and straightforward
in those days that I gained a feeling of comfort regarding
life in general and self-confidence when it came to handling
men in the future. One thing I should not have tried to
emulate was shaving with an old-fashioned cut-throat razor.
I damn near did . . ."

To my startled satisfaction she hooted with laughter; I hadn't
realized it was all that funny. But I must confess it made me feel
good.

"Go on, please! There *is* more?"

"Well, there is a little more, but—you know, it—"

"Oh do read on, Commodore! Please, just for me."

Quasi-reluctantly I leafed on and came up with one called
"Cabin Boys."

"The smaller the ship, the smaller the urchin. Freighters over
ten thousand tons have stewards, below ten thousand, mess-
room boys, and anything from a coaster down has a child
that picks his nose, touches his lips with the result, wipes it
on the seat of his pants, puts his dirty thumb in the soup
tureen while serving, washes up by wiping, sings lewd songs
in a choirboy voice, and in port has his scalp inspected by the
bosun, after which a liquid is applied, for sale in harbor
drugstores, called McNamara's Hunting Water . . ."

This one I read to the end. It was even more successful.
"Commodore, to think I never knew! I never knew you were a
writer! You can't stop now—go on, please!"

I leafed on and read another. I must have read six before I arrived at the one I had written just the day before. I hesitated. "This one you may find a bit sentimental. It won't make much sense to you at your age."

"Oh, please, Commodore! How long have we known each other? Twenty years? Do me a favor."

"Well, I called this one 'The Meaning of It All.' "

"Let's hear it."

"After your retirement, after you have said farewell to your last ship, and those you've loved most have died, you start crossing the desert of empty days and empty nights that make up the life of an old bachelor. Then the moment will come when the question arises: Dear God, what is the meaning of it all?

"The answer depends on where the question hits you. If you are sitting under a willow tree on the banks of a lake, waiting for a fish silly enough to bite, chances are that you'll let the question sail overhead like a cloud. If it hits you on a rainy day, when you are looking through your steamed-up window at the wet street and at Madame Bonnet tripping by with her umbrella, you may be tempted to answer, 'Nothing.' If you can carry the mood of the willow and the lake with you until you sit behind the window gazing at Madame Bonnet, you will have gone as far as you are likely to get.

"Some people find comfort in the hope that when their souls set sail like the ancient explorers, they will reach a distant shore, far from despair and grief, where old friends will meet once more. It is a comforting thought, but it is not the answer. The answer is this: Give up all thought of ever reaching land. Remember the joy of being alone at sea. You are fortunate among mortals, for, alone on your bridge on the oceans of the past, you have known happiness. You may find the same happiness on the longest voyage of all. If this is your hope and not the distant shore, you will have brightened the darkness of your desert night with a spark of the light of the sea."

I looked up. She was gazing at me, misty-eyed, then she leaned over and kissed my cheek. I turned away self-consciously, looked at the clock, and cried, "Good Lord, do you know what time it is?" We had been at it for nearly two hours. She too looked at the clock, then said, "Tell you what: I'll take the car and pick up something for us to eat at that little place in the square. We'll have that here, and then you'll have your nap—"

"Hey, listen!"

"You'd better have a nap, Commodore, for at six sharp we are supposed to meet my client in the bar of the Hôtel Réserve in Beaulieu sur Mer. He will explain it all to you in detail much better than I can."

"Look, Miss Bastiaans, thank you for listening to me and for your encouragement, but I don't want a job, and I don't want to meet your client. I am an old man, without—"

"Oh, don't be silly!" She rose and picked up her purse and headed for the door. "Afterward you and I will have dinner together, just the two of us, by candlelight. How's that sound?"

"Well—"

She opened the door, turned around, and said as an afterthought, "Listen, if you don't mind, do me a favor: put on whatever you use as an equivalent of your number-one uniform. This man is a stickler for conformity—shirt, tie, gray flannels, black shoes—you know, the uniform of the typical American businessman. Would you?"

"I'll see what I can come up with," I said uncertainly.

She left. The thought of dinner for two by candlelight got to me. It was a long time since that had last happened. The first time had been with Sylvia, years ago, our first dinner in that cellar restaurant with the red benches in Dover, April 1944, waiting for D-Day.

How young she had been. How—

2

IT WAS NOT QUITE in his number-one uniform that
the famous poet of the sea, Fancy That Harinxma, entered the bar
of the Réserve in Beaulieu. Baggy gray pants, a blazer that had
somehow shrunk since I last wore it, and a black cotton turtleneck
which brought to mind Groucho Marx's objection to movies in
which the hero's bust was bigger than that of the heroine.

The drive in Miss Bastiaans' infernal machine along the Cor-
niche had been hair-raising. She drove like a demon, the car took
hairpin bends at a speed that made it resemble a dog lifting its leg
on the edge of the precipices we were skirting.

We arrived. Valet parking, top-hatted doorman whisking us
inside through the revolving door. Then the bar: stygian darkness,
a tinkling piano, a maître d' with the shoulder tabs of a vice-
admiral who guided us through the blackout to what turned out
to be a booth with a man seated in it. The man, in his thirties—
blond, khaki suit—rose and stretched out his hand. "Hi there! I'm
John Buckram, also known as Rusty. Nice to meet you, sir. How
are you, Eleanor? Sit down, sit down, please!"

We sat down side by side. The velvet bench exerted such a
pull on my pants as I slid in that I wondered if I'd forgotten to zip
up my fly again, one of my standard numbers. I groped discreetly:
okay.

"Well, let's order something to drink," the man said.
"Garçon!"

The maître d' emerged from the gloom.

"What'll it be, folks? Scotch? Bourbon? Some of that French
stuff, Pernod?"

"I don't like their Dutch gin," Miss Bastiaans said. "I'll have
vodka on the rocks."

Though I might be wary of her in other respects, I trusted
her taste in Dutch gin. "I think I'll pass, thank you."

The blond man ordered the drinks. Then he smiled at me, a boyish smile that did not reach his eyes. Something, maybe his haircut, suggested to me that he was in the military, or had been until recently. Fairly high up, maybe a colonel. In one of those flashes of total recall that come with age, I saw the curved ceiling of a Nissen hut, a bar with an array of bottles, a notice saying AMERICAN COLONELS UNDER THE AGE OF 21 WILL ONLY BE SERVED IF ACCOMPANIED BY PARENT OR GUARDIAN, and a grinning English sergeant with a gold tooth behind it. Reykjavik, Iceland, fall 1942, after the disaster of my second Arctic convoy.

"Let me tell you what all this is about, sir," the man said. "I gather Miss Bastiaans gave up on you earlier today."

So there had been a debriefing, while I lay snoring on my bed. "Please do," I said.

"Does the name Robert Monroe mean anything to you?"

"Can't say it does."

"Well, we'll get to him later. First let me tell you about myself. I represent the combined manufacturers of the future space station *Freedom*. Twenty years ago, the last of the Lunar Rovers was deposited on the surface of the moon by *Apollo 17*, and left behind. You know what Lunar Rovers are, I presume?"

"You mean the little electric buggies the astronauts used on the moon?"

"Good for you. It carried among its instruments a dosimeter, a device that registers the degree of solar radiation to which the moon is exposed, lacking an atmosphere. It is of great importance to us to discover the amount of accumulated radiation recorded by the dosimeter over the past twenty years. The reading will determine the nature and the weight of the radiation shield needed to safeguard the health of the astronauts who will be using the space station as an observation post and, eventually, as a jump-off point for the exploration of Mars. The station is expected to remain in orbit for quite a few years. Alas, there is not going to be another manned moon landing in the foreseeable future, so we need to find some other way to read that dosimeter. We have considered a satellite landing with a television camera, but the experts tell us it would be impossible to get an accurate reading of so small a dial by those means. We tried various other things, and then we found out about the Monroe Institute, a scientific lab in North Carolina. I gather Miss Bastiaans has not mentioned this to you?"

"No."

The waiter, who had been discreetly hovering in the gloom, took this chance to put the drinks in front of them.

"Thank you. Well, you had better tell him, Eleanor. Cheers."

Miss Bastiaans looked at me appraisingly. "Are you ready for this, Commodore?" She took a sip from her glass of vodka, grimaced, said "Blah," and put it down. "Robert Monroe is an engineer, a sound engineer, who heads a scientific research institute in Faber, North Carolina. After years of experimentation, he has taken out a patent on a procedure that brings about an out-of-body experience by means of separate audio stimulation of the left and right sides of the brain. You are familiar with the phenomenon of the out-of-body experience, aren't you"

"In general terms."

"Well, it resembles the near-death syndrome in which some unconscious patients find themselves. Their awareness, or consciousness, or whatever you want to call it, becomes separated from the brain. They find themselves floating underneath the ceiling, observing the procedures below while physicians try to revive their inert bodies. Robert Monroe's institute has achieved this in many cases by putting a volunteer into an isolation booth, under sensory deprivation. There's no light, no sound, no physical stimuli, except for a set of earphones connecting him with the control room. He is then subjected to a variety of vibrations via the earphones, each side producing a different frequency. At a certain combination of impulses, which is different for every individual, the subject slides into an alpha state which eventually leads to an OOBE. His consciousness detaches itself from the body in the booth, and is able to move about, unhindered and unseen—

rather like a ghost. He can pass through doors without opening them, wander down the hall, and go out into the open. But that's not all: a large number of Mr. Monroe's volunteers managed to transport themselves to specific destinations determined by their own thought, or wish. In some cases, overseas—in one case, the moon. This may be where you should take over, Rusty."

"Well, when we heard this," the man continued, "we thought: Why not? Remember that we had exhausted all other possibilities. Why not subject a well-trained, well-prepared man, an astronaut or a pilot, to Monroe's procedure, separate his consciousness from his physical body, and direct him to find the buggy on the moon and read the dosimeter? We decided to try and form a team of men with navigational expertise, used to functioning under exotic circumstances—let them study charts of the moon and the videos made of the buggies in action, read the reports of the astronauts in question, from which they can gather the landmarks by which to locate the buggy in question. Let them study the Lunar Rover itself in the lab, for it *is* a fairly esoteric machine. Nobody expects miracles, but so much depends on our knowing the precise amount of accumulated radiation on the moon over the past twenty years that it's worth a try. We have tried everything else, this is our last shot. And this is where you come in, sir."

"I do?" I asked, managing to keep a straight face.

"It was decided after long conferences with psychologists and other experts in human behavior, that instead of going for a team of young astronauts or pilots, we should involve older men. I mean a lot older, veterans of the Second World War. Men who had taken part in commando raids, or, like yourself, sailed with the Russian convoys. I gather Eleanor has explained to you why."

"Sorry," I said, "I must have missed out on that too."

"Commodore," Miss Bastiaans said sternly, "don't be naughty."

He ignored all that. "Let me elaborate in more detail just how we envisage this working. You gather a small crew of old colleagues; let's say five or six. We'll ship you to the United States, all expenses paid. Your salary will be in the high five figures for the assignment. First-class hotels, VIP treatment, your feet will never touch the ground. Side trips to Washington—the Lincoln Monument, the Smithsonian—"

It sounded like sheer hell. "You must forgive me," I said, interrupting him, "but this is one crazy idea."

He seemed to take it personally. With some effort at intimidation he said, in his colonel's voice, "Many discoveries started out as crazy ideas, sir. One of the craziest at the time must have been Galileo's notion that the earth orbited around the sun rather than the other way round. And there are other examples. Einstein—"

"The crazy part is that team of men over eighty. I am sure you have picked the brains of many experts, but you may have omitted to consult an expert on old age. I don't mean a doctor of geriatrics in his forties, or some young woman psychiatrist who chose 'the senile personality' as her specialty in medical school. Your leaders of commandos into enemy territory are too old now, too weary of the load of our physical decay, to be of any use to you."

"But, sir, take yourself! Here you are, as bright as a button, knowledgeable, experienced—"

"Okay, take me. Since the death of my wife a year ago I have lived alone, by choice. I do not want to see or hear anybody else. I want no outside interference, not even a cat. Just my Moroccan maid, who comes once a week to wash the dishes and make ritual gestures with a broom. I used to walk two hours every day, even on the bridge of my ships, back and forth, driving mates and men at the wheel crazy; now all I can manage is twenty minutes, during which time I have to sit down and rest five times. When the telephone rings, I almost have a heart attack, not because I am a cardiac patient but because I am an eighty-two-year-old recluse who leaps out of his skin at sudden noises that shock him out of his state of suspension between two worlds."

"Worlds? Which worlds?"

For the first time, he seemed to be aware of me as a person, not just a subject for his experiment.

"At my age a man finds himself in a no-man's-land between memories and dreams. Not Virgil's 'misty marshes of Hades approaches,' but a state of awareness that comes upon him gradually, that the range of his perception is much wider than he has assumed all his life. I know this from firsthand experience. Left to my own devices, unbothered by the outside world, safe in my old parrot's cage, I found myself moving, with a growing sense of excitement and adventure, into the outer regions of our so-called reality. I began to discern mysteries never before revealed, perspectives never before perceived, states of mind more detached from our purblind human awareness than Mr. Monroe can bring about with his machine. I haven't the faintest idea where all this will lead me eventually, while I'm still, as you put it, in the body. But I'll tell you this much: despite my staggering walk, unzipped fly, palpitations at the sound of the telephone, solitary fits of laughter, senile rages with inanimate objects like teapots spitefully losing their lids, jammed cupboards that refuse to open, I have, usually late at night or in the early morning, the most extraordinary, exciting adventures, far exceeding the adventure of being fired from a cannon to the moon. Understand: I'm not minimizing the earnestness of your purpose, but I can assure you that the motionless voyages of discovery of the very old, voyages of exploration into the outer reaches of the mind, are more tempting —to me at least—than anything you could propose. Frankly, I cannot think of anything more exhausting, confusing, or haunted by panic than to be flown to America, stagger through customs and baggage claim, be forced to eat hotel meals and sleep in a succession of alien beds, to end up in an institution where, clad only in my underpants, I'll be put in a dark booth with earphones on my head and be subjected to a patented mechanical manipulation that will split me in half and release my soul to go gallivanting in space while behind my ghostly back my other half lies dying. I prefer my solitude, in which I sit quietly boozing and snacking, shedding peanut shells and cracker crumbs, far from lethal contraptions like the car this lady drives in a way that scares the wits out of cats, sparrows, squirrels crossing the road, and old men standing stock still at the curb because they have forgotten to empty their bladder before they left for the post office and are now caught halfway, knees crossed, eyes rolled upward, praying for mercy. No, I can't say where my solitary voyage of discovery will ultimately lead me, but neither did Ulysses. And at my age, one is closer to Ulysses than to John Glenn."

I don't know what exactly I expected—a respectful silence? A serious question? But Miss Bastiaans simply said, with that infernal silent determination which made her so mysteriously attractive, "Come, Commodore. We're going to have dinner." And she rose; so did Rusty.

"Where shall we go?" he asked.

She gave him one of her terminal smiles. "The Commodore and I planned to dine alone."

"I see." His smile was a sight to behold. "Well, have a nice meal."

"Come, Commodore." She put her hand on my arm.

On the way to the dining room, we passed the men's room. She stopped. "Go ahead," she said, "I'll wait for you."

I bridled, then realized that I had brought this upon myself. The only thing she had been able to identify with, from her own reality, was the old man overcome by urgency as he was about to cross the road.

3

WHEN WE ENTERED the restaurant, another pitch-dark vastness, this one with little islands of candle-lit tables in the gloom, I was ready for her. I knew exactly what she was up to: mollify me with wine and then start wading into me again about this damn-fool assignment.

We sat down at a table for two, and were handed menus. When I saw the prices my ears twitched. The simplest dinner for two was going to cost me a week's pension money. Next I was handed the wine list; one bottle of *vin du pays* would hold me up for another week's ransom. She said casually, without looking up from her menu, "By the way, Commodore, this is on the firm. I recommend the *canard à l'orange.*"

"Look," I said, "if I were in the bag for this I would accept that, but I have just turned the assignment down."

"Don't be silly," she said. "How about some wine? Let's try the Margaux '85. Or do you prefer red? In that case try the Chateau—"

"I'll just have one glass of red, please," I said. "Any old red. I want to keep my wits about me."

She looked up from the wine list. "Why? You're not expecting me to try and seduce you into doing something you don't want to do? That would be very crude, Commodore. What's more, I'm beginning to agree with you. The proposal *does* seem ludicrous."

"Are you serious?"

"Absolutely. After what you said, I realize just how ludicrous. Typical of a bunch of young space engineers without any experience of human relations, except with each other, like those Russian bright boys who launched the first rocket into space with a monkey inside. They would be able to tell you everything about that monkey, its heart rate, its brainwaves, rate of breathing, production of urine, its terrified defecation at liftoff—everything except its name. And why not? Medical labs are full of nameless monkeys experimented to death for the sake of mankind. You're right, Commodore. Just forget the whole thing." She turned to speak to the waiter.

I couldn't understand it at first; she had pleaded with me earlier with such utter conviction. Then I got wise to what she was doing. Sylvia and I, some years ago, had a fat old tomcat who would look at the food placed in front of him, sniff at it disdainfully, then turn his back and walk away, disgusted. The way to cope with this, we had discovered, was to pick up the dish and take it back indoors. Within minutes he would stand outside, meowing furiously, outraged, demanding his food. All Miss Bastiaans had done was take my dish away. I could not help smiling.

She gave me a quizzical look, then the wine steward returned bringing two bottles of wine, hers in a bucket. "I'm afraid there is a mistake here," I said. "I ordered only one glass."

"Commodore," she said, "in a restaurant like this you don't just order one glass. We don't have to finish both bottles, you know."

After we had tasted and our glasses had been filled, I raised mine and said, "Here's to the colonel."

She raised hers and frowned. "How did you know he was a military man?"

"It stood out a mile. Any moment I expected him to call the waiter 'son.' "

"But his rank, how did you know that?"

"Well, your boys in the back room, whoever they may be, would not send a captain or a major, and he's too young to be a general. But what about you? Are you staying with this assignment?"

She sighed. "I don't know. There are some things in it that attract me, some questions I'd like to see answered. On the other hand—oh, sometimes I wish he was still alive! He would have told me what to do."

It had never occurred to me that she might have really loved old Arnold Kwel. He was a horrible old man, devious, cruel; when you were with him you always had a sense of your own insecurity. He was so much wilier than you or anyone else around.

"I think of him so often, you know," she said dreamily. "I remember him every day. It's as if he were just in another room. Well, that's not quite true. As if he were on another continent, waiting for me to join him. That's probably why Mr. Monroe's experiment interested me so much. Maybe there *is* something to the ship disappearing over the horizon and your small happy crowd waiting on the distant shore. It's a lovely thought."

Waiters came with the soup. After we had spread our napkins on our laps and the plates were filled and put in front of us, I waited until they had left with their little chariot before I asked, "In what way would Mr. Monroe's experiment connect with the distant shore?"

"Oh, never mind," she said, picking up her spoon. "It's a thing of the past anyhow. Let's forget about it. *Bon appétit.*"

I wished her the same and we ate our soup in silence. Suddenly she put her spoon down and gazed at the candle flame. Her eyes looked moist with tears. "I really would have loved to find out if there is anything to it."

"I can't quite see how you could. Putting old men under hypnosis, or whatever, and sending their minds off to the moon —I don't see how that would make you any wiser."

"How could you know? He really didn't explain any of it. There is much more to it than what he told you back there. You see, what really happens—but you don't want any part of this, do you now? Be honest."

"Well, just because I, personally—"

"Look," she said, "let's leave it alone now. You've made a decision, and so be it. If you're interested generally in what they are doing these days, I can lend you a book I have with me, in the trunk of my car. It contains verbatim reports on the process of the out-of-body experience, spoken by the subjects themselves in their isolation booths, recorded in the control room."

It would have been churlish on my part to refuse, so I said, "Sure, I'll be delighted."

There was a silence, during which we finished our soup, then she asked, out of the blue, "How did you and your wife meet? It was during the war, wasn't it?"

"In England, a month before D-Day."

"Did she live there?"

"No, she was one of those Wrens that you see in the movies. Pushing little ships' models about on a chart of the Channel with croupiers' rakes. For the brass upstairs looking down to see where everybody was."

"You were in command of a ship then?"

"An old W-boat, an ocean tug, British. Good old soul, more like a cow than a ship, really."

"What were you supposed to tow on D-Day?"

"I, and a whole fleet of others, were towing sections of the Mulberry Harbors across the Channel—two breakwaters-cum-dock off the coast of Normandy. It seems that there are still bits of them left."

"I don't quite understand. What exactly were they?"

"Breakwaters, made out of prefabricated concrete caissons that had to be towed into place, flooded, and then put together. Mammoth do-it-yourself harbors for the invasion fleet. One British, one American."

"So where did you two actually meet?"

"Oh, I was hanging around in Dover, waiting for orders, like everyone else. The town was full of young sailors with rakish caps and gold rings halfway around their sleeves. They gave you only half a ring; there was such a demand for gold braid in that war, they had to ration it."

"And the Wrens?"

"The Wrens were there en masse. Many were good friends of mine. Occasionally we had meals together, seven, eight of us."

"And she was one of those?"

"Not at first. She'd been in the service earlier and had married an Australian bomber pilot who was shot down over Düsseldorf, three weeks after their wedding. Then she came back and joined up again, but she was a wreck. Not that you'd ever know. *Death where is thy stingalingaling,* remember? That was the form those days. Those nights. *Don't be gloomy, darling.* Apparently, the others told her that what she needed was another man in her life. Finally she said, 'Okay, find me one. As long as he isn't Air Force and he has his own teeth.' So they asked me."

"Why?"

"No idea. The town was full of young Navy types, all of them with their own teeth. They said I was 'mature.' I'd lost a ship and my crew, I knew about mourning—"

I was blinded by a flash and damn near dropped my wine glass. It was a photographer who had taken a snapshot of us. He peeled off the backing and there we were: she looking her age, me with my mouth open. It would go on the bill, he said.

I handed it to her. "Do you want this?"

She gazed and said, "Ugh! Do *you*?"

"No, thank you."

She tore it up and dropped it in the ashtray. "Well, go on. What happened next?"

But I no longer felt in a confessional mood. The flash had blasted me out of it. "Some other time," I said.

Unexpectedly, she put her hand on mine. "Let it be," she said. "That's what we both have to learn. To let it be. Let's talk about ships."

We did; she was a very knowledgeable companion. We talked about my ships, and the company, men we had known and what had happened to them, all through the rest of the meal. In the process we each knocked back a bottle of wine.

When finally the time came to leave and I rose from my

chair, my first steps felt as if I had just set foot ashore after a long voyage. The instinctive counterbalancing of the rolling of the ship stays with you for some time after you go ashore.

As we stood waiting for the car, I suddenly felt like taking her in my arms and hugging her—not her herself, but what she stood for: the company, my ships, my life, the dead.

I did not. The machine arrived, growling; the valet banged on the brakes and made the tires squeal. "Does your car do that to people?" I asked her.

"We'll take it easy on the way home," she said.

4

S H E D I D I N D E E D drive slowly this time, as if we were returning from a tryst. Empty road, full moon, shimmering sea far below; I wished I hadn't told her about Sylvia. Too damn close to the knuckle; Syl and I had sat exactly as we had tonight: a candle lamp between us in that one surviving restaurant in Dover after all the bombings. A cellar, with Cypriot waiters and red velvet benches and, like everywhere else, that neutral scent of dust from the buildings that had been bombed into rubble.

We arrived in front of my bungalow. I opened the door to get out, but she said, "Wait, Commodore, wait! I'll get that book for you." As she opened the trunk and rummaged through it, I managed to hoist myself to my feet and advance to my door, groping in my back pocket for my key.

"Here!" I heard her say behind me. "Let me do that."

"Well, okay, thank you." I handed her the key, she opened the door. I asked, "Would you like to come inside for another cup of coffee?"

She smiled. "No, thank you. Neither do you, I know. Here, let me give you this. I think you'll enjoy it. It's really what brought *me* into all this."

"Thank you." I took the book.

She then handed me a business card. "Look, I have to leave early tomorrow morning. If you ever need me for anything, anything at all, call this number in London. They'll always know where I am and how I can be reached, and I'll get back to you. Okay?"

"Look, Miss Bastiaans, it's very kind of you, but really—"

"As a friend. You would do the same for me, wouldn't you? If you found yourself in my position?"

"I suppose I would, yes, in your position. Thank you."

She turned away, walked to her car, very elegant in the moonlight, both she and the automobile. Then she gave me a last wave, got in, and took off with a roar. Several oldsters in neighboring houses must have been shocked awake, asking themselves, "What was *that*?"

I rather hastily closed the door behind me, leaned against it, and looked at the dismal room. Any room looks dismal with just the ceiling light, but this one really was depressing. Maybe because the talk about Sylvia was hard to shake.

I sat down on the couch and looked at her empty chair. How young she had been! How composed, how quietly desperate as she turned up in her number-one uniform, dolled up for dinner with a man with whom she would have to go to bed, such was the understanding in those days. She welcomed me with a smile, but her grief-haunted eyes were a threat to my composure. They brought back all the friends lost in their meeting with death and its stingalingaling. We had a meal in the restaurant with the velvet benches and the hunting prints in the candlelight, at a table for two, just like tonight. It was pretty awkward, as I remembered. I tried some jokes that didn't go down well, and wondered what else I could do. Show her my teeth? Demonstrate my maturity? I couldn't think of anything to say that did not sound ludicrous in front of those eyes. I pointed at a print on the wall beside our table, the etching of a reservoir in a rainstorm. As a joke, I read out the dedication. I still know it by heart. *This plate, with the most exquisite affection and the most profound respect, inscribed to the honorable Miss Talbot, benefactress of the Seawater Baths in the county of Essex. 1886.*

It was to become part of our lives. The honorable Miss Talbot came up several times over the years. I had written her letters signed, "With the most exquisite affection and the most profound respect." But that first time she did not seem to think it was funny. She stared at the dreary picture earnestly, as if it contained the key to a mystery that haunted her. The mere idea of making love to this grieving girl was appalling. So, after the meal, I suggested taking a bus to Canterbury and a movie, but instead we checked in at the Cathedral Hotel. We didn't spell it out, we both knew we had to satisfy the expectations of the Wrens who had sponsored us; but we stayed in separate rooms. It gave a conspiratorial aspect to our first meeting which seemed to reassure her, a hint of childhood and innocence. She did indeed lead the other girls to believe that we had a passionate encounter, as did I. But now we had to keep up the illusion. It became a game: pretending we had a torrid love affair, when all we were doing was having a meal and sitting through a boring movie, without so much as holding hands. Yet I was very taken with her and felt protective; and she obviously felt safe and unthreatened. This created a sense of kinship between us. We shared all kinds of odd, personal things, such as her telling me about Johnny, her husband, breaking a heel bone hurdling at school, so that he was left with a little click in his ankle. He had demonstrated it to her, walking up and down barefoot on the carpet before they had gone to bed.

On D-Day I sailed with the rest, towing one section of the British Mulberry Harbor. We met with surprisingly little enemy fire, but three days later my ship hit a mine that the sweepers had overlooked, or that had worked loose from the seabed. The old bucket went down like a stone, more to my surprise than sorrow. She had seen her day, it was an honorable way for her to go.

There were no casualties; we were picked up promptly by a Sunderland flying boat. A swaggering Air/Sea Rescue group captain fished out the lot of us, including the ship's cat, and delivered us to Dover, where she stood waiting on the quayside. We faced each other; she burst into tears and put her head on my shoulder out of shame. You didn't cry in those days. They'd say, "Fancy that! Not this time, eh?" "No," you would answer, "it didn't have my number on it."

We had a red-eyed meal in the cellar restaurant and stayed the night in an inn down the road. In one room this time, on a large double bed where we lay fully clothed, her head on my shoulder. We fell asleep that way, at least I did. We woke in the unearthly light of the dawn and finally made love. We did not get married for another year. Forty-seven years and three children later, she died in her sleep, without warning. I only realized what had happened when I kissed her in the light of the morning and there was no response.

Well, enough of this mawkish reminiscing. It served no purpose. Maybe I should chop our story into little episodes, roll them into little balls, and put them in the cookie tin. Maybe that would take away whatever it was.

I sighed, picked up the book Miss B. had given me, and headed for my bedroom, exhausted. In passing, I saw the little red light flashing on the answering machine and pressed the playback button.

"Dad, this is Helen. Dad, I've had it! Really I've *had* it! You haven't read my letter, quite obviously. You haven't answered, you haven't even *thought* about it! Look, you cannot stay in that sad little house without Mom. You cannot go on living the way you are. I saw for myself when I was there, it's heartbreaking. Well, obviously you're not going to make the decision. I'll have to do it for you. The two of us must talk about this face-to-face. I'm on my way. I arrive in Nice airport tomorrow morning at eleven-twenty on Air Suisse, via Zurich. It's the first plane out of London. We're going to take our time, talk over the whole thing, and then I want you to come back with me to England to look at the place for yourself. Please, Dad, just *look* at it! You can at least do that, can't you? My heart breaks over you, you stupid old man! So, meet me at the airport and we'll take it from there. And stop procrastinating, Dad. I love you, damn it!"

There were two beeps, then the sound of the spool spinning back and then five beeps. By that time I was beside myself with fury. God damn it! These damn women! What did they think I was, a drooling, senile old bastard? *Damn* them! I was fully compos mentis, a totally independent male! I would die on my own terms!

It was too late to call her back. She would have already left and was somewhere in a hotel near Heathrow. I picked up Miss Bastiaans' bloody book and sat on my bed. Should I call *her*? No, for God's sake! That would be disastrous. I would just be trading one animal trainer for another.

I stomped over to the table, flipped through the cascading file of magazines, bills, and old correspondence, and found Helen's last letter, clipped to a couple of brochures.

Well, she had certainly tried. I read her letter and it was pretty nice, really. I should have called her, but those brochures took care of it. *Golden Evenings* they called the place, for God's sake. *Charming conversation room, sherry bar at five in the evening, a little bus to town twice a day. Sorry, no pets, not even parrots accepted.* What? No parrots? That did it.

Well, I would have to meet the damn plane and go through the motions. Poor Helen. She really was a devoted soul, and she had always been my favorite. But *this*? No! No, no, *no*. Period.

I picked up the book Miss Bastiaans had given me. Robert Monroe, *Far Journeys*. Leafing through it at random, from the back, as was my wont, I came upon a page marked with a little sticker.

So that the picture is clear, the subject lies on the waterbed, in an acoustically and electrically shielded eight-by-ten booth.

The booth has its own air conditioning and heating controls; electrodes for monitoring physiological states are glued to head, fingers, and body. A sound microphone hangs about four inches above the face. Audio headphones completely cover the ears. Most important, the subject has just gone to the bathroom to be sure the bladder is empty.

The monitoring technician in the control room, one of several, communicates vocally through a sound system with the person in the booth. The monitor also feeds hemi-sync sound into the subject's headphones to test the responses to new frequencies and aid the subject in achieving the desired state of consciousness. Finally, the monitor observes and notes changes in instrument readouts on the subject's physiological condition. An assistant is present to help in the processing. Here is a typical "entry" report, the beginning of an OOBE, transcribed from an early file recording during the experiment.

SS/ROMC (OFFICE MANAGER) 7 MINUTES IN—TEST #188.

I am going rapidly now through a tunnel. I was standing straight up, but now I am just sort of sucked up through this tunnel. It is very narrow, and I am rapidly shooting through this tunnel. Now I can see a point of light at the other end. I am traveling rapidly toward this point of light. It is like I am on some type of light beam that is helping to propel me. I am coming out. I am going into a different dimension and I've just completely slowed down. I am right at the opening at this point. Now I am gently coming through. Everything is green. It is so bright that it's almost blinding because of coming out of the dark tunnel. It's a different feeling. Now it is a real strong energy that seems to be pressing against me. It's a great feeling now. This is a new energy level. I feel a strong—everything around me is green. It is so bright that it is taking me a minute to adjust and to absorb where I am.

There was one problem. Once our subjects passed through the tunnel to the light or achieved the out-of-body state, they were not interested any longer in hour after hour of dull searching for new effective sound-frequency patterns. They would still perform the tasks, but beyond the tunnel and into the light was Paris. Keeping them down on the farm was certainly no trivial problem. We had to play a little to achieve that. For instance, we sent our subjects to explore the moon, which they found a very dull place. Nothing but mile after mile of craters and mountains, no vegetation, no sign of life, nothing to truly attract our human attention.

So this was where the colonel and his cronies had picked up the idea of sending men's souls to the moon! But why old men? Well, the hell with it. Meanwhile, there was Helen—all the pressure of love and concern and female tyranny. Would I be able to stand up to her? Or would she strongarm me, in the way that only favorite daughters can, into relinquishing my parrot's cage for the conversation room, the mini-sherry bar, the daily little bus to town? Golden Evenings for the rest of my days?

I awoke in the middle of the night, fully clothed, on top of the bed, with Helen's letter and the brochures spread all over me, and was hit, of all things, by a terrible homesickness for the sea. It was the blueness before the dawn in the window that did it. The blue hours before dawn were when most oceangoing tugs made their departure. The ship was a mess until the strangers and relatives of the crew had said their good-byes, full of sobs and hankies and nasty little dogs on leashes driving the cook around the bend because of his panicking cats. It usually was the yapping dogs that made me press the button of the ship's horn to give the long, protracted blast: *All visitors leave the ship.*

There they would go, the wives, the girlfriends, the parents, the widowed mothers with only one son. They would leave the ship behind in a state of shock: candy wrappers on the deck, toilets overflowing, the gangway rumbling as they made their hasty exit. Exiting also would be the owners' representative, the customs officer, the skippers of the two little tugs that would nose us out. There would be a secret excitement in the air: the moment was close when I regained control of my ship and became Master after God again, and the small universe of the ship would regain its comforting harmony. The pilot would come on board, and then, at long last, I could nod to the mate on the bridge, who would yell, "Let go aft!" I would put the telegraph on *Standby engines.* The aft moorings would be lifted off their shore bollards by the dockers, splash into the water, and be hauled in by the crew on the deck. I would nod to the mate again, who would yell, "Let go for'ard!" In the days before the thrusters, once these moorings were on board, a third nod would bring the shout, "Belay the spring!" and I would tell the helmsman, "Hard port, son." The helmsman would repeat the order, then I could give the ship its first gentle hint of life: a brief burst of *Dead slow ahead*, enough to make the stern slowly swing out. Then I would say, "Midships." The helmsman would repeat it and I would put the engine-room telegraph on *Dead slow astern.* The huge bulk of the massive ship, now alive, awakening, eager, waiting, would shift away from the quayside. The keen little tugs would take over; true to tradition, oceangoing tugboats were put under way by their captains, not by the pilot, a privilege we all staunchly defended. There she would go, slow ahead, with the little for'ard tug straining at the leash like a dog being let out, the aft one hanging back desultorily, letting itself be dragged along.

She would be almost mine, almost. The excitement of the departure mounted; finally the pilot was ready to leave. He would be given three roars of the ship's horn in farewell, then at my nod the mate would pick up the phone and order coffee for the bridge. They always coincided: the arrival of cook on the bridge with four mugs of coffee and the ship passing the outer buoy. That moment brought a silence which never failed. The helmsman would stand still, the cook would stand still with his mugs, and the mate too, looking at the captain with the envy of mates, which I knew, as I had been one myself. We all would stand still, gaze over the side at the outer buoy slowly slipping by, and then: there was the sea, all mine now, all mine.

Memories full of melancholy. What days they had been! Ah well, enough of this. I'd better undress, get properly into bed, and do some serious sleeping; I would need to be rested before entering the ring for the battle that would determine the course of my last years.

5

I **OVERSLEPT.** When I saw the time I cried "No!" and swung my legs out of bed, too fast. I stood up but had to sit down again and wait until I could see straight. The first thing I did was head for the telephone in my drafty pajama pants and T-shirt with the legend BEST GRANDPA IN THE WORLD; my grandchildren had given me six of them for my eightieth birthday. I called Nice airport and enquired about the status of the Air Suisse flight out of Zurich. Ten minutes late. Terrific!

While suiting up for the meeting with my daughter, I had to pause frequently to catch my breath. Then I called a taxi and ate a banana and a bunch of cookies while waiting. There had been no time for coffee—maybe at the airport? God protect old men from domineering young women! Why didn't they leave me alone? I wanted to sit down every morning at ten o'clock and write sentimental little pieces on life at sea between the wars; now here was a whole new war, the War of Independence.

The taxi came. I was carted off to Nice airport where I loitered outside customs at the newsstand, reading tabloid headlines: SPACE ALIENS DISCOVERED IN PET SHOP. ELVIS ALIVE AGAIN? FERGIE OF THE DANGLING BOOBS UK'S NEXT REPRESENTATIVE IN UNITED NATIONS?

She emerged from customs looking rather shabby, lugging a huge shoulder bag stuffed to the gills: a professor's wife shopping for a family of five and eight animals. When she saw me she gave a shrill cry: "Dad!" and we wept in each other's arms. At least I did; in the act of throwing her arms around me she had dealt me a sledgehammer blow in the crotch with her bag, which must have been filled with stones. The result was that, after we had hugged and kissed, I staggered to the taxi virtually with my knees together.

"Are you all right, Dad?" she asked, worried, putting her hand on my arm.

"Sure, sure, fine!"

Then there we sat, side by side on the back seat. I gave the driver the address of the Réserve, which I had decided was the most suitable place for the coming battle: Miss Bastiaans gone, a quiet corner table, wine, exquisite food, and the hell with the prices.

The taxi took off with small jumps, like a kangaroo warming up. "Well," she said, "isn't this a surprise?"

"It is," I agreed.

"Aren't you glad to see me, Dad? Tell me. Just say, 'Helen, lovely to see you.' Okay?"

I looked at her young, lined face: she looked the way Sylvia had when I came home from my first long trip after she had given birth to Tom, future bank manager. "You are exactly like your mother," I said. "Just as pretty, and irresistible, and bossy as hell."

She laughed, lifted my hand to kiss it, and said, "I will not rest, Dad, until you live in civilized conditions. I can't tell you how—"

"Love," I said, "keep all this until we are having lunch. First let's enjoy each other's company and prepare for the wrestling match at our ease. I need time to catch my breath." I shifted my position, painfully.

"Why a wrestling match, Dad?" She sounded astonished. "It's just a matter of coming back with me to see the place for yourself! I have plane tickets with me. I knew you would try and duck it, but you must, Dad, you *must* for the sake of all of us, for the sake of Mam, who would have done the same, I promise you. We'll fly back tomorrow—I really have to get back—and you can have a look at the place with me. It's not the kind of prison you have in mind, you'll see!"

I tried to shut her up by saying nothing and staring grimly out the window at the sea, two hundred feet below. But she carried on, a half-hour commercial for Screaming Evenings, or whatever the place was called. The bar, the bus, the running poker game, the interesting people, the dinner with her and the family once a week. If I had to go to town she'd take me, help me with the shopping and—"The apartment they're keeping for you is adorable, Dad. The last occupant died suddenly a week ago, and they've promised me—"

The top-hatted doorman was welcomed with undue warmth on my part. He delivered us to the rear admiral, who made a great show of recognizing me and took us to a table for two in a far corner.

When we had made our choice and the wine was on the table, she started up again about her luxury prison for last-time offenders. I raised my glass, which shut her up for a moment, and said, "Helen, look, you know I love to see you, but it's a pity you didn't warn me a little earlier. The place sounds terrific, but it's way too early. The fact is, I've been offered a job." I took a gulp of wine.

God only knew what made me say it. I had not planned to, I had just been reaching for a gambit that would give me a chance to regroup; it was totally unexpected, like glancing at yourself in the mirror and seeing you have forgotten your tie.

I looked up to find her gazing at me, mouth open, flabbergasted. "*What* did you say?"

"A job, love. I may be going to America. It's sweet of you to come all this way, but we'll have to wait for my visit to—well, whatever the place is called—until I come back. Maybe in two or three months."

"Dad! . . . What on earth . . . You're eighty-two years old!"

I told her. Once I had regained the upper hand, so to speak, I felt ashamed. It was a fantasy, a lie. Not one hair on my head considered swimming into wily Bastiaans' net. God knew what was in it for her, other than a fat fee as a headhunter; her effort had been, it seemed to me, disproportionate to the cause. But I told Helen the whole story, with ample quotes from Mr. Monroe's reports, and made it plain that I was in the process of deciding.

A little too plain. She instantly went into the attack again: I had to put a stop to this. "Love," I said, putting my hand on hers to soften my stance, "you must understand: you cannot bully old people. We're like mules. If you come at me carrying a harness and clanging chains, you turn me into an immovable object. Can't you see? The fear of all old people is that someone—out of love, tenderness, what have you—will take away their independence."

"Dad, I—" Suddenly she went silent and stared over my shoulder.

I turned around. It was Miss Bastiaans. Damn her! What was she still hanging around for? Damnation! How *dare* the woman stick her nose in my—

"Hello, Miss Bastiaans," I said, stiffly. "Forgive me for not getting up. You know my daughter? Mrs. er—"

"We've met," Miss Bastiaans said with a ready smile.

"So we have," Helen said. It sounded like the unsheathing of a sword.

"Mind if I sit down and have a cup of coffee with you?"

I did mind, and then again I didn't. Maybe it was the solution: let them fight it out between themselves. All I wanted was to sneak on board, cast off, and pass the outer buoy. Ah! What days those had been!

The maître d' turned up, coffee was ordered; then the two ladies, after a pause, took up their positions. One thing was clear:

they were not going to fight by the Queensberry rules. How the hell had I ended up in this situation? Who were these women, to fight over the rest of my life?

"My father told me about your offer to him of a job in America. I hope you don't mind my saying so, but I think it's madness."

"I'm afraid your father must not have made himself clear. He turned it down."

Helen was confused for a moment. "Did you, Dad?"

"Well . . ." I said, feeling as if I was ten years old and caught lying. I must have looked guilty and confused; Helen felt the need to defend me.

"I'll tell you why it's madness, Miss Bastiaans," she said, eyes flashing. "My father is an *old man*. When I saw him walk out of that airport to the taxi this morning, I was shocked to see how much older he has become since I saw him last. He could hardly walk!"

Well, hell. It had been *her* bag! "Now, let's all calm down," I said, "have a cup of coffee and—"

"I don't need calming down," Helen snapped. "I am as cool as—as—"

"A cucumber," Miss Bastiaans stated, like a teacher. My God, there went the cigar into the gunpower. Helen froze for a moment, then said, with the calm she had inherited from her mother, which even the dog had come to recognize, prompting it to hide under the bed, "At his age it is cruel, and quite simply madness, to think that he could even begin to undertake such a— a stupid assignment."

"Do you agree, Commodore?" Miss Bastiaans asked, so sure of herself that I felt prompted to mutter, "Up to a point, yes. At my age—"

Suddenly the woman said, with the voice of Arnold Kwel, "God dammit, Harinxma! Stop flirting with old age, *get back on the bridge!*"

After a moment of stunned surprise, I felt as if a surge of the sea had just swept through my soul. I grinned, then I said, "Aye-aye, ma'am."

We all sat in stupefied silence for a moment; Helen was the first to realize what had happened. She threw her napkin on the table, rose, said "Excuse me," and stalked out.

I made a move to go after her but Miss Bastiaans put her hand on mine as I was pushing myself up at the table. "Let her be for a moment," she said. "She's upset, but this is a matter between her and me, not you. She and I—"

I shook off her restraining hand, said, "Miss Bastiaans, that will do, I'll speak to you later," rose, and went after my fugitive daughter. I could understand her emotions; what I marveled at was her perception. She had spotted at once, the way Sylvia would have done, that something familiar had happened: the old tomcat had come back for his food.

I caught up with her outside. The doorman had called a taxi for her and it arrived just as I emerged. He opened the door. She climbed in and I followed.

I should have slipped him a coin or a banknote, or something, but the really rich don't go in for that. He closed the door without waiting for a tip.

One more morning like this, and I would be ripe for Golden Evenings. The angel of death, beautiful young woman in the doorway, had turned out to be my own daughter. The angel of life, in the startling guise of Miss Bastiaans ordering Harinxma back to the bridge, had won the day.

6

H E L E N, jaw set, was determined to be taken back to the airport. There was a London flight at four o'clock and she intended to take it.

For some reason I was filled with benevolence and fatherly love for the desperate girl, who could not hide her tears. During the long drive to the airport, we arrived at a compromise that astonished myself. I agreed with her that I had turned into a neglected old man, a batty recluse, and suggested she accept my American assignment on condition that, on my return, I would move into the little apartment she had selected for me with such care. It took a while, but in the end she herself suggested that she would arrange and supervise the move while I was gone, if I would trust her with it.

I was so full of warmth and closeness that I was ready to agree to anything to dry her tears and temper her desperation, anything, that is, except give up my assignment in America. For the die was cast: madness it might be, my mind was made up.

All things considered, we had a quiet hour at the airport until her plane was called. We said farewell with an embrace and another flood of tears, as if I were leaving on a long voyage. But then: I was. She had always cried when I left in the past. At first that had irritated me; then I had felt moved by it; I had ended up by expecting it. On one occasion she had remained dry-eyed, and I remember saying testily, "Glad to see me go, I gather?" I had not improved with time.

When, finally, the waving was over and she had disappeared into passport control, I sighed and turned away, overcome by exhaustion. All I wanted was a couple of snorts, peanuts, crackers, maybe a bit of cheese, and then to bed, after turning off the sound on the answering machine.

But the gods had decided otherwise. When I came out of the terminal there was the damn sports car with its shark's grin waiting for me. For some idiotic reason I remembered an American wartime comedian who, when told that sharks did not like human flesh, had answered, "But, then, they may take a bite and spit it out again!" Well, here was the shark, confident, opening the maw of her hellish machine.

"Hop in, Commodore," she said, "we're going to have dinner and set the whole thing up. Sorry I gate-crashed your lunch with your daughter, but my departure was delayed."

"I am whacked," I said, "let's make it tomorrow morning."

"Tomorrow morning I'll really be gone. Tell you what: I'll take you home, we'll have a couple of snorts, some peanuts, crackers, cheese—you'll be a new man."

She really was one of the boys! Or had been, like myself. What got to me, when all was said and done, was that she and I were the only survivors of what had once been called "Holland's Glory." When I retired, the Dutch had a fleet of nearly three hundred oceangoing tugs. With the near total loss of the market for straight-line towing in recent years, it had almost vanished. KITCO and its bitterest rival, Van Dalen, had merged; between them they had two oceangoing tugboats left. The rest of their fleet was composed of salvage vessels.

We had a couple of drinks with the works in my bungalow. I changed into the gray flannel trousers and blazer, and then, magically revived, joined her on her motorized broomstick for the ride to the top-hatted doorman and the rear admiral at the Réserve.

When we were at table, after I had chosen the *canard à l'orange* and the same wine as the previous day, she said, as the wine was being served, "Now let's discuss a few details, Commodore." She proceeded to run past me again everything said before: limousine, luxury hotels, VIP treatment, and my feet that would never touch the ground. She behaved exactly like old Kwel giving dinner to one of his captains before a major job, dotting the *i*'s, crossing the *t*'s, making his guest yearn for the freedom and peace of the sea.

When she was through, I said, "All right. So I'll start by making a list of candidates. I'll have to give it some thought. I can come up with a few names, but I have to check if they are still alive. After that I'll visit them to see if they are blind, deaf, have Alzheimer's, or are already in diapers."

"All of that would be okay, except the Alzheimer's," she said. "Who tops your list, do you think?"

There she went, exactly like old Kwel. You open your mouth, he sticks a cigar in it, has it lit for you by his secretary, and proceeds to give you the third degree.

Did I really want this? I don't know what triggered my sudden moment of doubt; maybe the fact that the memory of old Kwel and his cigar made me want to add another little ball to the collection in the cookie tin: "Captains and Owners." That was what I should be doing: writing a little piece every day, at ten A.M. sharp—not just for the sake of the writing, but because I had discovered that those little pieces were keys to the gate of that other dimension: the no-man's-land between memories and dreams, where old men were the only explorers. I felt caught in a trap set by women, or fate, or the wrong side of the process of aging—I had no business going in for this nonsense. Unless it were to turn out not to be nonsense, but indeed another reality beckoning me with its promise of a far journey to the distant shore. In which case my moment of unnerving doubt was a moment of fear . . .

"Sorry, Commodore—who did you say?"

"Excuse me?"

"Who tops your list? You were about to tell me."

I gathered my skirts, so to speak. "A bit early yet," I answered. "But one man comes to mind. An ex-Marine, Dutch, who led three commando raids into France. He and his crew blew up the U-boat pens at Saint-Nazaire, which you may remember."

"Sorry, before my time."

"Of course, yes. His name is Frans van Texel—we knew him as 'Tex.' An absolute bastard, but just about the most coura- geous man I've ever known. He lives somewhere near The Hague."

"Tell me when you want the limousine, and where. I'll take care of the rest."

"That would be splendid," I said.

She gave me one of her ravishing smiles. "Well, what shall we order for dessert?"

"A bit early for me," I said, staring down at my duck, which was the size of an ostrich.

"If we want to order the soufflé we have to do it now. I recommend it, it's excellent here."

"Aye-aye, ma'am," I said. "Soufflé it is. I am souffléd myself."

It was a poor joke, but I was spoiled. During the past year I had had the most appreciative audience in the world for my jokes: myself.

She beckoned the waiter, ordered the soufflé, then turned back to me and said, "All right, Commodore, the day after to- morrow you and I fly to The Hague. We'll put you up in the Hôtel des Indes and do a bit of an overhaul on you before you venture into the open. Now that you're representing the builders of the space station, you can no longer walk around in the get-up of Grock the Clown."

"Gee, thanks," I said, attacking the ostrich with what looked like a fruit knife.

"I'll take you to a tailor, but some things we may be able to get ready-made. We'll definitely get you a haircut—"

"Why?" Now I was on edge.

She smiled. "Because you can't, in your present function, go around as the working man's Einstein. And it won't be the first time. Remember? Kao-hsiung, ten years ago? I sent a tailor to measure you for some decent clothes on short notice because you were about to leave for home in Bermuda shorts, the jacket of your tropical uniform with commodore shoulder tabs, and a canary in a cage."

"No shoulder tabs," I reminded her, "I had given those to Ma Chang, the cook. And she instantly sewed them on to the shoulders of her smock."

"Ma Chang, that's right! She was the one who cut your hair during the trip, wasn't she?"

"Yes, with a wok on my head."

"Well, you are about in the same state now. I took you to a barber then, I'll do it again."

I put down my knife and fork and looked at her.

"I must warn you, Miss B., you may be living in a fool's paradise. This is all very well, but the cold fact is that I am eighty-two years old. All I am *really* good for, as long as it lasts, is sitting on my butt and writing tiny memory exercises. I'm too old to take on a new war. You should respect reality. And so should I."

"Harinxma," she said, with demonstrative patience, "I lived with a man who ran a world concern at the age of ninety. That's eight years older than you are now. He could run it because I took care of all the aspects of old age you are indulging in. Yes, you *are* indulging yourself, damn it! The show is over. It's time to wipe off the greasepaint, take off your wig, drop the quavering voice and the faltering steps. When I'm through with you, tomorrow or the day after, you'll be—"

"Young again?" I laughed. "Dear Miss B., I think you are terrific, but what you are doing right now is just that, in reverse. You are putting on my greasepaint, kitting me out with a blond wig, ordering a youthful costume, trying to turn me back into Commodore Harinxma, chief captain of the fleet, age thirty."

She gave me a pensive look with those all-seeing, loveless eyes. "Let's say, sixty."

And there came the soufflé.

It was indeed excellent. Halfway through its voluptuous ministrations I asked, "As a matter of interest: Suppose I were to kick the bucket over there? What would you do then?"

She smiled. "Meet you on the distant shore." Then she opened her purse and took out a typed sheet of paper. "That reminds me," she said. "The other day you mentioned you felt closer to Ulysses than to John Glenn. I came across this and thought it might interest you. It's a poem by Tennyson, about Ulysses as an old man. It says things I have been unable to convey to you. No, no, don't read it now! Read it in bed tonight. Now, how do you like the soufflé? Delicious, isn't it?"

It was.

7

I READ THE POEM as ordered, that night in bed, alone. I was tipsy and cross-eyed with fatigue, but at the same time curiously elated. I took out my teeth, put them in the glass by the bedside, and, yawning luxuriously as I unfolded the paper, began to read the poem about Ulysses as an old man.

It started with a description of him as the aging king of a boring little country, with a boring old wife; it did not really get hold of me until I came to the final section.

> How dull it is to pause, to make an end,
> To rust unburnished, not to shine in use! . . .
> There lies the port; the vessel puffs her sail:
> There gloom the dark broad seas. My mariners,
> Souls that have toiled, and wrought, and thought with me—
> That ever with a frolic welcome took
> The thunder and the sunshine, and opposed
> Free hearts, free foreheads—you and I are old;
> Old age hath yet his honour and his toil;

Death closes all: but something ere the end,
Some work of noble note, may yet be done,
Not unbecoming men that strove with Gods.

Ah, if that were true!

The lights begin to twinkle from the rocks:
The long day wanes: the slow moon climbs: the deep
Moans round with many voices. Come, my friends,
'Tis not too late to seek a newer world.
Push off, and sitting well in order smite
The sounding furrows; for my purpose holds
To sail beyond the sunset, and the baths
Of all the western stars, until I die.
It may be that the gulfs will wash us down:
It may be we shall touch the Happy Isles,
And see the great Achilles, whom we knew.
Though much is taken, much abides; and though
We are not now that strength which in old days
Moved earth and heaven; that which we are, we are:
One equal temper of heroic hearts,
Made weak by time and fate, but strong in will
To strive, to seek, to find, and not to yield.

I lowered the paper with a sense of admiration and awe at this closing move by a champion chess player, with daft old men for pawns.

8

WHEN THE LIMOUSINE turned into the driveway of the sumptuous villa on the outskirts of The Hague, I saw an elderly lady with a shawl around her shoulders waiting for us on the front step. After I had introduced myself, she said, "I'm so terribly sorry, this happened after you telephoned, but I'm afraid he's having one of his bad days. Well, even so—do come in." She sounded nervous.

The interior of the baronial house somehow felt empty. She led me to a drawing room dominated by the heads of stuffed animals on the walls, trophies from previous bad days of the master of the house. Among the heads I spotted the painting of a young woman, beautiful and full of self-confidence—my hostess at an early age. Another trophy. Somewhere in the house sounded a monotonous male voice on radio or television.

A tray with afternoon tea was waiting on the table in front of an empty fireplace.

"No sugar, only milk, please."

She poured me a cup from a huge silver pot which, like the sofa and the room itself, seemed to suggest a past full of big men. Then she glanced over her shoulder and whispered, "He's so *angry*. Apart from his legs he has so much going for him, compared to others your—I mean, our age." She handed me the cup. "Cucumber sandwich?"

She moved me because of the confident young girl among the trophies. She was so frail now, so frightened.

"You said you knew him from the war, Commodore. Were you friends?"

I smiled. "Wartime friends." The truth was, he had been a cold-hearted bastard who, though he never said as much, seemed to enjoy the killing. But we had to get along in the line of duty, so we did.

"He was such a darling man," she said wistfully. "Now he's on a short fuse all the time. He gets furious with me for no reason at all. And he has such odd bugbears, like perfection. You would think that a man with his past would demand perfection, but quite the reverse: it makes him mad. Our young GP talked to him— you don't mind my being frank with you?"

The young GP must have been aged about twelve, the kind of man Tex would have had for breakfast while waiting for H-hour in May of '44.

"Go on," I said, smiling at her.

"The doctor told him to try to relax and gave him pills, and arranged for a psychiatrist to come and see him. An excellent older man who talked to him for nearly an hour. He was so kind; when he was leaving, he patted my husband on the back and told him to take it easy; for some reason that made him throw something . . ."

I could well believe it. The good doctor was lucky not to have ended up among the wildebeest on the wall. Tex had been in his element when "maximum violence" was the key to victory. Young GPs and middle-aged psychiatrists in love with themselves are not the ones to advise the over-eighties.

"Maybe he'll talk to you," she said nervously. "He won't talk to me any more. He stays in his study all day watching stock-market results on television, morning, noon, and night; until bed-time. He has no interests, no friends, hates everybody." She laughed nervously. "He just sits staring at that screen all day in a sort of silent craziness. I don't know, he was such a good man. . . . May I take you to see him? Oh, forgive me, finish your tea first. By the way, I didn't tell him of our telephone conversation, so he's not expecting you. It seemed best . . ."

I doubted that, but finished my tea and followed her down a long corridor toward the sound of the monotonous male voice. The door at the end stood open; she pointed to it, then fled sound-lessly down the carpeted passage like a frightened animal fleeing from the gun.

The room I entered was steeped in gloom. A flickering screen was the only source of light. In front of it sat an old man in a wheelchair. Tex in a wheelchair. It was totally incongruous and, for some reason, menacing. It would be like talking to a prisoner manacled to the bars of his cell.

"Good afternoon, Tex," I said.

He looked up irritably. "Now what the hell is it this—" He peered at me through the gloom, then froze. The ghost of the old Tex stared at me; all color had been leeched out of his face, and his hair was not white but had lost its color. The only things unchanged were his eyes. The voice of the announcer droned a list of figures.

"Nice to see you. How are you?" Stupid question.

His face changed. "Jesus, Holy pissing—*Fancy That*! I thought you were another goddamn doctor!"

"You did?"

"Where the hell did you come from? What are you doing here? Who—" His face darkened. "Don't tell me she called you in!"

"No, no," I said. "I have come to offer you a job."

He frowned. The commando's eyes narrowed. He said calmly, "Go to hell," and turned back to the screen.

I found a chair, sat down, and proceeded to tell the back of his head about Miss Bastiaans, the manufacturers of the future space station, the Monroe Institute, America, and my quest for old veterans of World War II who were prepared to have their minds separated from their bodies to go to the moon, find a lunar buggy, and read a dosimeter. When there was no reaction, I stood up, switched on the light, and turned off the set. That did it: he exploded. Curses, abuse, obscenities—he tried to rise from his wheelchair rabid with rage, then slumped back, powerless. It was a pitiful sight.

His wife came running, put her arms around him, cried, "Darling, darling, what happened?" He told her to fuck off, in a voice that would have made a bosun flee. She fled; he looked at me with the eyes of the old Tex and said, "You are out of your goddamn mind."

It had been quite a show, but it left me unmoved. I went on to tell him in brief terms about the travel arrangements, the luxury hotels with room service, the limousines, the feet that would never touch the ground.

"How the hell did you get sucked into this?" he asked.

"Tex, look. At our age, after our kind of life, it's only natural for us to become lone wolves. We turn inward, we think we don't need anybody—we each end up as a sort of hermit, a recluse, in the darkest corner of the forest, the only place where we feel secure. It so happens that I've been coaxed out into the open—"

"By whom?"

"Well—the—the young woman I told you about, Miss Bastiaans, the headhuntress."

"Sounds more like the tooth fairy to me."

I decided to plow on. "It suddenly gave me the chance to have a last shot at life before I pack it in. Yes, it probably is crazy. The whole scheme may be a chimera. But I tell you, Tex, it's like a shot in the arm. It's rejuvenating, reenergizing . . ." Who was I trying to convince? Myself? Maybe he would tell me. If he accepted it, maybe the last element of doubt lurking in the back of my mind would be eliminated.

"What do *I* have to do with your rejuvenation cure?"

"I have been asked to take some old friends with me. You are the first one I thought of."

"Fancy that," he said with a grin. "How many old suckers are you trying to catch, Fancy?"

"Five or six. Strictly veterans of the Second World War."

"Why?"

"As I understand it, the principle is that our wartime experiences never became a homogenous part of our lives. The war, according to the boffin who dreamed up this whole thing, is like an island in the river of our daily lives. We remember details and moments of the war with a clarity never achieved by other memories later. The war remains an island that we can visit, but in order to carry on with our daily lives we have to leave it."

"Hmm," he said. "Not stupid. But not for me, thank you very much! Bye-bye."

"All right," I said, "as you wish." I turned to leave.

"But why *me*, for God's sake?" he cried. "Look at me, God damn you! Here I am, in a wheelchair! I piss in a bottle strapped to my leg! It takes two people to screw me onto the pot! I have the temper of a wounded tiger! Why *me*?"

"Let me tell you," I said. "I didn't know what I'd find when I came here. I only knew that you were still alive. I expected you to be an old man. And you are, with a vengeance. But in reality you are the same man you were when I knew you in Dover. You always lacked charm, but you were the bravest man I ever met. You're the one I want for my second-in-command. As a matter of fact, I won't do it without you."

"You should be committed," he snarled. "Now let me have a dose of sanity." He tried to turn on the television, but couldn't quite reach it. "God dammit! God damn the whole lot of you! Leave me alone, you bastards! Leave me alone!"

I turned on the set for him, and once more turned to leave. He stopped me by asking, "What was the name of that blonde you had an affair with in Dover? The young Wren."

"Sylvia."

"Whatever happened to her?"

"We were married for forty years."

"You were? Then . . ."

"She died last year."

"I see. Well . . ." I waited for him to say, "It's all part of the deal"—the war had moved that close while we were talking. But he said, "I see," and concentrated on the television screen.

At the end of the corridor his careworn wife was waiting. "How was he?" she whispered.

I started to reply, but she silenced me with a gesture and led me back to the drawing room with the glass-eyed trophies and the empty chairs. He must once have filled the place with his presence. She made me sit down beside her on the couch.

"When I left him he was in good shape," I said. "I gave him something to mull over."

She stared at me, then her eyes filled with tears and she whispered, "Wonderful."

"It may all lead to nothing," I said, "but if it works out he may have to go to America."

She stared at me, nonplussed. "But he won't even leave the house!"

"It's a long story," I said. Then, relenting, I started to tell it to her.

In the middle of it an angry voice rang down the corridor. "Helena! Helena! *Helena! God dammit! Helena!*"

She flitted out of the room toward the angry voice. There was a lengthy silence, during which I sat worrying. She came back with a piece of paper. "He asked me to give you this," she said, and held it out to me.

It read:

The man we want is Pjotr Warszinsky. Remember him? The Polish deep-sea diver who fell in love with a grouper he called Louise. I think I'll be able to trace him, somewhere in Paris. Give my wife your address and telephone number and I'll be in touch.

Another old tomcat had come back for his food.

9

I WAS SURPRISED by my reaction: I found myself wishing he had not sent me that note. Earlier I had been surprised by my own remark that I wouldn't do it without him. I had no such sentiment when I went to see him; now it turned out that I was disturbed by his acceptance. Why? Maybe because of the responsibility I had taken on for a handicapped man of obvious physical frailty? Or because, in my heart of hearts, I had hoped he would turn it down and thereby give me the excuse for backing out myself?

Those were questions I had to answer before I went any further; it was time to take a break. I told the driver to take me to the nearby park of Wassenaar Castle; he could pick me up in an hour or so, there was no hurry. Ten minutes later I found myself standing, alone, in the square facing the castle, wondering what the hell I was doing there. I couldn't walk for more than five minutes at a stretch. The park seemed sparsely sown with benches for the breathless.

I set out for a walk in the woods, be it a short one, to think things over. I tried to, but for a while I was distracted by birds hamming it up in the trees, warning all wildlife of the approach of a prowling predator with glasses and a fedora. A woodpecker, undisturbed by the hysteria of the lower classes, went on hammering somewhere in the green dusk under the elms. A squirrel thought it necessary to investigate by crossing the path ahead of me, and then, obviously not believing its eyes, crossing back again. It was years since I had last strolled in a Dutch forest with its chattering tenants; I had become used to silent pines and scented lavender bushes with only the hum of bees to break the silence. I was a water-Dutchman myself, born fourteen feet below sea level and reared on plains reclaimed from the sea; yet this gentle green forest with its whirling bird gossip and single-minded woodpecker felt like home, to the point where I said to the squirrel, as it crossed my path for the third time, "Hard to believe, isn't it?" That was a new phase of my voyage of exploration: the old dotard addressing squirrels and raising his hat to the woodpecker who had finally come to investigate. "You should be committed," Tex had said. He had been closer to the truth than either of us realized at that moment.

Why did his acceptance bother me? Was I indeed looking for a way out? What was it that scared me in this whole thing? Maybe "scared" was not the right word. If not, then what was? Suspicious? Reluctant?

Something else: a sense of having been waylaid on the road to some discovery, some growing awareness of the true values in human life. Sounded pretty pompous for the occasion—true values, my foot! I had been happy and content in my old parrot's cage in the South of France; I had been writing little sailorly essays and felt like Honoré de Balzac with webbed feet. Then two damn women had queered my pleasant private journey around my own quarters—terrific book, that, for the elderly: *Voyage autour de ma chambre*, by—don't ask me to remember names at this point in my life.

But, all kaffeeklatsch aside: Why had I hoped that Tex would turn me down? Damn, I needed to sit down somewhere and think, but not a bench in sight. A low branch? I set out to find one; the birds now realized that their foam in the bath had substance: here he comes, the predator, huffing, puffing, looking for something feathery to eat, so sure of his power over all Creation that he made a racket of crackling twigs and groans growing into curses. Ha! A branch. I sat down on it, arthritically, and landed on my behind with a bang and a scream of splitting wood.

Dead silence. The birds had fled. Had I broken something? No. Twisted a hip? No. Well, hell! They should have provided benches. Why—oh, come on, Harinxma. Own up!

All right, then: I wanted no part of the assignment. What I

wanted to do was go back to France, take up my life again, my own routine, be it messy and hopeless as far as the women were concerned, and resume writing my little stories about life at sea between the wars. Here was a new one to add to the collection: "Walks in the Woods." *The old sailor should be warned that, although tempting, walks in the woods are not for him. For one thing, there is nowhere to sit down. Low branches may seem to be the answer, but before he knows it, he'll find himself*— Oh, for God's sake! Shut up, old bore.

The fact was that I had painted myself into a corner. Confused, flattered, feebleminded with age, I had promised my daughter she could move my belongings during my absence to Golden Horizons, or whatever was the name of that storage facility. To extract myself from Miss Bastiaans' clutches was more than I could handle. I wasn't interested in dealing with *any* of it, not even the disentanglement. What I really wanted was to disappear. Sneak back to France, collect cookie tins and writings, disappear into the woodwork. Where, you old idiot? I'd be easier to trace than a leaking tar barrel. Those two women could have me locked up before I could—Ouch! Dammit, I *had* torn something. . . . No. Just the seat of my pants. And where the hell was my hat? . . .

While I looked for my hat, the birds came back, in noisy disagreement as to the danger of the old animal, now snouting for truffles among the dead leaves. The racket became so deafening that I shouted, "All birds: beat it! Fuck off!" After a short silence, they burst into cackles and twitters again, obviously splitting their sides. Even the woodpecker shrieked with laughter. The squirrel, squatting on his haunches, peered from the shrubs. Suddenly it struck me how much more fascinating all this was than for my soul to visit the moon to look for somebody's old golf cart. I had never had a dialogue with birds before, never even dreamed that it was possible. The hell with Mr. Monroe's book; the book I wanted was the one I had given away to a couple of young weathermen on the uninhabited island on the way to Taiwan: *Kinship*

with All Life. It had belonged to "Spooks" Haversma, my prede-
cessor on the *Isabel*, who had died in Aden and left me his psychic
library.

Well, well, no musings too nonsensical as long as they postponed the confrontation with the truth. Did old Ulysses *really*
want to sail, or just talk about sailing while gazing out the window at the ships in the harbor? All the poem said, in effect, was,
"Come on, Uli! Get on with it!" But he never sailed again after
that long first voyage; the whole thing was a fantasy indulged in
by Alfred, Lord Tennyson.

Only as I joined the driver in front of the castle did I realize I
had walked for over thirty minutes, and felt fine. I had lost
weight, maybe a pound or two, gained energy, and received a
new lease on life in the physical sense, thanks to Miss Bastiaans.
But that was neither here nor there. What counted was my promise to Helen. My life in the South of France was over, it was time
to turn a new leaf anyway. So let's go and visit Fons van Buren—
the only one besides Tex who turned out to be still alive of the
seven I had tried to contact.

"Where next?" the driver asked.

"Antwerp," I said.

"Today? It's nearly six o'clock."

"The Scandia Hotel, I'll be visiting my next client tomorrow
morning. Early."

"Okay," he said, started the engine, and drove me out
of Eden.

1 0

FONS VAN BUREN was a former Sabena pilot with whom I had shared a billet toward the end of the war when stationed in Bristol. He was a poetic man, most unusual for a pilot, a sort of Dutch Saint-Exupéry. He had managed to retain a gentle, caring humanity, totally free of stress and anger. During the war he flew for KLM, which ran a regular route Bristol–Lisbon–Gibraltar–Cairo; every time he returned he brought bananas and tiny bottles of cherry brandy for the lonely old ladies among us. Our hotel had been requisitioned by the Navy for the duration, but they were lifetime residents, placed there by their children before the war, and paid for in advance. Their tables were little islands of gentility in the roughhouse of a dining room full of boisterous pilots, boffins, Air Sea Rescue characters with handlebar moustaches, and captains of OTWA (Oceangoing Tugs Western Approaches), who picked up the "lame ducks," disabled cargo ships left behind by the convoys from America after U-boat attacks.

It was Fons who helped me the one time in my life I was emotionally frozen in desperation, after I lost my first ship, the original *Isabel Kwel*, and most of her crew on the Murmansk run. I was caught in a wordless state of bewilderment, rage, and revulsion that made me forget what life before the war had been, in the bleak conviction that it would never return. The world would never be the same, all beauty, joy, and innocence lost forever.

Fons spotted my condition, and although we barely knew each other, he handed me a book one day and said, "I think this may interest you. I found it fascinating. It's a volume of correspondence between Ellen Terry, the actress, and Bernard Shaw, dating from the end of the last century." I felt like tossing the book back at him; the last thing likely to speak to my condition was the correspondence of two theater creatures in this world of death, destruction, and inexpressible loneliness. But I did read it finally, and for some reason, which I fail to understand even today, it set me free. Those love letters, with their intimacy and humor and self-conscious tenderness, proved utterly absorbing, and thereby lifted me out of the purgatory of the damned, dissolving my state of mute despair. Good old Fons, I had not seen him for so many years. All I knew was that he had married a famous Belgian soprano, prima donna of the Royal Flemish Opera in Antwerp. Now I had to try and find him before my next appointment with Miss Bastiaans, three days away.

To my surprise, Fons turned out to be quite difficult to locate. Everyone in Antwerp knew who Madame Elvira Boeykens was, but they showed an awed, almost religious reticence when asked where she lived. They either did not know or would not divulge the information. Finally, my Dutch driver suggested we ask at the Opera itself. There the reaction was more than religious, it was evangelical. "Madame Boeykens? My God! You can't just walk in on her!" When I told them I wanted to see her husband, there were frowns. Was she married? Was I sure? Then my driver shouldered his way into the conversation, took one reluctant bureaucrat aside, walked him slowly backward until he hit the wall, and involved him in a whispered conversation.

"Twenty-two Boulevard Roosendael," he reported when they came out of the clinch.

The chauffeur was becoming like my last bosun: protective as a mother, aggressive as an irate father whenever someone got too close to me. He even called me "Ome"—Uncle—the Dutch sailors' name for old captains.

We arrived in front of the residence of Madame Boeykens, the "Antwerp Nightingale." It was an impressive pile, one of the art nouveau buildings that at one time made up most of Brussels and Antwerp, many of which had since been destroyed to make room for office high-rises built by English developers.

The chauffeur rang the doorbell. I was ordered to stay where I was while he found out if there was anyone home.

There was; the door was half-opened by an obviously angry old man with a finger to his lips.

The chauffeur mumbled something. The old man's face went blank. The chauffeur pointed. The old man looked at the car, open-mouthed, then seemed to put a question. The chauffeur nodded and pointed again. The old man gaped at me, wide-eyed with bafflement. The chauffeur came over to me.

"It's him," he said. "You'll have to be quiet because Madame came home late from the boondocks and is asleep."

Fons? It couldn't be! I got out of the car and approached him.

"Hello," he whispered unsurely.

I still could not believe it. "Fons?"

"Fancy That!" the old man said, gazing at me as if he were dreaming. "You aren't a ghost, are you? Come in, come in!"

I followed him into a huge lobby with Roman busts in niches, one of them wearing a woman's hat. He started up a stairway with a jade-eyed snake for a banister that led to the second-floor landing. I was about to follow him when he changed his mind, came back down and, whispered, "Better in the kitchen . . . Elvie hears everything. This way . . ."

The kitchen in the basement had an old-fashioned brass pump over the sink and a large black stove with bulbous pink doors. A table in the center was laid for two. He pulled out one of the chairs and whispered, "Sit down, sit down . . . Would you like some coffee?"

"Well, to tell you the truth—"

"Shh!" he warned, his finger on his lips.

"No, thank you," I whispered. "I just had some."

"Fancy That!" he said. "Fancy!" He reached out to touch me, then he sat down himself. "Tell me, what are you doing here?"

I told him in whispers. It was not easy; the invisible presence of the sleeping prima donna was oppressive. During the briefing he glanced frequently at the steps leading down from the door, as if he expected her to descend upon us at any moment. He was not really listening to me, he seemed to concentrate on my face, my mouth, my hands. He was, literally, unrecognizable: old, stooped, his white hair untidy like a discarded mop—but his eyes, taking me in, all of me, were those of a boy gazing at a new bicycle, not yet believing it was his., My coming had been a mistake; he was so vulnerable; to separate his consciousness from his body would be like stealing candy from a baby.

"You look just the same," he said, gazing at the new bicycle. "Do you miss the sea?"

It was a genuine question, not the standard polite inquiry. "Not the sea *per se*," I said. "Aspects of sailing a ship, maybe."

"Like what?"

"Passing the outer buoy on your way out to sea, for instance."

"Yes," he said, nodding. "I know. In my case, the takeoff. Lose touch, pull up wheels, a rose for Icarus."

"Excuse me?"

"I tried to describe it in a poem. That is the title: 'A Rose for Icarus.' "

"Ah, I remember you did some writing," I said.

"Once I was grounded, it all came back, especially at night. The joy of leaving the earth, the feeling of ecstatic reckless-ness . . ." His face lit up.

"Could you read it to me?"

"Would you like that?" He scrutinized me.

"You gave me Shaw's letters to Ellen Terry to read. I . . ." But he was no longer listening.

When Icarus geared up to leave the earth,
I watched him strap on his wings, his ailerons
To his ankles. I was full of love for him, and fear, and
A sense of doom, of irrevocable fate. But not
A destructive fate, not mere annihilation; a fate

So complicated, so merciless and yet so tender, that
When he crashed among the hay wagons wallowing home,
And the straw-hatted scythers, I placed a rose—

"Who is that?" a forbidding voice at the top of the steps demanded.

Fons sprang to his feet, and so did I, for some reason feeling guilty.

The woman looking down on us was huge. I had heard her sing Mimi's deathbed aria once and forgotten her mega-bosom, her immense girth; now she looked awesome.

"This is Captain Harinxma," Fons stammered, "an old wartime—"

"For *breakfast*?" the Valkyrie asked. She had her hair up in curlers and wore a man's silk robe and large Chinese slippers.

"I must apologize, Mrs. van Buren," I said. "I did not realize that in your profession—"

"Mrs. van Buren? In my profession," she trumpeted, "we are addressed by our *maiden* names. My name is Elvira Boeykens. How do you do?"

She came down, the most intimidating female I had ever been exposed to. "Well," she said, heading for the table, "why don't you join us for breakfast, since you're here. Mr.—what did you say your name was?"

Time for me to assert myself, before I became part of her breakfast. "In my profession, Miss Boeykens, we are addressed by our rank. I am Commodore Harinxma."

She loved it. Smiling, she sat down on the chair Fons had pulled out for her and asked, "Are you related to the dear Queen's Commissioner, Baron van Harinxma Thoe Sloten?"

"Wrong side of the tracks, Miss Boeykens. Our families may have been related a century or so ago, but my branch lost the 'van,' the 'Baron,' and the 'Thoe Sloten.' My father was an officer in the Merchant Marine."

"Is that so? Tell me about your mother—No, no! Eggs and

bacon? You know I am feeling bilious. Make me some porridge."
She turned back to me again.

I started to tell her about my mother while Fons set about
preparing a porridge in a copper pan on the stove with the pink
cheeks. Old men are at a loss as to what to say about their mothers, of which she must have been aware, for as I sat there, waf-
fling, she contemplated me with obvious enjoyment. Then she
said, "Don't let me intimidate you, dear man. I am, as Fons will
tell you—*Brown* sugar! *BROWN!*"

"Yes—yes, my dear."

I was overcome by anger. Fons had been an inspiring presence in our darkest hour; I would never forget the faces of the
marooned old ladies at their little tables when they saw the banana, the little bottle of cherry brandy. Now he was the slave of a
female bully whose only claim to immortality was the capacity of
her lungs and the vocal cords with which she had been born.

I sat through breakfast, submitting to the interrogation although it was obvious that she did not listen to the answers.
Finally she rose, put down her napkin, and said, "I will now get
dressed. Don't forget, my car comes at twelve sharp. Nice to have
met you, Mr.—sorry—Admiral—ah, yes: Harinxma, of course.
The baron. Such a darling man. Hope to see you again." She
swept out.

I helped Fons clear the table and do the dishes. When we
were through with household chores, we sat down at the now
empty table. I was struck by his serenity. "How do you manage,
Fons?" I knew it was a stupid question even as I put it.

He looked at me with the eyes I remembered from the war
and said, with a smile, "I am not here, really."

"Ah."

"Let me finish the poem I was reading to you when she
came in."

"Start from the beginning."

He closed his eyes, his face took on a euphoric expression;
then he recited once more, in that secretive whisper:

When Icarus geared up to leave the earth,
I watched him strap on his wings, his ailerons
To his ankles. I was full of love for him, and fear, and
A sense of doom, of irrevocable fate . . .

Hearing it for the second time made me realize it was written by a pilot rather than a poet. "Strap on his wings, his ailerons to his ankles." It sounded as if Icarus had been about to fly to Paris against a headwind and needed to be reminded to stay above the railroad tracks so the passengers would not notice that the train was faster than the plane, as indeed it was in the early days.

"Lovely," I said when he was through. "I loved that." Then I tried once more to explain to him the purpose of my visit. The space station. The dosimeter. The institute. The adventure. I even quoted T. S. Eliot to him: "Old men ought to be explorers." He gazed at me from his private world, as at a child repeating the contents of a movie he had already seen.

Finally I took my leave. The chauffeur, who had been reading a paperback called *The Lust Pigs* while waiting, asked, "How did it go?"

"No luck this time," I said.

Only when we were well on our way back to The Hague did it occur to me that I had never discussed these visits with the chauffeur. He must be part of Miss Bastiaans' private FBI.

11

WHEN I ARRIVED at the hotel I found a message from Tex: *I expect you tomorrow at 1000 hours.*

I went. He was sitting in his wheelchair in his study, not in front of the TV set but behind his desk. "Okay," he said, without preamble. "Who else is on?"

I told him about my visit to Antwerp. He shrugged his shoulders. "Fons always was a bit of an airhead," he said. "Once he had survived the war, it was merely a matter of who caught him first to put him in a cage."

It sounded callous; there was no room for poetry in his warrior's soul. He was as single-minded as a Roman centurion, emissary of the Pax Romana, massacring barbarians. He approached the assignment of a platoon of dotards about to have their consciousness extracted and sent to the moon in the same way he had approached the raid on the U-boat pens of Saint-Nazaire fifty years earlier. "All right," he said, "I found out where Pjotr is: an old men's home near Paris, run by the French government. Probably as nutty as a coot, but that won't matter."

"Why not?"

"I read most of the stuff you gave me on OOBEs. There's a lot of hooey written about the subject, down to some hippie in California who wrote a manual on how to make love to your girlfriend out of the body. But it sounds a lot like deep-sea diving. Pjotr will be perfect. You know about his fish?"

I did indeed; it was one of the strangest stories we took from the war. In the Mediterranean, as Tex's commandos were hanging around in North Africa waiting for the invasion of the South of France in August '44, Pjotr Warszinsky, while fooling around underwater to stay in practice, had made the acquaintance of a grouper that was said to be as large as a Volkswagen, though that may have been partly due to the underwater distortion. The grouper fell in love with him, and he with the grouper; he called her "Louise." Every time he dived, there she was, waiting for him, awesome in size but playful as a kitten, following him everywhere he went, nuzzling him, playing tag; to see the two of them cavort under the sea had really been something to watch. After VE-Day, Pjotr—so the story went—had gone back to the Mediterranean looking for Louise. I never heard the outcome.

"Depends how nutty he is now," I said.

"All deep-sea divers are nutty. I mean, to them the underwater world makes sense, and you have to leave them to it. Judging from the books, the out-of-body world is a perfect fix for the deep-sea diver: a whole new ballgame to anyone else. In any event, have a look at him and see for yourself."

"Okay, I will. Anything else?"

"I'd like to propose a second man: The Amazing Dubonnet."

"Who is he?"

"A circus magician. Escaped to England in '43 via the underground. Some Army type sent him to me; for once they were on the money. He's the most inventive guy I ever met. When it came to decoys to fool the opposition, he was hard to beat. I owe him a success or two. Brilliant mind."

"What would we use him for?"

"After reading the books, I accept the premise, but to my mind the procedure is marred by hocus-pocus. Might be a good idea to have a master conjurer with us, somebody who would spot a con game at a glance. What's more—well, never mind."

"Where is the man now?"

"Still part of a circus, now near Orléans. You could catch both birds in one sortie."

I hadn't heard that word used since the war. He had changed since a few days ago: the anger was gone, he seemed younger, more like the Tex I had known: bright, decisive. He would be of enormous help to me.

"Okay, what else do you want me to do?" he asked.

"Come along with me to France, as my second. Where exactly is Pjotr living these days? Paris, you said."

"Someplace called Clamart, on the outskirts of Paris. In a government institute called Les Cicades."

"This is going to involve a lot of travel, Tex. Are you sure you're up to it?"

He smiled happily. "As long as you don't ask my wife."

12

I HAD TO. I found her hovering at the far end of the long corridor, wide-eyed with anxiety. "Can we sit down somewhere?" I asked. "I would like to talk to you."

We talked in the drawing room under the self-confident eyes of her younger self among the trophies. She listened with mounting dismay. Finally she said, "You can't do this! It will kill him!"

"It will bring him back to life. As a matter of fact, it has already done so. At this moment he is—"

"But he cannot survive outside these walls! You don't know him, not as he is now! He is very, very frail, a draft could kill him . . ."

I asked peaceably, "How old do you think I am? Don't you think you could leave the decision up to him?"

"He's not fit to judge his own condition! You have given him delusions of youth, of things being unchanged. They aren't. You're still in good health, you'll be able to get around. He could not possibly do this and survive. I—I will not allow it."

"What if you came along?"

That took her by surprise; in her eyes, the real aim of the

operation had been to take him away from her. Maybe it was. Maybe the one to be sprung from prison was not Pjotr, but Tex.

"No," she said, "I cannot accept that responsibility."

"What if we asked his doctor? Psychologically it would do him a world of good."

"You don't know what you're talking about," she said bitterly. "He hurled a paperweight at his doctor the last time. The poor man needed five stitches in his forehead."

"In this instance I think he would welcome a doctor."

For some reason she suddenly caved in, as if to a plumber who had given her an estimate she knew was too high but she was too tired to go on haggling. "I need help myself," she said finally. "I am told it is terminal. Leave everything as it is, please, until—until circumstances decide it for us." When I remained silent, she added, "Maybe it would take another woman to understand."

I had no answer, for the simple reason that at our age we were all terminal. But then, poor woman, she did not know the secret call of the sirens that, according to Tennyson, had lured Ulysses into passing the outer buoy once more, to lose and find himself in the infinity of the ocean.

"I'll ask the director of our program to come and see you, Mrs. van Texel," I said, getting up. "It's a woman."

An expression of deep alarm changed her face, for a brief moment. Then she said, "It will not make any difference. Any difference at all."

I took my leave. The chauffeur found the nearest telephone. I managed to get hold of Miss B. in her London club, where they accepted my collect call without demur. She told me not to budge but stay in my hotel. She would take the next plane and go to see Mrs. Van Texel that very same day.

13

SHE DID. I was baffled by the ease with which she flew from one country to another; to her it was like taking a taxi.

She went to see Mrs. van Texel with flowers; when we met in my hotel later, everything had been settled. After her husband was collected the next morning, Mrs. van Texel would leave for Switzerland and stay with her sister until further notice. She had virtually handed over the man.

It made me feel, surprisingly, as if I had helped destroy something fragile and precious to two old people, separating them at a crucial time of their lives. She picked up on it, as was her wont. "Don't be sentimental, Commodore. She was right, it needed a woman. In my book, I helped the old lady escape, not her bully of a husband. Are we going to have anything to drink or are you a teetotaler now as well as a missionary?"

I told her she was a heartless man trader, like old Kwel; she loved it. She ordered the usual, with the works. "Let's make this an early night," she said. "I have to leave at the crack of dawn. You look great, by the way."

"Thanks to you."

"And the angina?"

"Gone. How did you know?"

"When I first met Arnold Kwel he was your age, and his grandson was in the process of taking over the company. He was old, bad-tempered, had all the usual things wrong with him: a decrepit old man who had stayed in the business too long. It took me six months—less, four. Then he was ordering everyone around again, screwing the competition, taking on tows that would make anyone's hair stand on end, except his captains'."

"Thank you, I was there," I reminded her. "But what did you do with little Jim Kwel?"

She smiled. The Dutch gin came, in little iced glasses, delicious.

"Well?" I asked. "What *did* you do with him, or to him?"

She speared a sausage, as if that were the answer, raised her glass, and said, "Here's to eternal youth."

I raised mine. "To the distant shore."

"Don't be gloomy," she said. "First, we have work to do."

Ah, the Wrens in Dover. "The full formula is 'Don't be gloomy, darling,' " I said, loving her.

She picked up on that too. "Don't get any ideas, Commodore; you'd be heading for icy seas. Now, where were we? We have Commander van Texel, we are going to have Pjotr Warszinsky, if he is compos mentis; how about your henpecked pilot?"

"No go, I'm afraid. He's off on his own, like Icarus."

"Excuse me?"

"A poem," I said. "Not by Tennyson, this time; by Fons van Buren."

She looked as if this were not a recommendation. Later that night, the telephone rang in my hotel room. It was two o'clock in the morning.

"Commodore Harinxma?"

"This is he."

"You had better come and get him. I can't handle him any more."

"I'm afraid I don't understand, Miss Boeykens. What happened?"

"You destroyed him, that's what happened," the voice said dramatically. "His mind wanders, he is talking about the moon, rockets, somebody splitting his brain. He is totally out of control. He wants to leave. Do you hear me? *He wants to leave me!*"

"To go where?"

"To join you, you evil old man! What did you tell him to poison his mind?"

"Would you please turn this from an aria into a conversation? Tell me what happened."

There was silence, lasting so long I thought she had put the phone down. Then she said, in a normal voice, "He wants to join you in whatever you are up to. I cannot cope with this; I have my obligations, my schedule, I cannot break contracts just to talk some sense into his senile head. He's behaving like a child, he wants to go and play outside, with you and your gang of old rascals. Well, you're welcome to him. Come and collect him, or he'll climb out the window and start walking down the yellow brick road. If he doesn't break his neck."

"Miss Boeykens, I cannot do this, and you know it. This needs to be discussed—"

"My dear man, *I do not have the time*! Can't you get that into your poor fuzzy head? My days are programmed by forces beyond my control down to the last minute! I have just come from a recital in Nivelles, tomorrow at ten my car will pick me up for Luxembourg. Come and get him, take him off my hands!" This time she did put down the phone.

I called Miss B.'s room.

"Yes, Commodore?" It had taken a while before she answered; she must have been asleep too.

I told her.

"Well, well," she said, "you're leading a rebellion of henpecked husbands, it seems. What do you want me to do?"

"Okay his participation and pay for it."

"All right. Does he need a nurse?"

"Possibly."

"Well, that can be arranged. But first, let's see how he comes out the other end."

"Of what?"

"Of the rejuvenation process. You'd better pick him up in the morning."

"Will do." I put down the phone. A moment later it rang again.

"Harinxma?" The dramatic woman's voice asked.

"Miss Boeykens."

"He has locked himself in the bathroom, so you'd better

bring a locksmith with you. If you come after ten, the front-door key will be under the mat." She broke the connection.

Fons barricaded in the bathroom? Dear God, what had I done?

14

AS IT TURNED OUT, we did not need a locksmith: the next morning, the moment he heard the key in the door, Fons let us into the house. "Good morning," he said. "Come in, come in."

I did not quite know how to handle this situation; then the chauffeur, who had come along to help break down the door, said with calm common sense, "You gentlemen had better start packing."

There wasn't much to pack; Fons proved to have taken it all in yesterday, while I thought he wasn't listening, and packed his bags already. It was a different situation from that of Tex and his wife, but I felt the need to say, "Look, Fons, it's none of my business, but your wife . . ."

He smiled. "My wife likes to dramatize things. I have to humor her at times. You don't seriously believe I'm so senile that I make a habit of locking myself in the bathroom? This is the way she likes her marital conflicts: sword fights, deathbed arias."

"But she said on the telephone—"

"I can imagine. What she said to me was, 'Do as you wish, dear. If you want to go to America and dabble in the occult, that's fine with me. As long as someone else foots the bill.' She can be reasonable, despite the dramatics."

I looked at him as he stood there: an old, old man, only

partly of this world, gazing at me with a slightly puzzled smile, as if he were dreaming me. Wings and ailerons. War and lonely old ladies.

"We'll not be dabbling in the occult, Fons," I said. "I told you, it's a technical procedure invented by an engineer who has taken out a patent on it."

His smile broadened. "That's it," he said. "That's what interests me."

"What?"

"The technical part. It must be like flying."

"Ah?"

"At a certain amount of revs the kite starts to roll, at a certain speed it takes off—a technical triumph, after a billion years of evolution. We have as little business flying as a fish, and yet: look at us! I find it reasonable that the next step should be our minds taking off solo, without our bodies. Flying has been degraded, we are now using it to kill people. The next step! I can't wait! Blocks away, rev up—do you know how we felt, how I felt when I looked down for the first time from seven hundred feet upon the procession of ants of which I had been part? Love, hate, loneliness —all that was ant stuff; nothing down below applied up there, nothing. Nobody who hasn't been airborne himself in the early days of open cockpits can possibly know what it was like. The sense of beauty, the—the only time I've heard its equivalent on earth was when Elvira sang Richard Strauss's *Four Last Songs*. That's why I married her."

The driver coughed discreetly at the bottom of the stairs.

15

I REGISTERED HIM in my hotel in The Hague and phoned Miss Bastiaans, who was now back in London.

"All right," she said. "What's his condition?"

"Physical or mental?"

"Both."

"Mentally he seems not to be present where he is at all times, but I find that, even so, he takes in every word you say."

"All right, what is going to be his role in your crew? If this was a ship, what would you see him as?"

"The cook."

"Explain that to me."

"A ship's cook does not just prepare the food. Usually, he is not *cordon bleu,* rather the reverse. I have heard it said about one cook that his chicken à la king could cause blindness; if followed by his *banane flambée,* idiocy."

"All right, very funny. Now, would you like to come to the point?"

"The galley on board a small ship like a tugboat becomes, on long voyages, its village square. A meeting place, occasionally a confessional. The cook is always there, doling out coffee, advice, consolation. If the captain is the father, he is the mother of the crew. You'd be surprised at the intimate knowledge he has of every single man on board; not just factual knowledge but character knowledge. Every crew needs that: an always open ear, an eye for everyone's problems, a cool hand on the forehead, a human presence in the darkness of the midnight of the soul."

"You could talk a pack rat out of its hoard, Commodore. What about the physical aspect? Is Mr. van Buren likely to collapse at some time during the assignment? He sounds pretty delicate to me."

"To appear frail is the cook's secret. You tell him your problems in part to shore *him* up. It's a subtle process: confession to make the priest feel better."

"All right," she said with a sigh. "Now what about Mr. van Texel?"

"What about him?"

"He too seems pretty frail, and emotionally unstable."

"Miss Bastiaans," I said, my patience showing, "your client ordered World War II veterans. I presume they did not expect Olympic athletes?"

"No need to get touchy, Commodore. I know you are the commanding officer, and that the choice of crew is your privilege, but I'll have to defend it to my clients."

"During the war, Tex was violent, and emotionally unstable, if you consider a string of sixty curses, most of them obscene, a symptom of instability. But he did blow up the U-boat pens of Saint-Nazaire, an operation officially declared impossible by emotionally stable headquarters. So why don't we say, 'You do your job and I'll do mine,' and get on with it? We have a lot to do in a very short time."

"You're right," she said. "You're scheduled to sail a week from today, Southampton to Port Elizabeth, New Jersey."

"I understood we'd be flying?"

"It was decided otherwise. You'll sail by container ship, British, the *Atlantic Maiden*. Captain Alleyn-Smith."

"Doesn't leave me much time, does it?"

"America set the date."

"I'll see what I can do."

"Details like additional clothes, help with packing, etcetera, I leave to you. We'll take care of expenses, including medication."

"About our expedition to France, tomorrow—"

"I won't be able to join you for that. Who are you taking?"

"The chauffeur, Tex, and Fons. Pjotr needs Tex, and Tex needs Fons."

"Why?"

"To look after each other. Good for both."

"All right. You leave for Paris tomorrow. I'll tell the driver which hotel and join you there day after tomorrow. I'll be flying in from London. Go ahead and explore the situation, but don't decide anything until you have talked it over with me."

"What do you mean?"

"Didn't you tell me that Mr. Warszinsky is in a government institution for elderly men in Clamart? I don't want you to take him out of there before you've had a look at him and discussed it with me."

"Yes, you're right."

"Good," she said.

"So, Tex and Fons van Buren have been approved?"

There was a pause. "What would happen if I said no?"

"I'd walk."

"I say: yes. Now, about Orléans. I understand you want to vet a conjurer in a traveling circus?"

"This is Tex's idea. I'll let him do the vetting."

"I'd rather you did."

"I'll have the last word anyhow, Miss B. But I don't want to spook Tex on his first assignment."

"All right, Good night, and hats off. You are living up to expectations."

"Thank you, ma'am."

"You can call me Ellie."

It was a curveball; I fielded it. "I'm honored, but I am an old-fashioned man. I did not call Mr. Kwel 'Arnold,' either."

"Bullshit," she said, "but as you wish. Good night."

She certainly was one of the boys.

16

THE VOLKSWAGEN BUS, ordered to accommodate Tex's wheelchair, was a sturdy vehicle but rather noisy, which meant shouting. Also, its seats were rather utilitarian, certainly not designed for the elderly. As a result, the three of us were pretty well bushed by the time we arrived in Paris, after a five-hour drive. It became obvious we were all lone wolves indeed, who had spent the past years in the darkest corner of the forest; our minds might be at their best, our bodies were old and stumbled under the whip. By contrast, the Dutch driver was as fresh as a daisy when we got to the hotel, all set for dinner together.

He was disappointed. All three passengers passed out on their beds; Tex had to be undressed, Fons slid into what looked like a coma. I myself collapsed in my underwear, too tired to telephone Miss Bastiaans; I left that to the driver. She had the good sense not to telephone me herself.

The next morning, the two others were still down for the count; I took a taxi to Clamart. Pjotr's old men's home turned out to be a red brick edifice at the far end of a dead-end street lined with dilapidated storefronts. The mere sight of the place was depressing; once inside, gloom and hopelessness descended upon me.

There were a few old men shuffling about, none of them aware of my arrival, or anything else it seemed. There was a penetrating smell of urine. In an office with an antiquated safe and a roll-top desk sat a stern middle-aged woman who looked up as I entered.

I asked for *mon ami* Pjotr Warszinsky.

"What do you want with *him*?" she asked, in the voice typical of the French concierge.

"I'd like to visit him."

"Are you a relative?"

"We are—were—good friends."

"How long ago?"

"Oh, forty years or so."

She turned away and went on writing. "In that case you can save yourself the trouble, monsieur. He won't remember."

"Do you mind if I find that out for myself?"

After a silence in which she continued to write, she said, "I see no reason why. He won't remember. He does not remember, period. Goodbye, monsieur.

Well now. "I'm sorry, madame, but I insist. I am Commodore Martinus Harinxma, his old commanding officer." I put down on her ledger the business card Miss B. had had printed for me.

She looked at it as if it were a cockroach. Then she picked it up with a scowl, handed it back to me, and said, "Even if you were *le président de la République,* I'd tell you the same thing. I cannot allow him to be disturbed by questioning, or any other form of provocation that would cause him distress. *Au revoir, monsieur.*"

I took the coward's way out. "Thank you, madame, for your cooperation."

Back in the hotel, Tex was lurking in the lobby in his wheelchair with Fons in smiling attendance.

Tex listened to me the way he must have listened to dispirited reports by point men, then he said, "All right. The question is: Is the woman right? Is Pjotr beyond reach? The only way for us to find that out is to interview him in person. Has your Miss Bastiaans enough clout, here in France, to get away with it?"

"I don't understand what you have in mind."

"Kidnap him."

"How?"

"Surely, at a given moment the inmates are aired? Single him out, charge, whisk him away."

I was overcome by melancholy. He was sadly out of touch

with reality. This must have been the kind of operation in which he specialized: *single out, charge, whisk away*. But kidnapping a senile old man who could not remember? With the three of us as kidnappers? It sounded like a Marx Brothers movie.

"Interesting idea," Fons said cheerfully.

I said, "I'll take it up with Miss B."

Tex shook his head and gave me a look of contempt. "You and your tooth fairy. Can't you do anything off your own bat? You commanded ships once. What happened to you?"

"He grew old—like the rest of us," Fons said appeasingly.

"Speak for yourself!" Tex scoffed. "Okay, go call your sweetheart. Ask if it's all right with Sweetie Pie that we snatch Pjotr from the jaws of French bureaucracy. Big deal!"

"Will do," I said.

How can one honor the dead and those still alive who live in the past? Fifty years ago I had never thought I would come to care for Killer van Texel; now I felt the urge to put my arms around his frail shoulders and hug him and whisper, "Tex, you're terrific. Terrific!" I didn't. Maybe I should have.

Miss Bastiaans, when I got hold of her on the phone in London, listened without comment while I relayed to her Tex's insane plan. To my astonishment she said, "Good idea! Put everything on hold. At eight o'clock tonight I'll be in the bar of the hotel."

"Good for her," Tex said when I told him. "I have been thinking: this *does* need a woman. Okay, let's hit the bar, if they admit the over-eighties."

They did. Fons, who now shared a room with Tex and had quietly taken on the role of attendant to the cantankerous old bully, wheeled him in, then said he had to go and write his daily letter to Elvira. Despite the early hour, Tex proceeded to get drunk and aggressive, and had to be held down in his wheelchair when he wanted to hit the snotty barman in the snoot. I thought of calling Fons; this needed the view of a bird-man looking down on us ants from seven hundred feet up. When Tex went on yelling, I put my arms around his frail shoulders and said, "Hush, Tex, hush, you're terrific, but calm down now. You're terrific . . ."

He became still in my arms, looked up at me with the eyes of fifty years ago, and said, "You bastard, don't patronize me!"

All I could say was "Sorry."

Soon thereafter, Fons turned up for lunch. "I'd like a word with you," I whispered.

"I heard that," Tex said. "To hell with both of you."

Fons, in a radiant mood, said, "I'll take you up." Writing to his wife had a euphoric effect on him. "I'll be down presently."

"Oh, fuck off!" Tex snarled as I walked with them to the elevator. "I don't need you and your charity! And I don't need *you* either!" he yelled at a total stranger who joined them just before the doors closed.

When I came back, the occupants of the bar fell silent for a moment, in commiseration. Invalid brother? Handicapped old friend? Any man in a wheelchair was allowed to spit in fate's face. They sympathized briefly; then the hubbub of voices resumed.

After a while Fons joined me so unobtrusively that I would not have noticed his arrival but for the brief quiet that descended on the bar as he came in.

"Is he okay?" I asked.

"Oh yes," Fons said happily. "All tucked in and sputtering away. Never heard that before."

"What?"

" 'God's snot.' What are you having for lunch?"

"He should try poetry," I said.

Fons contemplated me with those airman's eyes. "You mustn't allow yourself to be upset. He still is what we all were once, that's his problem."

"You never were like that, Fons."

"Then what was I like, to you?"

"The same as you are now. Looking at the world from seven hundred feet up, with a love of ants."

Our lunch was a silent affair: Fons lost in his own thoughts over his *croque madame*; myself very, very tired. I had not recovered yet from yesterday's drive, and this morning's visit to the old men's home had not exactly cheered me. Again, I doubted the sanity of the whole expedition. It was all very well for men in their fifties, spoiled by the arrogance of command, to decide that old dotards in their eighties were the right fodder for Mr. Monroe's miracle machine; in reality, our physical and emotional resilience was so pathetically low that a seven-hour drive and a visit to a government institution for superfluous old men left us in tears. How happy I had been in my parrot's cage, writing tiny prose poems about lamplighters, cabin boys, celestial navigation, and how to wash oneself in one of those turn-down basins found in cabins on board freighters! None of those subjects had any substance for today's sailor, other than as historical curiosities. Yet that was my world, even if I was its last inhabitant. How fortunate I had been, safe in my little bungalow in the South of France, living in my own reality as on an island, with that charming Moroccan maid, A-hu'a-u'abi (or sounds to that effect), as my only visitor who arrived, and left, with her face covered by a veil, as if we were carrying on an illicit affair. The parrot's cage was Paradise Lost.

And look at the others! Poor old Fons, aged ninety or thereabouts by the looks of him, munching his toast as if his dentures were milling it, and grim old Tex in his wheelchair—both of them insecure and lost when released from their private prisons. Pjotr? I had not seen him yet, but the concierge had given me the clear and alarming picture of a gaga old man who had lost his memory. Some crew! And then a conjurer from a circus, also in his eighties, called The Amazing Dubonnet? Not to mention myself: Fancy That, cross-eyed old poet of the sea?

I contemplated handing in my resignation to Miss B., if indeed she did turn up tonight. I formulated in my mind the order of my arguments, starting with: too much of a change, too much mental, emotional, and physical effort. Exhausted, aching, confused—

"Birds are strange creatures," Fons mused.

"You're not kidding," I said.

This exchange should convince any unprejudiced observer of the lunacy of sending nutty, fragile old men to America to be trained for an out-of-body expedition to the moon.

17

MISS BASTIAANS did indeed arrive at eight sharp that evening. She walked into the bar exactly as I had seen her striding up my garden path: red-haired, blue-eyed, slender, modish; image of exquisite femininity. A touch too much, perhaps; she was garbed for action in the forties. Toque hat, boa, long gloves, the works.

Tex sat waiting for her with determined contempt. The sight of her clearly came as a shock; she must be the embodiment of all the Dover girls he had made love to as a youth daring death on the beaches of France. She shook his hand, pulled up a chair.

"Well," she said, after ordering a drink, "Pjotr. Rusty is in the process of finding out if he's a zombie. If not, if he is likely to be useful, Rusty will fix it with the French, no problem. You just stay on standby here in the hotel, while he takes care of it."

"What role do you have in mind for him in America, if he's okay?" asked Fons, who had joined us in his unobtrusive way.

"Well, the commodore said that an out-of-body experience is like deep-sea diving. Weightlessness, dusk, a different element—"

"But will he be able to memorize a set of coordinates?" Fons persisted. "Suppose his mind—or whatever—arrives on the moon, how do we know that he'll be able to recall what he is supposed to do there?"

"That's what Rusty is finding out."

"Suppose we take him," Fons went on. "What is to become of him when you are through with him?"

"I don't get the point." She sounded briefly thrown.

"He'll have no passport, no identification, no home. What—"

"I leave all that to Rusty," she said briskly. "That's *his* department. All I'm supposed to do is recruit him. If he is competent, that is."

"I see," Fons said.

She rose. "Well, I have a few phone calls to make. Let's meet again for dinner. Nine o'clock in the restaurant. See you then." She left, followed by male gazes, archetype from our collective past. The one thing lacking was a cigarette between her gloved fingers as she walked out of the bar. In the background, one of the big bands would have been playing "No, Don't Say No," mellow with muted brass. The hiss of soda water squirting into glasses. The rattle of a cocktail shaker. The memory had a total reality, brief and fleeting: the past was alive, here, now, sliding along with us like the shadow of an airplane across the landscape.

"Where are you off to?" Tex asked when I got up.

"Back presently." I walked off, to the elevators.

She must be psychic, for when I knocked on the door of her suite, wondering if she was in a condition to receive visitors, she called, "Come in, Commodore!"

It was a sumptuous suite, aggressively luxurious, but as uncozy as an expensive surgeon's waiting room. "Sit down," she called from somewhere. "Be with you in a minute."

She appeared dressed in a sort of caftan, her hair pinned up. "Drink?" She walked over to a table with bottles, glasses, and an ice bucket.

"No thanks," I said, "not for the moment."

She poured herself a stiff one, sat down in the easy chair opposite mine, and said, "All right. Out with it."

If she was that knowledgeable, I might as well make it short. "I'm afraid I'll have to back off," I said.

She took a sip. "Tell me why."

I did tell her, exactly as I had planned during lunch. Too much of a change. Too much mental, emotional, and physical effort. Exhausted, aching, confused.

She listened, and drank.

"And then, Tex turns out to be quite a handful, more than I can cope with. And poor Fons, I'm afraid, is lost in the no-man's-land between memories and dreams. All he said during lunch was 'Birds are strange creatures . . .' "

She finished her drink.

"That's about it," I said.

"In short, you have decided to give in to old age after all," she said calmly.

"At eighty-two I had better, I now realize."

"All right." She put down her glass. "Let me rephrase that for you: after a tiring drive and an upsetting visit to an old men's home, you have given up on the rare adventure offered to you, to tackle a task that no one else—I repeat: *no one else*—could possibly fulfill, for which you are uniquely suited."

"Come on, Miss B.! Let's be honest—"

"If I'm anything, at this moment, Commodore, it's honest. There you were, locked away in your little bungalow, mourning the death of your wife, preparing, if not wishing, to join her, writing little memoirs while waiting. In comes a woman from your professional past, who offers you a professional assignment: to take command of a platoon of elderly veterans and tackle the greatest adventure any man of your or any other generation could be offered: to explore—"

"Miss Bastiaans," I said, "there's no need to sell it to me all over again. If I were sixty, even seventy years old—"

"You would have been no good to me. This assignment calls for a man your age."

"I not only doubt that, I think it's balderdash. Each of us three is too damn old to stand the strain and stress of all this. We ludicrously underestimated our limitations."

"All right," she said. "let's approach the facts from another angle: you turn down the assignment because of fatigue, and instead you agree to let your daughter take over your life."

"Nonsense. All that needs is for me to say no."

"Will you?" She smiled.

"I'll decide that when the time comes."

"Commodore . . ." she leaned over and put her hand on my knee. Her eyes were blue and close. For the first time I saw the wrinkles around them. But there was something about her, a power, an emanation, that made me vulnerable to what she was about to say. I knew what she was about to say.

"You know you are *not* going to say no, Commodore. You are making the wrong decision. You'll get over your exhaustion, you'll conquer your uncertainty, which is simply a captain's self-doubt before any new voyage."

"Nonsense. I never had that problem."

"Don't lie, Commodore. Don't fight the truth that stares you in the face: you are choosing death over life, because life is too much of a challenge. Totally legitimate, but the wrong choice, for *you*. We all, certainly I myself, accept your physical limitations and are prepared to adapt to them. But you refuse to accept that you are ideally suited for the task ahead. Have a good night's rest. Take the day off tomorrow. Go to the Louvre. If we were in Rome, I'd suggest you go and look up at the ceiling of the Sistine Chapel."

I looked at her huge blue eyes, the wrinkles.

"Miss Bastiaans, the truth staring me in the face is *you*. Compared to you, my daughter is a pussycat."

She smiled. She had the most beguiling smile. "Good," she said. "Consider yourself seduced. But not by me, by your own better sense. You know as well as I do that you are going to do it. I am glad, and honored, that I'm the one to whom you confide your doubt and uncertainty."

"I confided to you my resignation," I said.

She said, "Balls!" and let go of my knee. "Drink?" She rose and headed for the table with the bottles.

God knows how, but she had done it again. "All right," I said, "Bols it is."

18

PJOTR'S "RELEASE" had been okayed by head-quarters, we heard from Miss Bastiaans when we convened for dinner. A French-speaking woman sergeant would do the talking; the men were a commando and a French policeman. It seemed a lot of hoo-ha for one old hobo, which Pjotr appeared to have become, but it was Rusty's contribution to Operation Soul Flight, the code name our assignment had been given for administrative reasons. Tex thought the whole thing extremely funny. *"Female Sergeant Soul Flight.* Wish I'd had *her* in my bump-and-tinkle set to distract the Jerries!"

"Be that as it may," Miss Bastiaans said, "after his arrival, we'll convene in my suite here for debriefing. The real obstacle may turn out to be Pjotr himself. If he is as confused as Rusty seems to think, he might panic at the sight of an unknown woman advancing on him crying *'Oncle!'* Even if he were not."

"If everything else fails," Tex said, "we can always send his fish."

He was given a mortifying look by Miss Bastiaans which

failed to impress him. "Don't be gloomy, darling," he said. For-
tunately, she knew now where that came from. She was learning
fast; the bells of hell go tingalingaling.

"First of all, we'll have to find out for ourselves if he is fit to
take part in the experiment," she stated.

"What will be the deciding factor for his being turned
down?" Tex asked. "Incontinence? Rambling? Singing dirty Polish songs?"

"Tex," I said warningly, as I saw Miss Bastiaans' face freeze.

"I mean it! All he's expected to do is stretch out on a waterbed in the dark with earphones on his head, to have his spook,
or whatever, detached from his body. Does he have to be continent for that? Or even compos mentis? That man has the courage
of a lion. The rest, we'll take care of—'we' being the rest of the
crew."

"I must confess—" Miss Bastiaans started.

"What if he has a pet?" Fons asked from his own world.

"In an old men's home?" Tex said scathingly. "All he's likely
to have is a spider."

"Anything else, Commander van Texel?" Miss Bastiaans
asked.

Tex blew her a kiss. The ancient miracle was taking place: a
crew was being born, more exclusive than a family. She would
never be part of it; she was head of operations for the owners: a
bunch of Americans rich enough to keep our feet from touching
the ground and powerful enough to arrange for the release of a
Polish deep-sea diver in his eighties from a French government
warehouse for confused old men.

I explained it to her later, when we were alone. Oldtimers of
the fleet had told me, when I was young, how Mr. Kwel had tried
to hobnob with his crews and was given the cold shoulder.

"But why?" she asked, not understanding. "Does a crew
form by exclusion? By putting up a united front against the owners and their representatives, who are more involved in getting all
of this together than they are themselves?"

"There is always the master," I said. "He's the man in the

middle. Soon they won't admit me either, at least not to the galley where they convene. The bridge can be a lonely place too, you know."

"Well," she said, "that makes two of us."

"Hmm. Perhaps we should hoist the flag-signal 'L.B.' "

"Meaning what?"

" 'Let us stay together for mutual support.' It was the motto of the Atlantic convoys."

"Did they object to my presence at dinner?"

"A restaurant is not a mess room."

"So I was welcome?"

"More than that. An honored guest."

"Hell," she said, "who needs that?"

"They do."

She looked at me with a melancholy I could not fathom.

19

THE AFTERNOON of the operation we gathered in the lobby of the hotel: Miss Bastiaans, Tex, Fons, and myself. Pjotr's release had been set for 1600 hours, when inmates of the institution were free to receive visitors. It seemed few of them ever did.

At 1625 two taxis drew up in front of the hotel. Out of the first came a stern, middle-aged woman with a butch haircut, followed by a man who startled by his size: he emerged slowly, there seemed to be no end to the limbs. The woman and the man approached the main doors and indicated to the outdoor staff that the other taxi should remain as it was, where it was, no eager opening of the doors.

Miss Bastiaans looked frail in her slim elegance compared to the two military bureaucrats who shook her hand with wincing force. Neither I nor the others were introduced; this was brass time. She received a terse report, signed a chit presented to her, and nodded her approval to some suggestion; the two marched out and went to open the second taxi. Out came a French policeman leading a middle-aged man of jolly mien and jaunty movement. Tex muttered, "My God! They got the wrong one!"

The man was escorted in; at the sight of us, he grinned and cried, "Hi there, Tex! How've you been, Fancy? And you must be Fons. Nice to see you!" He shook us all by the hand; his face turned out to be old at close quarters. Then he headed for Miss Bastiaans, who was talking to the policeman. "You must be Ellie, right? How do you do?"

"Who *is* this?" Fons whispered, nonplussed.

"Pjotr," Tex answered. "Ten years younger than either of us."

"But how—"

Miss Bastiaans and the man headed for the elevator. When we pushed Tex's chair along to join them, the policeman held us back. "Let them go first," he said, in French.

"Are you with the Opéra Comique?" Tex asked.

The policeman frowned.

"I am Commander van Texel, this is Commodore Harinxma, and this Group Captain van Buren. Get us an elevator, son."

He did. I would have too. Despite his wheelchair, Tex packed so much authority that the policeman even held the doors open as we pushed the wheelchair through. Just before the doors closed the man almost saluted, but managed to suppress the gesture in the nick of time.

"Bloody folderol," Tex said. "They carry on as if they had kidnapped General de Gaulle."

"How is it possible?" Fons asked. "Are you sure this is our man?"

"I'm having a problem there too," I confessed.

"They must have been feeding him hormones," Tex said. "He looks exactly the same as when we went to take out those U-boat pens; just as loony. But guts? He planted the limpet mines while we took care of distracting the Jerries, and then he had to swim all the way back to the submarine. God knows how he did it; he must be part fish himself."

The elevator arrived on the fifth floor. We wheeled Tex to the door of Miss Bastiaans' suite. It stood ajar; I knocked.

"Come in!"

We went in. Pjotr was leaning on the bar, holding a tall glass with ice and what must be vodka. He said, grinning, "Sorry to have kept you waiting. When the woman turned up to take me out on the town, I had to get dressed first. I was in my pajamas. Now—what is this all about? The woman told me, but I didn't take it all in. You're planning a commando operation?"

"Fancy, you'd better explain," Fons said. "You're supposed to be running this thing."

"Good to see you," Pjotr said, turning to me. "You don't look a day older, Captain."

"I should be so lucky," I said. "I'm eighty-two."

"Well, so must I be, but no one has been able to find my records. My French identity card says I'm seventy. Tell me— what's going on? I started to test the woman by reciting '*Se le h'm de mon amie n'était pas si petit-petit,*' but no dice. It would have made things easier if you had given her the password."

"Sorry about that," I said.

"Okay, I'm here. Seen *this?*" He pulled up his right trouser leg to show us one of those plastic bracelets they give patients in hospitals, only heavier. "It's electronic," he said. "At twenty-one hundred hours they'll start to trace the signal. Can I use your head, Ellie?"

"Head?"

"The bathroom," I translated.

She opened the sliding doors to her bedroom and took him there. When she came back she said, "I'm afraid I may have to take him back. I have read his record; he suffers from senile dementia; his mind is stuck in '44. I suppose he thinks he is wanted for a demolition job."

"There but for the grace of God," said Fons.

"We'll have a meal, then I'll take him back." She sounded tough and determined. Too tough.

Pjotr came back, rubbing his hands. "I hope you don't mind my rummaging in your toilet bag for a pair of scissors, Ellie. It was on the counter."

"What did you want those for?" Miss Bastiaans asked, frowning.

He stretched out his right leg, pulled up the trouser leg, and grinned. The electronic bracelet was gone. "I flushed it down the toilet." He beamed with satisfaction. "Now, if they want to find me, they'll have to go down into the sewers of Paris. Well, what's up, you men? What do you want me to do? I may need a refresher course, but, like biking or skating, it's a skill you never forget."

"It's not a demolition job this time, Pjotr," Tex said with unexpected gentleness. "It's more subtle than that."

"Ah? I'm dying to hear." He crossed himself. "Figuratively speaking."

With an edge to her voice, Miss Bastiaans said, "Before this goes any further, I want to have a brief talk with you gentlemen in private." She took the bewildered Pjotr by the arm and went to open the sliding doors to her bedroom again. "If you don't mind, wait in here for a few minutes. There are magazines. We won't be long."

Pjotr seemed about to dig in his heels, but I said pleasantly, "She's with headquarters, Pjotr. She wants to pass on something for our ears only."

"But—but aren't I part of this outfit now?" he asked suspiciously.

"You will be, but there's obviously some matter that has to be dealt with first, in private. After that, no more secrets, old boy."

Pjotr allowed himself to be shepherded back into the bedroom. She closed the doors on him and turned around, ready
for battle.

What she got must have come as a surprise to her, although
she never flinched. Tex gave her a piece of his mind, no punches
pulled. We were not sold into slavery to her sponsors. We were
free agents who had accepted to do a job and agreed that Fancy
would be in command. We, the participants in this cuckooland
scheme, were the ones to decide if we wanted Pjotr on our team
or not. The choice was up to us; we would be responsible for him.
If she or Rustbucket or whatever the man's name was decided to
make that a problem, she could take us all straight back to where
we came from. He, for one, was damned if he would accept high-
handed dictates from some invisible Mafia; we were a team of
wartime experts who had earned gongs for doing a professional
job under the worst circumstances at the risk of their lives. So
take it or leave it, lady.

It had been in the best Patton tradition, but if it had shaken
her, she did not show it. "In that case, would you please tell me
exactly what you have in mind for this man to *do*?"

Tex took a deep breath before pulling out a few more stops:
it was time I took over.

"Don't worry, Miss Bastiaans. It's simply that Pjotr must at
least be given a chance to show if he's up to this. The plan would
be for Tex and Fons to take him with them when they go to the
circus to interview that conjurer. He'll be safe there, and Tex and
Fons will put him through some tests and questioning and find
out just what he's capable of. They'll soon know if he is up to
this. I'm happy to leave it to them—and so should you be."

Before she was able to respond, the doors to the bedroom
slid open and Pjotr appeared, with painted lips, wearing her feath-
ered toque and her boa around his neck. He gave a coy little wave
and chortled, "Yoo-hoo!" He was wearing the black evening
gloves as well.

Poor Miss Bastiaans: despite her dress and language of the

period, even the perfume of the forties, she could not possibly fit in with the undergraduate humor of Spitfire pilots and officers of the invasion fleet. All of us had, sick with secret fear, cocked a snook at death and its stingalingaling by engaging in nauseating practical jokes. She was dealing with the last survivors of D-Day, who now resumed the old private jokes and catch phrases, because, this time, whatever way you looked at it, our number was up.

"Good show, old chap," I said to Pjotr. "But what we really want to see is the lingerie."

"I'll take a rain check," Miss Bastiaans said, and fled.

20

I CAUGHT UP with her in the bar, sat down on the stool next to her, and replied to the barman's raised eyebrows with "The same, please."

"It would seem I have bitten off more than I can chew," she said, without looking at me.

My glass was put in front of me; I waited for the fizz to die down. "Don't be sidetracked by the bathroom humor and the juvenile carryings-on, Miss B. I'll explain them to you one day."

"Okay," she said, raising her glass. "Here's to that day." She took a sip, turned to face me. "Just for your information, your Pjotr *is* senile. Official medical diagnosis."

I thought about it. "Well, perhaps he is still living in the forties, but, then, that was when he was at his dazzling best. When it comes to executing the operation, he may out-dazzle us all."

"You are not having me on, are you, Commodore?"

"You are dealing with a man living in a world that is no more. The jokes are a part of it, so are the fears. Why not the courage and the brilliance? But leave it to Tex and Fons—they'll soon know if he is up to it."

We drank in silence. Then she said, "I'm beginning to wonder about my motives in all this." She shoved her glass across to the bartender. "Same again," she said, almost defiantly.

"Tell me about your motives."

She waited for her drink, took a first swallow. "I accepted this assignment because I'm turned on by old men. As long as they are intelligent, wise, and have authority. How's that for a motive?"

I said, "Don't let's play games, Miss B. You're in this because you were lonely, and about to slide into depression. You'll get over it, the same way I did."

"Depression? Why should I be depressed?"

"Because our world is gone, presumably forever. I mean: the world we shared."

She smiled. "Ah, the tugboats. Well, we'll have to find another one, won't we?" She raised her glass. "Here's to Holland's Glory. May they rest in peace."

We drank in silence, with a brief, agonizing sense of loss. She had been so good at her job, so unique, so dazzling. Well, so had I, without the dazzle. "Farewell to all that," I said.

We shared another toast. Then she asked, "What do I hear about your taking the same plane to London as I tomorrow?"

"I was planning to interview a Group Captain Harrison. He lives in a village called Nether Wallop, he's the last on my list. Then there are a few other things I want to do before we leave for America."

"Who is *he*?"

"A flamboyant Air/Sea Rescue type. He picked us out of the drink on D-Day-plus-three, after my old W-boat hit a mine off the Normandy coast. Came soaring down in a Sunderland and collected all of us under enemy fire, even salvaged the ship's cat."

"What's a Sunderland?"

"A seaplane. Was."

She opened her purse and took out a notebook. "Give me his name again."

I did.

"Address?"

She finished her notes, put the little book back in her purse, snapped it shut, and said, pushing herself away from the counter, "Well, the early plane leaves at seven, that means wake-up call at four-thirty. Meet you in the lobby."

"Right," I said.

She signed the bill for the barman while I stood idly by her. Surprising, how quickly you get used to being a kept man.

Late that night I was wakened by the telephone beeping on the bedside table. "I had him checked out," her voice said, factually. "Group Captain Harrison is blind, deaf, and, according to my informant, mad as a hatter. He needs a guide dog, has a piece of garden-hose-with-funnel for a hearing aid, is incontinent, and has to be put to bed each night by the district nurse. So, without wanting to intrude on your territory, I suggest you scratch him."

"That's too bad, he seemed ideal. But you're right. Even so, I'd like to join you tomorrow morning. I have some other business in England that I need to deal with."

"Could you be more specific?"

There was a short pause, then I said, "I intend to say good-bye to my daughter in Exeter and visit her mother's grave with her. Sylvia died in England a year ago tomorrow."

"I see."

"I also want to have a look at a residential home Helen has picked out for me. Mainly for her sake; you and I were pretty rough on her that day in Beaulieu. I want to make up for that. I'll pay my own way, of course."

It was her turn to pause. "Are you sure about this?"

"Excuse me?"

"Don't you think you'd better take it easy now while you

have the chance? You've done a remarkable job so far, but you *are* eighty-two."

Impossible woman! At the first sign of my daughter reentering the picture she goes into action. "Miss Bastiaans," I said, "I am at your beck and call, but I must insist you leave me the rudiments of a private life."

"At least let me offer you the limousine and book the hotel for you."

I might have accepted all this a few minutes earlier, but by now she irritated me beyond measure. "Miss Bastiaans, when I say I'll foot the bill this time, that is what I intend to do. I'll take the train to Exeter, just like anyone else, and my daughter will meet me. I can be back for a luncheon appointment in two days' time, if you wish to see me in London."

Another pause. "Very well, Commodore. Suit yourself."

I was about to put down the phone when she said, "The best hotel in Exeter is the White Hart. There will be a room there for you if you need it. As for the limousine—"

"Thank you, Miss Bastiaans. I'll take the train." This time I did put down the phone and lay there fuming until I arrived at a gratifying conclusion. I would roll this whole syndrome of Miss Bastiaans and her ilk into a little ball, drop it in the cookie tin, and write an essay on the effect of overbearing females on male crews about to leave for long voyages. Smiling, I fell asleep.

2 I

SHE AND I were whisked to the airport at an ungodly hour the next morning in a local taxi, in silence. I was careful to buy my own ticket for London, which meant that she traveled first class and I economy. It gave me a crazy satisfaction, like sticking your tongue out at teacher. My seat was damned uncomfortable, but everything has its price.

At Heathrow I went through the baggage claim and customs unaided, aggravated my arthritic shoulder by lugging my bag, but what the hell? Independence was a heady brew. I did not catch sight of her at all, she had disappeared in the world of the airport.

When I finally joined the queue for taxis, I was whacked. The wait took forever, and in the end I had to share one with a very large woman wearing one of those hats with false fruit that are the dream of old horses, not to eat but to wear. She told me all about her intestinal disarray on the way to Paddington Station. When we finally arrived, I wished her well with her surgery; she replied stiffly, "That's all behind me, sir."

I said, "Oh yes, of course! Good luck all the same!"

The long journey to Exeter brought home to me that I had not traveled by train in a long time. I should have treated myself to a first-class ticket; the second class was stuffed to the gills, people were standing in the aisles. Making room for the elderly was no longer in vogue; I had to stand, suspended from a strap, as far as Salisbury. I nabbed the first available seat; then an older woman, be it younger than I, stood beside me in the new crowd. Well, you are what you were made into as a young man: I got up and gave her my seat. So, off again, dangling from a strap; I should have accepted the damn limousine. I should have accepted the hotel. I should—at least I got my seat back at Taunton.

At Exeter St. Davids I was beat, and delighted to see Helen waiting on the platform. But once I got out, heaving my old bag after me, I saw that she was not alone. I was welcomed by three grandchildren, the pompous professor himself, and a dog that kept up a hysterical struggle to escape from its leash. There were kisses and hugs and fending off of canine enthusiasm; as I did so I momentarily lost my balance. Luckily, eager hands caught me and set me upright again. Not a promising beginning.

I would have liked to lie down for a while, but the cemetery was closing, said Helen. With our escort watching from a distance, we went to Sylvia's grave.

Arm in arm, we stared down at the gray tombstone. There was total silence within me, an emptiness not to be described. They say it gets easier with the passage of time. Maybe it does, but not when you stand, arm in arm with her daughter, at the foot of the awful slab with her name in the featureless row of the dead.

I was overcome by the urge to join her, to have done with all this. Then Helen turned to face me, and kissed me, and we cried together for a while, her slender body pressed against mine, her hair touching my face.

"Love," I said, "oh, love."

She looked at me with her mother's eyes and said, "I love you too, Dad. *Do* stay with us for—for—"

"We'll talk about it," I said.

After a last look at the awful slab, we slowly walked away, exhausted.

We rejoined the others, were loaded into the station wagon, and, with the dog breathing hot air down my neck, drove to the professor's house.

22

GERBILS, KITTENS; when I went to the bathroom I missed the target because of a sudden *croak* by my side. There was a terrarium in the bath, and in it a frog trying to escape. I spoke to the frog, said, "Now don't do that again!" and wondered if she had booked a room in the hotel for me after all. No harm in finding out.

While the family was involved in an interchange between generations one floor below, I sneaked into the marital bedroom, checked the telephone book, and dialed the number. Yes, there was a room reserved for Commodore Harinxma; would he be arriving in time for dinner? I said, "No, no, thank you," and went down to meet my fate.

Fate it was. Instead of a peaceful cocktail hour and a snort or two with my feet up, I was told that Mrs. Williams was waiting for us at Golden Evenings to show me, and whoever else wished to come, the little apartment they were holding for me.

I did not have the sense to postpone it until the next morning. Feeling the symptoms of imminent collapse, I climbed back into the bloody station wagon and there we went, five strong, to have a look at Opa's future. It was too damn much; it seemed just minutes ago that Helen and I had turned away from the grave with swollen eyes and red noses, and now here we were—

The less said about it all, the better. It was not only exactly as I had imagined, it was worse. Mrs. Williams, the administrator, was a Siamese twin of the concierge in Pjotr's institution for confused old men. The little apartment had aspects of a humane cage for elderly orangutans: everywhere you looked there were pulleys for alarm bells, stainless steel hold-bars screwed to the wall, peep-holes for the keepers . . .

Helen loved it. I got the impression she would have liked to be locked up in there herself. What a relief! No more pompous husband, no teenagers, no doggies, pussies, parrots . . . She looked around her like Alice in Wonderland, poor soul. I kept up my show of sincere interest, even more so when Mrs. Williams, her eyes those of a funeral director viewing a corpse, quoted the price of the humane cage in Green Evenings—enough to set up a mistress in an apartment in town, furs and jewels included.

By the time we got back to the house, I was fit to be hospital-ized. My so-called rejuvenation had been a drunken dream; I was back where I had been before Miss Bastiaans turned up at my door. Worse; I had palpitations, shortness of breath, pain in the chest, and a splitting headache. I survived the meal, but after that, I told Helen I had a room at the White Hart because I had to leave early the next morning for London, for a conference. She was terribly disappointed and not a little suspicious; she asked if Miss Bastiaans was going to be there, at which I rolled up my eyes and went through the protestations of an adulterous husband.

The room was pleasant, quiet, and welcome, but by the time Helen finally left I just staggered to the bed and flaked out. Normally this would have done it. On previous occasions a lie-down had solved the problem. But not this time. As I lay there, exhausted, the terror mounted. In the end, I sat up, pulled out my wallet with trembling hands, leafed through the bills, banknotes, a last will addressed to a doctor in case I was found unconscious in the street, and ultimately found Miss Bastiaans' emergency card. I dialed the number where she could be reached at all times, day or night; a male voice answered, then, "Okay. Hang in there, she'll call you." I had no idea who it was, maybe her lover.

I lay there gasping, staring at the ceiling, sticking Nitrabid pills under my tongue, but they kept getting lost under my dentures. Then I was overcome by the urgent need to use the bathroom, and there, squatting like an elephant in extremis, I heard the telephone ring. It sounded close by. I discovered there was one right next to me. I grabbed it and said, "I'm in the bathroom!"

"I guessed you would be, one way or the other," her laconic voice stated.

Before I had an opportunity to work that out, she said, "Is your door locked?"

"I have not the faintest idea. Why?"

"Because I'll be there in a few minutes."

"A few—?" I heard the phone being put down at the other end. Minutes?

I was in the process of zipping up when there was a knock on the door. I staggered out, opened it, headed straight back for

the bed, and crashed. The door closed, there was a discreet tinkling which sounded familiar; after I had opened my eyes and
managed to focus, it turned out to be ice in a tall glass.

"Here," she said, handing it to me. "Normally you shouldn't
drink this stuff in your present condition, but under the circumstances I think it's the answer. Cheers!" She lifted hers. It was as
if she had just dropped by for a casual visit. Where the hell had
she come from, I asked her.

"I have a room here in the hotel."

"You mean—you were *here* all the time?"

"Sure. Only, I took the sensible means of transportation and
came by limousine. How are you? How's the stingalingaling?"

I felt like weeping. Hamming it up a little, just a shade, I
said, "I met my moment of truth today. I think you had better
find another centenarian for the assignment: I'd drop dead on the
floor even before we were within sight of Mr. Monroe and his
machine."

"Commodore," she said calmly, "I tried to warn you, but
you had to find out for yourself. Believe me, I know the syndrome, intimately. For you to travel second class, and then to
expose yourself to a busy private household after a harrowing
visit to the cemetery, was taking unnecessary risks. You must
understand that your rejuvenation holds good only as long as you
are professionally involved. You can handle any crisis with your
crew, or with the assignment, but the moment you venture into
the realm of old grandfathers, you collapse. It's as simple as that.
Why didn't you trust me? I'm an expert, you know."

"You're telling *me*," I grunted.

"So, tomorrow we go back to London in the limousine. I
have booked—"

"Miss Bastiaans," I croaked, "I appreciate your concern, but
this time—"

"This time, Commodore, you've had a warning that you
should not ignore. You must have felt worse than you ever felt
before. True or false?"

I grunted.

"The secret of returning to active life at your age is that you must have the good sense to pace yourself. Have *some* sense, for God's sake."

"Miss Bastiaans," I said—then I was overcome by a terrible wave of tiredness. It was not terror, not shot through with the lightning of approaching death. It was homesickness for Sylvia. I did not *want* another woman stroking my hair, not want—

At that point I must have fallen asleep.

23

THE NEXT MORNING I was as good as new. She and I had breakfast together in the dining room; she had her briefcase with her and took out a sheaf of typed papers. Not a word about what had happened the night before.

"I have here your instructions for the crossing," she said, "by which I mean a list of activities, a list of subjects to study—you'll find study materials in your cabin—and so on. There will be a physician, an older man, ex–ship's doctor, to keep an eye on you gentlemen during the ten days to Port Elizabeth."

"You are not coming with us?"

"I'm afraid not. I have other irons in the fire, you might say." She handed me the typewritten sheets one by one, and for a moment it was as if I had never been away. We were on board one of KITCO's tugs ready to sail, and there she was at the very last moment with a sheet of instructions that made you wish you had joined the circus instead. But it was all well thought through, complete, and in a sense reassuring. "Full program," I said, using the tea to wash down my pills.

"Commodore—" she suddenly put her hand on mine.

"Don't spend your energy upholding an adolescent independence. Remember Arnold Kwel, he was—"

"Ninety years old, in a wheelchair, with glass eyes and cloth ears, and you were the puppeteer—"

That was the moment Helen came in. She made straight for me, said, "Dad?" and then realized I was not alone. Her mouth tightened. "Excuse me," she said, turned, and stalked out. This time I did not go after her. This was becoming ridiculous. I would telephone her later.

Miss Bastiaans said, as if she had not noticed, "I took the liberty to arrange the packing for you, as time is getting short. I told them to look out for a tin box marked 'Ye Olde Dutch Windmill Cookies.' They will also pack the exercise books it was sitting on."

I was impressed. "It would have been nice if you could come along for the crossing. I would love to read you some more."

"The time will come," she said. "Once we are in the States. Now"—she put down her napkin and rose—"I think I should try to have a word with your daughter. Do you need to go up to your room? We'll leave in an hour or so."

"But how are you going to find her? She may be—"

"I'll find her," she said. "See you anon." And there she went, pulling a wake of admiring glances.

I hung around in my room and then in the lobby, reading idiotic magazines like *The Staghunter* and *Seventeen,* for over two hours. Finally she came back, looking as if something had been settled. "Right," she said. "She's waiting in the tearoom across the road, to have a cup of coffee with you before you leave."

"How did it go?"

She smiled at me, just as she used to smile before leaving the ship with her briefcase. "All's well," she said. "Go and see for yourself. She's a nice child."

Child—? I had forgotten how old she was.

24

I T W A S a silly meeting. The whole situation was silly. To bring our relationship into line with reality would have taken hours; in fact, it was impossible. It would have meant my owning up that I was not about to enroll in Golden Evenings, that I would go crazy with her family and its animals as a regular stopover, that I considered her husband a crashing bore with the marital pretensions of a desert sheik, and those teenagers—well, never mind. We did not touch on any of that. She acted heroically, accepting the late-winter infatuation of an old man, and referred to Miss Bastiaans as "the lady." Her sad, lined young face expressed total misunderstanding: her own father, going with her to visit her mother's grave on the first anniversary of her death, meanwhile hiding from the family that he had that floozy waiting for him in a hotel room nearby, spending the night with her doing God knows what—what *do* men in their eighties do?—and then being found in flagrante the next morning at breakfast—her own *father*—

It was all so hopeless. Miss B. had obviously talked her into seeing me again, but had only reinforced her suspicions by the very fact of making the arrangement on my behalf.

I tried to make emotional contact with her by taking her hand; but the way she looked at me made it clear that, superimposed on everything at all times, she saw a dirty French postcard.

It was sad, and stupid, and would have been tragic had it not been so ludicrously silly. Our kaffeeklatsch ended with my saying, "By the way: I hope you aren't assuming that Miss Bastiaans and I are having an affair?" at which she cried, "Dad! Whatever gave you *that* idea?" If it had been a tryout for an amateur theater show, she would have got the role of curtain puller.

On the way out of town I told Miss Bastiaans I would need to have another conversation with my daughter, before leaving for the States. She suggested I do so by telephone from Holland; now we had to get to Heathrow and catch the Amsterdam plane; I had to meet the doctor and okay him later that day.

I met the doctor that afternoon in the hotel. I had little time for him, and after five minutes I decided I had no time for him at all. He was pompous, condescending, and would have imposed himself totally had I not been back on the bridge. With that character on hand, the crossing would have been like a traveling ambulance with five patients. I informed Miss Bastiaans by telephone that I had nixed the doctor; when she started to protest, I said, in a moment of inspiration, "How about Bosun Schoonmaker?"

"Bosun who?"

"That big hearty fellow I had on board the *Isabel*."

"But he's not a medical man, Commodore!"

"Miss Bastiaans, Bosun Schoonmaker is far more experienced in the moods, ailments, and idiosyncrasies of aging males than your doctor friend. I know him, he'll be worth his weight in gold, and if anybody starts to kick the bucket out there, I assume medical help will be available. Now—"

"Yes, but—" she started.

"No 'yes but.' Either I organize my own crew or you find yourself somebody else. Good night." I slammed the phone down and sat waiting for her to ring back. She didn't.

25

IT TOOK ME some time to run down Bosun Schoonmaker. He lived in a boardinghouse near Amsterdam, was retired now, and had something to do with selling fish. I phoned and spoke to a woman I presumed to be his landlady, giving her my name and telling her that I expected him that night at five o'clock to discuss a job I had for him.

"But he has a little fish shop, sir."

"Well, so he has a little fish shop. If he'd rather sell fish he can give me a telephone call, I'll look for somebody else. Thank you very much." I was really getting the taste of it back.

He was there at five. I was waiting for him in the bar and spearing a sausage when a voice cried, "Ome!" Everyone fell silent and craned their necks.

There he was. I remembered how I had first interviewed him, also in a bar, before we left with the *Isabel*. It was déjà vu all over again: a huge hulk loomed over me, I looked up and saw a Nordic face with high cheekbones, right off the carved pulpits of seventeenth-century churches. He held out a hand the size of a frying pan and said in a voice loud enough to stampede cattle, "Hi there, Ome! How are you?"

"Sit down, Bosun, sit down."

He sat down, the barman turned up to take his order. "Beer?" I asked. "Gin?"

"What are you having, Ome?"

"The usual."

"I'll have the same," he said loyally. The barman departed.

"Mrs. Bouman told me you had a job for me. She must have got that wrong?"

"As a matter of fact, she didn't. Let me explain."

I did; he listened carefully. I remembered how he had always listened carefully. He even had a little book in which he made notes. He was, without doubt, the most comforting man to have around, worth fifty ship's doctors radiating bliss after a long happy marriage with themselves. "Do you drive a car, Bosun?"

"Well, car, Ome—a pickup truck. Why?"

"As I told you, we will be five old parties, to be carted halfway across the United States. We have been offered a minibus and I don't want an American driver. With you at the wheel, and mopping up after us, seeing to it that we are comfortable, occasionally getting some food in the nearest eatery for those who want to relax in their hotel room, I can't think of anything better."

He looked at me with such radiant joy that I almost blushed. "You know I'd do anything for you, Ome," he said, heartfelt. "I don't know the other gentlemen, but I know *you*. Let me tell you, I could have strangled Captain Fransen when he sent me home in Talcahuano and let you cross the Pacific alone with that bunch of Chinese. And just look what happened!"

"Yes, Bosun," I said, "look what happened. How about your fish-and-chips shop?"

"Don't you worry. I've got somebody who'll take over. Even if I didn't, I'd still come with you."

"That's really—er—nice, Bosun, but let's get to the serious business. You'll be looking after not just one old geezer, but five. What's ahead of us, God knows, may be tougher than a typhoon in the South Pacific. You would be taking on a big responsibility. Are you ready for that?"

"Yes, Ome," he said. The expression on his face was clear: he was not going to listen to any more warnings or protestations, he was going to sail, if it had to be that same night. I hoped he did indeed have someone to take over his shop.

"Okay, I know the others will be happy to have you," I said. "It's a job like you never tackled before, but then, that goes for all of us. This is going to be the *Isabel Kwel* all over again, with knobs on. Okay?"

"Okay, Ome. What are you going to do now? It's nearly your bedtime."

"Bosun, hold it." I couldn't help laughing aloud. "It's five-thirty. Now let's talk about money."

We talked about money, reluctantly on his part, as if he would rather have done it for nothing. God knows what I represented to him. Youth? The sea? Probably just loyalty. A lifetime ago, I had hired him as a young man, and, some years later, promoted him to bosun. At least, that's what he said; I have to confess that I did not remember. But then, that came with age; a month or so before Sylvia's death we had gone for a walk with friends, and I had been holding forth about something and wanted to involve her, at which point I had said, "As I told my—er— my—well, whatever she is." She had taken it with a smile and kissed me.

"Ome, you look like you're tired," the bosun said. "Why don't you let me take you to your room and settle you down for a nap? I'll bet you haven't had one today. If you like, I'll hang around and see that nobody barges in."

I gazed at him with an indescribable feeling of—hell, bad writers like myself begin by saying something is indescribable and then try to describe it. It was good to have him back.

"Okay," I said.

"Do you have to pay for the drinks first?"

"No, it goes on the bill. Now stop fussing. Come upstairs and we'll talk some more. But, Jesus, man, hold back on the mother love."

I think it was he who put me firmly back on the bridge. The indescribable feeling was one of security: Bosun Schoonmaker would turn us into a crew in no time at all, better than I could. Miss Bastiaans' promise that our feet would never touch the ground had been shipowners' talk; with Bosun Schoonmaker looking after us, the commercial became reality.

26

HELEN CALLED that night. I don't know where she got the number. Miss Bastiaans, efficient at all times and on all occasions, must have given it to her during their tête-à-tête in Exeter. We had a nice conversation, but she sounded tired. I said all the right things. She said all the right things. Yet something was lost, maybe innocence.

Our farewell talk left me pensive, if that's the word. I was overcome by a sense of loss. Not the loss of Helen, something else. Before all this started I had been—how shall I say?—a straightforward old man. The little speech I had delivered that night in the Réserve had not been hot air blown for the occasion, it had been true. I had found myself, at that time, in the no-man's-land between memories and dreams, aware that the range of my perception had become much wider than it had been all my life. The first time that happened to me was at the age of seventy-five, when I had spent a few months in England together with Sylvia, tracing the footsteps of a Roman centurion in the fourth century A.D., a man with whom I had identified to the point of total recognition. I had not had an experience like that again, but the quality, the specific weight of my life had remained the same: a constant awareness of another dimension, a richness of inner experience that had made the empty bungalow and the shabby way of life of the old recluse more exciting than any active adventure could have made it. Now, despite the insight of my later years, I had answered the sirens' call to sail once more, and found myself caught in outward concerns and practical emergencies, but with that one dimension missing. I wondered whether Ulysses, if he had indeed sailed again with his old crew, would also at a given moment have—

The telephone rang.

It was Miss Bastiaans. She had just spoken to Commander van Texel, calling from Le Havre. The French conjurer they had gone to interview at the circus in Orléans turned out to have died six years ago. His place, even his name, had been taken by his widow; she wore his clothes and a male wig. She was not prepared to take part in the assignment, but she had agreed to take in old Pjotr until we sailed, when he and Fons would meet us on the quayside in Southampton. She gave me a number where I could reach Tex.

I telephoned him, heard the whole story once more; so we would have to make do with a crew of four. I told him about the bosun, though he did not really count, did he now? He was not going to have himself put under to visit the moon, he was just there to mop up after us and put us to bed, right?

The conversation left me with an increased sense of loss, heaven knows why. *Get back on the bridge, Harinxma.* That was when the whole thing had started: with the old tomcat coming back for his food. But surely, there was more to "the whole thing" than this?

I took the folded sheet out of my wallet, smoothed it, and read the poem once more:

Old age hath yet his honour and his toil;
Death closes all: but something ere the end,
Some work of noble note, may yet be done,
Not unbecoming men that strove with Gods . . .

It was, I decided, a matter of faith.

27

THE CONTAINER SHIP *Atlantic Maiden* looked, despite her romantic name, square, functional, and as carefully devoid of beauty as a moving van. She had no business gracing the seas. What she needed was wheels.

Her crew was made up of Lascars, as we used to call them in the past, Pakistanis, to whom we were obviously part of the Mysterious West. The officers were English, the captain aggressively so; he seemed more suited to be an Oxford don than Master after God of this giant floating truck.

The three others of our group were delivered on the quayside by the Volkswagen bus driven by our Dutch driver. He helped carry the luggage on board; the bosun hurried to assist him. The one who made the bosun nervous was Miss Bastiaans; she was, as always, efficient, thorough, and in command. She inspected the cabins and ordered the luggage to be put on the floor, which was stupid because old men would have to lift it back on the bed to unpack. The bosun asked, in a whisper, "Is that your daughter, Ome?"

"Hell, no, that's our head of operations."

"A woman?"

"Not *a* woman, *the* woman. Don't you remember? She was the right hand of old Mr. Kwel." He didn't remember, he had never got close enough to Mount Olympus to become familiar with the gods.

"Is she going to sail with us?"

"No, don't worry. You'll be in command."

He laughed. "Not with you around, Ome."

I began to feel uncomfortable in the glow of his adulation.

The others staggered on board in various states of decrepitude. Tex, in his wheelchair, looked the youngest and most sprightly. Fons looked haggard, deathly pale; he was obviously exhausted. Pjotr looked exhausted too; his jauntiness had not survived the trip to the circus, the long car journey from Orléans to Southampton. He collapsed on his bunk, lost to the world. I told the bosun to unpack his suitcase for him.

I was looking through the educational material, for want of a better word, which Miss Bastiaans had put in my cabin, when the bosun turned up, theatrically gloomy. "I'm sorry, Ome, but that woman *is* coming. I thought I was unpacking his bag, but it's hers."

"You're nuts."

"Come and look for yourself."

I did. There was the toque with the feather, the boa, the black dress, the evening gloves. I went to find her.

She was talking to the captain who rose respectfully when I was ushered in by a steward behaving like a headwaiter. Following the usual introductions, I asked her if she was coming along with us after all, because my bosun had been unpacking her stuff. She frowned, then laughed. "Oh, those are the clothes Pjotr put on for his little charade. I let him keep them. I couldn't wear all that again without feeling like a mad old man in drag."

The captain of the *Atlantic Maiden* looked, to coin a phrase, all at sea. I did not feel the need to enlighten him, neither did Miss Bastiaans. "Let's have a look at the schoolroom, Captain. It's important that there is enough space to unroll charts and the like."

"I don't think *schoolroom* is the right word, Miss Bastiaans. We have cleared Storage Number Two for you. The cook wasn't happy about it, but then cooks never are, are they?"

I agreed.

"I'd like to see it," Miss Bastiaans said.

We were shown Storage Number Two, a rectangular dark room without portholes with a large Ping-Pong table in the center and a blackboard on the bulkhead.

"No chairs?" Miss Bastiaans inquired.

"Well, I thought maybe the gentlemen would content

themselves with those benches I had put up against the bulkhead. They're anchored, you see. If we put in chairs and the ship starts to swing her hips, the chairs would go walking." His moving van had no hips to swing; obviously he was bent on convincing himself that the *Atlantic Maiden* was aptly named. The eyes of love. "Would that do, Commodore?"

"I suppose so. If they get tired we can always string a couple of hammocks and let them absorb their instructions horizontally."

Miss Bastiaans looked at me with the first sign of fatigue. That is the worst trait of the golden years: poor jokes. The only one likely to enjoy mine, apart from myself, was the bosun. He had no sense of humor, but he loved me.

"Well, if there's anything else you might want, Commodore, let me know," the captain said, rising, eager to get back to serious business.

"I will, sir." We were like two dogs sniffing one another, tails erect. It was time we sailed.

Three hours later, we did. Of the five of us, the bosun and I were the only ones on deck. I had been invited to the bridge, but preferred to stay with my crew. The captain seemed relieved.

The farewell from Miss Bastiaans was strained; I failed to understand why until I realized that she hated leaving me to my own devices. I had the impression that, had she foreseen her present mood, she would have made the crossing with us rather than meet us in New Jersey. At a given moment, when we were about to part, she looked as if she contemplated kissing me good-bye. To my relief she decided against it.

"Well, Commodore," she said, "off you go."

"Correct," I said.

"I still think it's very, very silly of you to have turned down the doctor."

"I know, Miss Bastiaans. But then, I'm a silly old man."

"I'm afraid I have to agree."

"Oh, get off the ship," I said, suddenly fed up with the whole thing. "Come on, move!" I pushed her to the gangway, where the pilot was waiting with whom she was due to return. With an expression of relief, she obeyed. As I saw her depart in the pilot's launch, I waved to her, all the while repeating in my mind the final line of Bernard Shaw's *Captain Brassbound's Conversion,* when Lady Cicely waves her pirate farewell: *Farewell, farewell, with my heart's deepest feeling, farewell!* Then she turns around to add: *What an escape!*

28

IN RETROSPECT, the crossing to Port Elizabeth was the happiest time for me, compared to what was to follow. It did not have to do with being back at sea; to my surprise, that didn't mean a thing to me. To wallow inside this floating moving van on the great briny had nothing to do with sailing a ship the way I had done most of my life. Even the Atlantic, which I had come to know in all its fickle beauty and unpredictable temper, seemed dull and pedestrian, morose at having to carry this caricature of a ship after, once upon a time, windjammers and ocean liners had graced its horizon. "Being at sea" did not mean a thing because I wasn't: I was part of the contents of a moving van.

The true joy was getting to know the others again. It seemed as if youth were once more within our reach: Tex, tough and cynical, with an instant grasp of any situation; Fons, pensive and frowning, more attentive to the needs of others than to his future task of looking for a buggy on the moon; Pjotr, as nutty as a fruitcake, turning up for classes with Miss Bastiaans' toque and occasionally her boa, to the jaw-sagging astonishment of the Pakistani crew.

Once everyone had recovered from predeparture exhaustion, we started our daily study of lunar charts, the *Apollo 17* astronauts' video of EVA Number 1, site 4, and their verbatim report of Operation Crumpled Fender. We spent hours in Storage Number Two absorbing it all; rather than making the assignment more realistic to us, however, it made it seem more off-the-wall.

It turned out that none of us fully believed in this stuff. We had signed on for reasons other than eagerness to be split in half and explore the moon as spooks. The state of disembodiment, exhaustively described by Mr. Monroe and other experts of the phenomenon, sounded to us like being drunk. The plan concocted by Colonel Rusty and his gang of boffins was like the plot for a science-fiction series on television. But we had signed on for it and were ready to give it a shot; none of us contemplated backing out, even though we agreed among ourselves that this was one harebrained operation. We compared memories, and could not find a loonier one in our combined wartime experiences. The bosun, for his part, never quite understood it; I suspect that in his darker moments he thought a bunch of mad scientists were about to subject us to secret tests in a search for the serum against some outlandish disease.

We dutifully carried on with our daily training sessions. We became familiar with the lunar sea where our buggy had been left behind and could, each of us, draw the landmarks from which to take our bearings when the time came. The buggy itself had an interesting aspect distinguishing it from the others—hence the (retroactive) name of the operation. While being unfolded on the moon after the landing of the module, one of its fenders, the left-rear one, crumpled. As there was no atmosphere and the dust in that area was very fine, the wheels of the buggy were likely to throw up a cloud of particles that would remain suspended, unless deflected downward by a fender. The astronauts, in their clumsy outfit, had managed to execute an emergency repair with the aid of charts and, so the rumor went, chewing gum. Should, in a million years' time, another civilization explore the moon and wonder what the creatures were like that had left those mysterious instruments scattered about, the left-rear fender of the Lunar Rover Number 9 could tell them more about the human race than anything else they would find.

All seemed to go smoothly as we carried out our daily routine. Our relationship with the English crew was polite and remote; we ourselves were in the process of becoming a tightly knit unit. Then, one night, the bosun woke me, whispering, "I think there's something wrong with the commander, Ome. You'd better come and have a look."

I dressed hastily and found Tex on deck in his wheelchair, gazing at the sea with a bottle in his lap. He belched loudly before he became aware of my presence. Then he looked up at me the way drunks do, and said, "Oh, shit! It's you."

"Depends who you are seeing, Tex." It was pitch dark; in his condition all men would become demons wearing masks.

"I see a fatuous old ass," he said, "like myself. What the hell do we think we're doing? Why are we *here*? The whole thing is balls! God knows, I didn't enjoy watching the stock-market results on television all day and doing battle with my fainting wife, but this . . ."

He took a long swig from the bottle. I saw it was English gin.

"Thank you, Bosun, we'll be all right," I said.

"Yes, Ome." He withdrew discreetly.

"All right, Tex, let's have it. What's the problem?"

"If I had any sense," he said, "I'd get out of this goddamn contraption, which I still can, up to a point, hoist myself onto the rail, and take a swan dive into blessed nothing."

"That's neatly put. Any particular reason why?"

"You're so snotty, Fancy, fooling yourself with this rigmarole of being the skipper of a crew! You are the victim of a hoax. God knows what they want from us; whatever it is, it is the fevered vision of some mad boffin. My God, we deserve better than this at the end of our lives!"

"Do we?"

He tried to focus on me, found it too much of an effort, and took another swig. The problem would be to get the bottle away from him.

"I think you are doing yourself and the lot of us an injustice," I said, reasonably. "I think what we have been asked to do must make some sense, otherwise why would they spend all that money on us?"

"They've been known to spend money on sillier things. Can't you *feel* that we are on a dead-end road?"

"At our age, Tex, we're on a dead-end road whatever we do."

"That I don't believe, you see. I believe there is some way, some hope . . ." He burst into drunken tears. I contemplated taking the bottle away from him then, but it was a shade too soon.

"Tell me more," I said.

"About what?" he asked in a tear-choked voice.

"About hope. A moment ago you were talking about taking a swan dive off the rail. That didn't sound very hopeful to me. What hope are you talking about?"

"The goddamn distant shore!" he cried. "The fancy stuff about old friends meeting once more! That was something I did not believe in and yet hoped for. *Now* look at us! Here we are, we're on that distant shore. Here are the old friends meeting once more. And what *are* we? A bunch of old loonies, boring the bejesus out of everybody, including ourselves. Is that what the distant shore is going to be like? Give me oblivion!" He groped for the bottle but didn't find it because I had snitched it during his moment of bathos. He was too drunk to care, he just waved his hand; he had forgotten what he had been looking for.

"Tex," I said, "I don't know if you are in the right condition to discuss this sensibly, but—"

"Oh, for God's sake! Spare me your skipper's monologue! I've not only heard it all before, I've given it. How many knock-kneed ratings do you think I had to drag out of the diarrhea of gloom by their furry ears?"

It was a good speech, as drunken speeches go. I particularly liked the furry ears. "Tex," I said. "I don't know if it means anything to you, but to me and the rest of us, this operation is a return to the island."

"Island?" he asked with a hiccup. "What fucking island are you talking about?"

I put my arm around his shoulder, which almost launched him to his feet; I had to grab hold of the chair before it capsized. "I can't stop you blatherskiting to me, but I'll be goddamned if I'll let you French kiss me!" he yelled.

"Can I be of any help?" the Oxford voice of the captain of the *Atlantic Maiden* asked. I had not noticed his approach; it was an unfortunate moment.

"No, thank you, sir. I think we have matters well in hand."

"Maybe—er—some Alka Seltzer?"

It was so well meant and so clumsy, that even Tex in his cups couldn't help bursting into laughter. "If there's anyone I'll allow to French kiss me, it's *him,*" he howled, emerging from the diarrhea of gloom.

"I'm so sorry," the captain said, mystified. "If there's anything I can do, medication or whatever, you know where to find me."

"I do indeed, sir. Thank you very much."

"Don't mention it. My pleasure."

He disappeared into the night. "Now you see? You're frightening the horses. Cut it out, Tex. Where did you find that bottle?"

"Bottle?" he said. "I found no bottle. I'm *looking* for it."

But he was over the worst. I called the bosun, who appeared at once; he must have remained within earshot. "I think the commander is ready to go to bed," I said. "Thank you for calling me on this."

"Oh, for God's sake," Tex moaned. "Skippers!" He said it in the tone in which men say "Women!"

Back in my bunk, I worried about him. He was a realist. He owed the fact that he was still alive to his incorruptible realism during those hair-raising operations he had been ordered to engage in. No wonder this time he was overcome by unease: he had to believe in what he was being asked to do. The fact that this time he couldn't must have been the reason for his drinking himself silly in the dead of night.

I thought about this. Did I believe in our assignment myself?

I believed in the rationality of Mr. Monroe's experiments. I believed in the reliability of the reports of the many subjects he had put through their paces while out of the body. I saw no reason why at least one of us would not share that experience. I had obviously failed to transmit that belief to Tex—and, who knows, the others as well.

I would call them together the next day, after Tex had slept it off. We would go through the whole procedure again, with the understanding that if something came up that one of us could not believe in he would speak up. I would, somehow, have to make the assignment sound acceptable.

I had been asked to do worse in my time.

29

I TACKLED the problem the next morning in the schoolroom. Tex must have felt rather sheepish about last night because he was, by the mysterious chemistry of old men, grimly defiant. Fons smiled as I supposed he did at Elvira when she was being particularly unreasonable. Pjotr wore Miss B.'s hat but not her boa this morning, which may have indicated that he was aware of the seriousness of the coming discussion. The only one ready to listen to me without reservation was the bosun.

I began by saying that I had reason to believe there was some doubt among us as to the realism, for want of a better word, of the assignment for which we had signed on.

"Realism my arse," Tex snarled. "I have handled plenty of surrealist assignments in my time. That's not the problem, the problem is I don't *trust* them."

"Who?"

"Let's begin by analyzing the situation. Fancy here, happily hiding, as I understand it, in the darkest corner of the forest, is seduced into coming out into the open by a smashing redhead who could seduce an elephant into believing he can dance with a mouse. Radiant, rejuvenated, he puts on a zootsuit, gets a marine haircut, high-shines his shoes, and makes the rounds of his few remaining cronies from the war. And what is he offering? What the redhead told him: that we can all, if we put our minds to it, dance with a mouse."

"Come on, Tex," I said, "forget about the wisecracks and get to the core of the thing. You don't believe in the assignment."

"Fancy, there *is* no assignment. There is a creed to which we are asked to subscribe, namely that man is made up of two equal parts. His mind, or his soul, and his body, of which the brain is a part. The creed is that the two can be separated so that the body remains unconscious on the bed and the mind detaches itself and heads for the moon after having been programmed to do so. Now that, clearly, is a matter of faith. If you don't believe the basic concept of the mind being separate from the brain, you have no assignment, you have signed on for a different thing altogether. Now, let's talk about *that*. What do they want us for? Why are we here?"

"Tex," I said with commendable patience. "we *know* the reason why we are here. We are here because, as old men, we could not believe that we really were as decrepit as we appeared to be. We always had in the back of our minds the concept that circumstances forced us to act old. We always believed that if only we were touched by some magic wand—"

"Like a redhead," Tex interrupted.

"—a magic wand, we would reveal ourselves as we really are: not *that* old, not *that* decrepit. We acted old only because nobody had any use for us. If anybody thought about us at all, it was about where to store us so we'd be looked after. Golden Evenings, Happy Days, Safe Haven, you name it; they wanted to feel they had done what they could to salvage us from what, to them, was an old buzzard's nest. My daughter never really grasped that after my wife's death my environment didn't matter any more. So my front garden, which once was manicured according to the conditions of our retirement village, turned into a patch of weeds, fertilized by the neighborhood cats—"

"Fancy," Tex interrupted again, "that is your own private situation. Why don't we—"

"Why don't you shut up, Tex, and let me finish? Dammit, you are a member of a crew under my command, now shut up!"

"Sorry," he said.

"So the reason why I took on this assignment was not the assignment itself. I was prepared to give that my full attention when the time came, but I wanted to avoid the warehouse my daughter was about to put me into. Do you understand?"

"I love to hear you talk," Fons said. "You should write poetry."

"Fons, come on! Step out of the stereotype for a moment and answer the question. The reason you signed on was—what?"

"I wanted to find out."

"What?"

"If indeed my soul is eternal and death is the horizon, which is no more than the limitation of our sight, as two thirds of the world's population believe. If Icarus did not fall into oblivion, but his soul was free to try again even as his body burned. I gathered from what you told me and from what I subsequently read from the books you gave me, that there is a man in America who has found a way of separating the mind from the brain by technical means, so my mind would be free to go to the moon and perform a task agreed upon beforehand. I signed on for the spiritual experience. That does not mean I am not aware of the fact that by signing on I undertook to collect a specific reading on a dosimeter, if I can find it. Does that answer your question?"

"Very well. Pjotr?"

Pjotr woke up from the opening stage of a snooze. "Huh?"

"Why did you sign on, Pjotr? Have you any idea what we're supposed to do in America?"

"I don't give a damn," Pjotr said, yawning. "I'm not about to understand what it is before I am asked to do it. I'd forget, you see."

"All right," I said. "So let's talk again about the details of the assignment. Let's make sure we know exactly what we are supposed to do and how we are supposed to do it; and as to our personal motivations—"

"Whoops," the bosun cried, making a dash. He caught Pjotr, falling sideways off his chair, in the nick of time. "I'd better put him to bed," he said apologetically.

"Sure, Bosun." He really was the one righteous man in Gomorrah.

After they had left, I said, "All right, let's go through the procedure again. This time, anyone who is unsure of any move at all, speak up, please. Okay. We are given the coordinates prior to the operation. We have studied the lunar chart. We know exactly what the buggy looks like, how to recognize it . . ."

"Let's go back a few steps," Tex said. "We receive our instructions, then lie down on a bed in a booth where a number of tabs are stuck to our skin with leads to some instruments. Then we get fitted with earphones, locate the mike so we can address it in the dark, then the light is turned off. Then a voice, presumably that of the controller in the control room, speaks through our earphones and starts the procedure of putting us in the alpha state—"

"One day, when I was in the alpha state, my soul appeared to me," Fons began softly.

"Fons, what the hell?"

"Sorry. The first line of a poem."

"All right, men," I said, "let's continue."

For some reason, this meeting had me worried.

3 0

*Dear Angel of Death: As I am supposed to keep you posted, here is my
report on the latest meeting of your crew.*

*For the first time, I was acutely aware of the fact that we—all four
of us—have no business being involved in any assignment other than the
search for the bathroom in a roadside hotel. I may not be a fair judge of my
own condition, but as to the others: today has proven, beyond the shadow
of a doubt, that they are as gaga as coots. Pjotr goes without saying. Fons
does not absorb anything that he cannot transfer into meter and rhyme.
Tex, despite his heroic past and present panache, could not outthink a
dachshund if he tried. Which leaves your essayist, Fancy Harinxma, who
pens little pieces of life at sea between the wars but has no clue as to life in
the present. The question that arises, irrepressibly, like a bad smell, is:
Why? Why were we chosen? For what?*

*You are, without doubt, the brightest woman I have ever known.
Compared to you, my dear Sylvia, who could run rings around me any
time she chose, was of a childlike simplicity. It is totally impossible that
you should have chosen the four of us in a haze of "guesswork." You must
have had a specific reason; my problem is that I cannot for the life of me
figure out what that might be.*

*Cause for my nervousness is that we have been here before, you and
I. Once before the old man—which by that time meant you—sent me,
knowingly and without a qualm, on an assignment that was not merely
life-threatening but intended to do away with me and my forty-man crew,*

when the sick Isabel *would meet her inescapable fate. And why? So a Chinese investor might collect the insurance money and you and your old man could be rid of the lemon. So, even though I am hopelessly charmed by you (who would not be?), I ask myself: What the hell is the joker in the pack this time? What fate do you have in mind for us four this time? . . .*

This was one nutty letter. *"Dear Angel of Death"?* I might as well have written *"Dear diary."* There was no point in writing all this down, much better to spring it on her while we were having a quiet booze, somewhere in America.

I crumpled the letter into a ball and went out on deck to toss it overboard. Doing so brought me to the fringe of a memory. Once before I had thrown a crumpled-up letter overboard, to prevent my mailing it. A long time ago. A long—Mary?

Mary. The boy Tyler's widow, after our wild and desperate lovemaking in the chartroom of the old *Isabel,* in Halifax. When? Must have been '42, after the first Murmansk convoy, in which her husband died. Old memories, old sins. And alongside, in the fog, another vision: a huge ship, a crew of old friends. *Another one, skipper! At two o'clock!* A sense of fulfillment, of—gone.

This was what I meant when I told Miss B. that old men live in a world between memories and dreams.

"Ome?"

"Yes, Bosun?"

"Old Pjotr is acting real strange."

"Coming."

I went. Pjotr was dreaming, and talking. "Perfectly normal," I told the bosun. "Only, not everybody talks."

"But who's he talking *to,* Ome?"

"Probably a fish."

The bosun withdrew quietly.

I stayed with Pjotr for a while, listening to his end of the dialogue, which did not tell me much, other than the name Louise. He dreamed in Polish.

3 1

IN PORT ELIZABETH we were whisked through customs and immigration by an escort of gray-flanneled taciturn men of mysterious authority, presumably Colonel Rusty's crowd. We were told by a smiling Miss Bastiaans, over lunch in a restaurant called McDonald's, that there had been a change of plan. We were not going to the institute in North Carolina. She could not tell us why; Colonel Buckram and Mr. Monroe must have had their reasons. Instead, we would be going slightly further afield, a matter of a day or three or four, to a small community in the hill country west of San Antonio, Texas, called Big Owl. A temporary lab had been prepared there, identical to Mr. Monroe's, only the technical stimulus to achieve separation of mind and body would be different. We would not be using Mr. Monroe's patented hemi-sync procedure, but a different method which would have the same effect. The leader of the technical team was a brilliant young scientist who had earned his laurels, a Dr. Wildeman. We would not be staying in the facility itself, but in a first-class hotel nearby, where all our needs would be taken care of. Now we had better be prepared for a slightly tiring four-day drive across the United States; everything would be made as comfortable as possible.

The transportation was comfortable enough, a large Ford van with plenty of room for Tex's chair. The bosun, after driving it around the block, said it was going to be a breeze. We never drove more than a few hours at a time, then stopped for lunch in one of those fast-food restaurants you find all over America. Then back into the bus, half-asleep in our seats until an early stop at some motel off the freeway, where we collapsed on strange beds and slept the sleep of the dead until the bosun served a piece of pizza and a soft drink.

Old, old, old: I had not been fleet of foot for quite some time, but during that drive I staggered and collapsed each night—panting, gasping—into the nearest chair. Fons grew older by the day; he was sprightly enough, but his face became so lined, so desperately tired that I was overcome by a feeling of guilt. In a rush of what now looked like megalomania I had lured these poor dotards into a dream of youth with the poetic idea that old men ought to be explorers. I felt guilty, seeing Fons's exhausted face; Pjotr asleep on his bed with his mouth open, wearing Miss B.'s hat like a child of ninety; Tex, the toughest and most realistic of us all, slowly having his precious energy drained away by being carted from one American motel to the next. The bosun, lured from his fish-and-chips shop by the delusion of a revival of the old days at sea, now discovered that at the age of seventy he had been asked to do a young man's job. He did it joyfully, obviously trying to convince himself that he was having a wonderful time, but there were moments when he sagged behind the wheel when the car was stopped, like a deflated doll. What had possessed me? What evil star had lured me into this night, taking four guileless old dreamers with me into what was turning into a nightmare?

Miss Bastiaans was the only one who could answer, the only object in the desert of guilt behind which I could hide and cry, "Not me, Lord! No, no, not me! It was her. *Her.*"

So where would she and I end up? The image that came to mind at that moment was of her, standing in her 1940s mourning outfit at the foot of a grave somewhere in Texas, on the ready to hunt another head.

Jackson, Mississippi. Alexandria. Kirbyville. Houston. San Antonio. We arrived in the town of Big Owl at the end of an afternoon of unrelenting heat. We were too whacked by then to take in much; the bosun made sure we were all comfortable in a motel called Mother Billie's. Miss Bastiaans was there to welcome us, and despite my state of near collapse, she and I had a drink in some saloon where country-and-western music whined from ceiling speakers and ten-gallon-hatted customers stamped out the beat with their cowboy boots.

Miss Bastiaans put her hand on mine. "All well, Commodore?"

It was one of those questions which made you wonder why the hell you were not allowed to go to bed. "Yes, thank you, all things considered. Why do you ask?"

"You are of particular interest to me. After all, it's you who heads this expedition."

There was something else. There were no symptoms; she looked just as convincing, ravishing, all-seeing and blue-eyed and loveless as before, but—well, if it was anything serious, I was sure to find out in due course. "When do we start?" I asked.

"Tomorrow morning you are expected to present yourselves in the testing lab, at eight-thirty. I've given instructions to the bosun. He knows where it is and he will see to it that you are on time. You'll be lectured to by Dr. Wildeman, who will explain the procedure. Then I suppose he'll start straightaway with some initial tests."

"Tests of what?"

"Of the separation of mind and brain. Don't ask me how he'll go about it, it's esoteric territory to me, but I do think that within the next week the first effort will be made to send one of you to the moon." She sipped her drink. "Any idea of who should go first?"

"Of course it's up to the person in question."

"Pjotr?"

There she went again, reading thoughts as if they were tea leaves. "Given his diving experience and his readiness to go, he would seem a good first subject."

There was laughter and clinking of glasses. The speakers overhead boomed a new song: *"Walk out backwards so I'll think you're coming in . . ."* I was overcome by melancholy—dear God, what are we doing here?—that old thing.

She put her hand on mine again. "I know, Commodore, it's a stressful time. I must say I admire you. I—"

"Miss Bastiaans, cut the crap. I don't need admiration, I need my bed." For some crazy reason, and it *was* crazy because it bore no relation to any real feeling or even thought on my part, I almost added, "with you in it." Bewildering, because I did not feel the slightest physical attraction to Miss Bastiaans. Maybe it was just the need of some human closeness.

"You know, Commodore," she said suddenly, if anything she did was ever sudden, "when this whole thing is over, you and I should let the others fly home while we take an easy drive through the American heartland to—wherever. I'd like the opportunity for us to just talk, reminisce, enjoy one another's company, without the stress and responsibility of an assignment."

I smiled at her. It was rare that she fouled up, an occasion to be honored. I said, "I know I'm an old donkey, but I don't need a carrot to see me through. Thank you all the same. Lovely idea."

She smiled, and ordered another double on the rocks.

3 2

THE BOSUN LAY in wait for me when I returned to the motel. He asked, "Are you ready to take a look at the others, Ome?"

I was ready to be crated, but this was part of the routine of the Master after God at times of stress: to visit each member of his crew last thing in the evening. I started with Tex who, grimly ensconced in one of the double beds in his room, with all available pillows at his back, was watching what appeared to be a porn movie. He was unwelcoming. "Thanks, but I don't need tucking in. Good night and fuck off."

One down, two to go.

Fons, to my surprise, was sitting fully dressed on a stool in the center of his room, staring fixedly ahead. I thought that he was meditating; then he looked at me and his eyes were so full of grief that I told the bosun to wait outside. I sat down on the edge of his bed.

"Fons, what is it?"

He smiled at me the way a guru would smile at an eager pupil. "I am a bit old for sudden changes," he said kindly. "Before going to bed after a day like this, I just like to sit for a while and adjust."

"To what?"

"To being without Elvira. To being lost in a continent as alien to me as darkest Africa. Wondering what death will be like."

"You don't think your number will come up away from home, do you?"

"Doesn't it always? How many friends died at home? I can't think of a single one. When we accepted to return to the island, which I thought was a wonderful idea, we forgot that the island was a place where most of us died. Didn't they?" He smiled.

I had better fall back on my captain's act. "Look, Fons, we are on an assignment which we accepted. There is no point in dwelling on our insufficiencies, or doubts, or fears—"

"Who said I was afraid?"

"That's not the point. The point is that we signed on for a job. Tomorrow at half-past-eight we have to be present and ready to do what we were hired to do. So let's get a good night's sleep and talk about all this some other time. The operation tomorrow will take all the vitality we can muster."

"Good old Fancy," he said, with a smile. "You must feel as lonely as hell."

"That's the skipper's lot, isn't it?"

I'd had enough of this slumber-party talk. "Go to bed, Fons. If you need the bosun to help you undress, let me know. Now I'll have a look at Pjotr; then I'm going to 'listen to the leak' myself."

"Sleep well," he said.

Two down, one to go. "Let's go, Bosun," I said.

We walked to the next room in the cool of the night. The bosun used a passkey; we entered and there was Pjotr, in bed, fast asleep, with his toque on.

"Looks all right," I whispered.

The bosun stared at the sleeping man with a frown. "I think I'll bunk down here tonight, if that's all right with you, Ome."

"Why?"

"He's been waking up in the middle of the night of late. That's when he needs a bit of company because he doesn't know where he is. He worries, he weeps."

"Weeps? You never told me."

"Well, it's not important. I mean, it's just like a child. He wakes up, cries, and all he needs is somebody to comfort him just by being there."

"All right, Bosun, if you think it necessary. Thank you."

"I don't need any thanks, Ome. I'm here to look after all of you. That's what I'm doing."

"And you're doing it very well. Thanks again."

I left. Enough is enough. I slogged to my own room, pulled out my key—but the door was open. There, in the chair at the makeup table, sat Miss Bastiaans, smoking a cigarette.

"Sorry to intrude," she said, "but there are a few things we have to discuss before tomorrow morning."

"I thought we discussed all that when we had our drinks."

"Not really. Do you want to get into bed? Shall I come back?"

"No, no, stay where you are, but let's make it short because I've had a basinful tonight."

"Of me?"

"Of being the skipper of this nonsense."

"That's what I want to talk to you about. You and the others have settled into a 'nonsense' concept of this undertaking. I want to correct that before we go any further."

I sighed. "Why don't you leave it to us? So we think it's

nonsense. That has never stopped any of us from doing what we signed on to do. What's more, I'm worn out. If you want me to make any sense tomorrow morning, you'll have to give me a chance to go to bed and sleep." I made a move toward the door to open it for her.

"I mean it," she said. "This is serious. The attitude is important in—"

"Miss Bastiaans, stop it! I'm the skipper of this bunch, it is my responsibility to deliver them tomorrow at the appointed hour and I will do so, never mind the mood they're in. Good night."

She gave me, for some reason, a satisfied smile. "Good night, Commodore. Sleep well."

When I closed the door I realized it had been a vintage performance on her part. She had just wanted to make sure before the whole thing started that I was back on the bridge. I would like to meet the man who could run rings around her.

33

THE NEXT MORNING I woke early and had breakfast in the eatery attached to the motel. I was so stiff after four days in the car that I went for a walk through town to stretch my legs.

It seemed a pleasant enough place. Rather insular; other people must find it so too, for in the window of the travel agent was a notice saying "Airline tickets to *anywhere*." A gas station carried a sign saying WE LOVE (*love* in the form of a heart) OUR LAW ENFORCEMENT OFFICERS. Among the stores on the main street was a flower shop that sold books; it was called Books and Blooms.

Everywhere I looked I spotted the town emblem: the image of a huge staring owl, even among the books and blooms.

The laboratory we ended up in later that morning was part of an abandoned school, a red-brick building with a weathered façade and window bars that looked as if they'd been installed to keep children in rather than intruders out. A uniformed security officer guarded the entrance; his presence seemed to be the only one in the echoing emptiness of the abandoned building. He took us to what must have been the principal's office; a surprisingly young man sat enthroned behind an empty desk in the company of two secretaries, each with an empty desk of her own. After one secretary had left he said to the remaining one, "That will do, Sergeant." Miss Bastiaans sat, knees crossed in unapproachable elegance, in a visitor's chair.

"I am Dr. Wildeman," the young man started. "Delighted to see y'all here. I gather you have had the opportunity to study the procedures and substance of your assignment during the crossing? If there are still questions that you wish to be answered, I'll be happy to do so now." Smiling, he looked about him. He obviously had no experience dealing with old men. A junior medical officer, more attuned to the problems of postadolescence.

"Are you the one who is going to put us on the plank?" Tex asked, by way of poking a stick through the bars at an animal he did not trust.

"I am," Dr. Wildeman said, pleasantly enough.

"Are there going to be any others, or are you by yourself?"

"There will be a number of others in the control room, but I thought that at this particular point in time a note of intimacy might be helpful."

"She had big gray eyes," Pjotr said. "Very unusual in a fish."

Dr. Wildeman frowned and muttered, "Quite."

It was time I took over. "Dr. Wildeman, obviously all of us are somewhat wary of what lies ahead. There are questions which were never answered to our satisfaction. I would like to put them to you now, as you suggested."

He gave me the kind of look that Pjotr had described as unusual in a fish and said, "Please do."

"What exactly are the reasons for the selection of men of our age?"

"That one's easy," he said. "You are what I was given."

"I don't understand."

"I am as unprepared for this as you are. I was brought in at the last moment when satisfactory arrangements with the Monroe Institute could not be made. I was called down from wherever I was and told to conduct this experiment. I feel competent to do so, and I am sure that you and I will get on well. After a few days of acclimatization we will get into the rhythm of this thing."

"Thank you. How about answering my question?"

He smiled a lawyer's smile. "I cannot answer any questions as to why you were selected, or how. I can tell you about myself, and maybe you can tell me about yourselves. My name is Wildeman, I am doctor of physics, associate professor at Rice University in Houston. I was asked by Colonel Buckram to conduct this experiment to survey the moon, either by distant viewing or by an out-of-body experience, in order to read a dial on a Lunar Rover. I have conducted similar experiments before. It has nothing to do with parapsychology; it is a rational, viable, and, to a physicist, an acceptable procedure. We at Rice University have not got as far with it as Mr. Monroe in his books would have us believe he did. My experiments in this field have been less romantic than his. But I'm reasonably sure that some of you, if not all of you, under the impact of a certain vibrational impulse, may eventually be able to absent yourselves from your physical body for a while and—who knows?—visit the moon. It sounds like science fiction, and I cannot guarantee that any of you will end up on the moon. I cannot even guarantee that you will have an out-of-body experience. But, judging by previous experiments in this field, it's reasonable to expect a positive result. One of the main conditions is that y'all relax, behave like normal human beings, and develop a less strained relationship with me. I'm sure that will be easy. I'll start by familiarizing myself with the degree of awareness and preparation at which you have arrived. After that, we'll start experimenting a bit. First with distant viewing; we'll take it from there in easy steps. Are you familiar with distant viewing?"

We were not. He explained that it was a well-tried procedure, one in which the Russians had made remarkable progress. For instance . . .

I looked at the others. Their suspicion and discomfort were obvious. What could I do to get through to this pleasant young man that he was the wrong person for this crowd? What was needed was someone much older, who could relate to men our age and to the concept of our returning to "the island." We needed an authoritative figure who could re-create the peculiar atmosphere of a wartime briefing; this goodwilled young man, trying to popularize what was obviously a highly technical procedure, would never overcome the suspicions of old veterans, to whom he would remain a keen young fellow trying to explain how simple a computer was.

We sat through that first session in a growing atmosphere of failure. In the end it became apparent to him that he was not communicating, so he called a halt, obviously earlier than he had intended to. I suggested that he, Miss Bastiaans, and I meet for a brief conference about procedural matters while the others were shown around the place by one of the secretaries.

When we were alone he eyed me with the beginnings of hostility. I tried to explain to him what he was dealing with; then Miss Bastiaans dealt with him in the way she had dealt with reluctant tugboat masters: ravishing, but to the point. "Would there be," she asked, "an old—and by 'old' I mean in his sixties or older—colleague of yours who could act as your spokesman in this particular situation?"

"I'm afraid I don't quite follow."

"You are faced with the difficult task of communicating with four men in their eighties, whom you are planning to put naked and in a state of sensory deprivation in an isolation booth, with earphones on their heads. It might make things easier if you could think of somebody older, to whom you could leave the social aspects of this and not have to worry about the psychology of the over-eighties. It's a matter of public relations, not of any doubt as to your qualifications."

I'm not sure how exactly she did it. His hostility slackened. "Well . . . my old professor—he's not only conversant with the whole procedure, he coached me in it—he might be available. I cannot speak for him. I hadn't considered bringing him in. But if you think it would help . . ."

"Describe him, would you?"

"Well, he's old. I mean, certainly in his sixties. He is"—he smiled uncomfortably—"a cantankerous—"

"Old bastard?" she suggested.

He gave her a startled look. "Yes, that's fair to say."

"Sounds okay," Miss Bastiaans said. "Don't you think so, Commodore?"

I grunted.

"Could you reach him, or shall we? I mean Colonel Buckram and his crowd."

He thought it over. "No, I think I had better approach him personally. If you like, I'll do it now."

"Perfect," she said. "Thank you so much. It's a comfort to find you are aware of our special problems."

"I hope you are aware of mine," he said testily.

"You and I should have a session on that," she suggested with a smile.

Oh boy.

34

PROFESSOR BARFIELD turned up two days later. He was so perfectly cast that it seemed as if he were a golem created by Miss Bastiaans: bearded, bat-eared, rumpled, in constant combat with his spectacles which went on sliding down his nose; but he had the authority of experience. There was no need to explain to him why he had been called upon. "Wildeman is a nice boy," he said when we had our first conversation. It took place in the Big Owl Barbecue, the town's favorite hangout. The antlers at the entrance were covered with ten-gallon hats, the place was packed with men; the loudspeakers moaned a lachrymose cowboy ditty played on a zither. "A bright boy," he continued, "but like all of them, snotty as hell. They haven't crashed on their chins yet. To them everything is still as plain as a pikestaff. My God! If I myself had been selected to work with men in their eighties I would have liked somebody with a bit of a beer belly and hair sprouting from his ears to guide me through this minefield, because that's what it is. A self-assured young scoutmaster like Wildeman doesn't realize that you folks must be—I won't say *crazy,* but slightly touched in the head to take on an assignment like this at your age. Explain to me why you did."

I explained the phenomenon of the return to the island, how we had turned into a cohesive unit like a crew, and the problems this posed to anyone who tried to manipulate us individually. He understood at once, and posed a few intelligent questions about each one of us. I liked him; and as those things are usually mutual, it was with a sense of relief that we walked back to the old school, past the gas station that loved its law enforcement officers and the dainty display of Books and Blooms. Like myself, he walked with some difficulty, which was heartening, and told me about an example of old age conspiring against him: he had asked for a

book in the university library; some teenage librarian had treated
him condescendingly, prompting him to tell her exactly who he
was, in crushing detail. She had been duly impressed, but, alas,
he then walked away with a series of little farts. A man to whom
we could entrust our fate.

In the meantime, Miss Bastiaans had taken care of Dr.
Wildeman, now pliable and pleasant, at least as long as she was
around. Professor Barfield called us together in the control room.
After some yawning and armpit-scratching, he explained what it
was all about. "It's nothing really. Scientists always make a
priestly song and dance about their procedures, but this has nothing to do with swinging incense burners or mumbled incanta-
tions. You folks are just going to lie on a waterbed—wonderful
for arthritis, by the way—there will be some music at first, then
some sleepy talk"—he yawned—"gradually you'll reach a stage
of relaxation called the alpha state. Because it's called alpha state,
a lay person may instantly be suspicious that it means sacrificing
his free will. Not so. It's a presleep condition in which the body
rests but the mind stays alert, it's that simple. We'll start with
some distant viewing. I'll have, in the control room, a picture in
front of me of a church, a desert, a deer, a mermaid, a bunny
rabbit, you name it; all you'll be asked to do, while you're lying
there, is tell me what you think the picture is that I have in front
of me. Nothing spooky about that. Sometimes it works, sometimes it doesn't. We have to start somewhere. It's the beginning
of a process that we will explore at our ease and in easy stages in
the days to come. Okay? Right then. Let's do just that. I won't
appoint anyone as the first contestant. You can draw straws."
Another long yawn.

To me he was every old wartime commander personified.
They used to describe the upcoming operation, which might leave
half of us dead and others limbless, as a cakewalk.

35

WE DREW LOTS. Tex was the first. The bosun helped put him on the waterbed; we all sat on kitchen chairs against the wall of the control room while Professor Barfield sagged in a director's chair, knees wider than humanly possible, glasses on top of his head, poking his nose. Dr. Wildeman, efficient, keen, worked the instrument panel.

"Let's hear it, Wildeman," Barfield said, yawning.

Wildeman recited the readings of the series of dials on the panel; the rest of the display was made up of knobs, slides, speakers, and small television screens, two of which showed, from different angles, Tex in his underpants, his body shriveled, startlingly old, covered with tabs and wires, lying on a bed, looking suspicious and apprehensive.

"All right, let's go," Barfield said. One of the secretaries, the sergeant, handed him a charcoal sketch of an elephant. "All right, Tex," he said, "do some guessing. First, tell me: what is the color of the control room? Do you remember?"

"Er—pink. Pinkish."

"Can you remember how we were sitting, in what sequence? Give me an idea of what you remember of the control room."

Tex did.

"Right. Very good. Now, look, I have in my hands a picture of something not very complicated. I'd like you to take a shot at it. Just a shot. What's your first thought as to how it looks?"

"A—a—a—something bulbous?"

"Could be called that, yes. What else?"

"A—a . . . a protrusion of some sort."

"How do you mean?"

"Like a—a—teapot."

"Good," Barfield said with a gesture at Wildeman and the

dials, indicating "just a shade higher" of something. "Very good. Tell me what kind of teapot."

"Well . . . a teapot. With a spout."

"What color?"

"I don't know. Gray? Blue . . . whatever."

"Try and peer over my shoulder." It was a strange suggestion.

"How can I peer over your shoulder when I'm locked in this box?"

"Well, let your imagination roam. Get out of the damn box in your mind, leave the bed you're lying on, and imagine yourself standing behind me in the control room that you described a minute ago. Here I am, beard and all, and I have in my hand the drawing of something like a teapot. Imagine peering over my shoulder, and try to give me a closer idea than 'teapot.' You're not far off. Just give it a shot."

"Hmm. Can't be a teapot, I don't see a handle. It's upside down, by the way. At least I think so."

"Right."

There was a silence which lasted longer than I expected. Then Tex's voice said, "Well I'll be damned."

"Tell me about it."

"An elephant?"

"Yes! Bravo! Terrific. Okay, next step."

"The next step is to let me out of this damn thing," Tex said. "I'm beginning to feel caged."

"You got out of the cage just now, didn't you? Sufficiently to tell me what I have in my hands: the drawing of an elephant. Where did that information come from, if you were caged in that booth? Your body may be, but your mind is not. Quite the reverse. Your mind has a chance to move about. So move about, man. Tell me more."

"What else do you want to know?"

"Anything. I hear somebody in the courtyard, I think. Any idea who that might be?"

"How could I?"

"Have a look, for God's sake!"

Tex laughed. "Okay," he said, "I'm making this up, but I'd say it's a car."

"What kind of car?"

"How should I know? A car. A passenger car."

"And who's inside?"

"No idea." Silence. "I'm lost now. Something isn't right. Let me out of here. Let me out! I've had it."

"Okay, Tex."

Barfield himself went to the isolation booth, turned on the light, took the electrodes off Tex's head, fingers, and body, swung aside the microphone, and helped him sit up on the bed.

"Jesus," Tex said, holding his head. "I thought I was going crazy."

"Why?"

"I don't know. It was eerie. I actually *saw* a car. Of course I didn't, but it seemed to me I saw it."

"Well, you described that drawing of an elephant—"

"That was just an educated guess," Tex said. "Let me get dressed."

"Right here, Commander," said the bosun. "Let me help you."

We left them to it.

36

WE TALKED IT OVER, the five of us, including Miss Bastiaans, in the Barbecue, which was becoming our watering hole. The noise was deafening, the place was filled to the brim with laughing males; yet I understood every word the others said.

Normally, the moment there was a background noise I became deaf; maybe my audiologist in Holland had been onto something when he said to me, "Are you sure you are not suffering from marital deafness?" When I asked him what that was, he answered, "That you are simply not listening."

Tex was excited about his experience and gave us an insider's view of what he had gone through. The whole booth business and the waterbed and the instrumentarium you were hooked up to were a bore, he explained, but the moment you managed to forget them and concentrate on what the earphones were saying, you did indeed have a sensation that might be the beginning of the detachment of the mind from the body. It wasn't at all what he had been led to expect: a process whereby he lay unconscious on a couch while his soul took wing. It was simpler and at the same time more subtle than that. You simply forgot your body because you were concentrating on the problem, and, believe it or not, that teapot had come out of nowhere. Now what the devil had made him think of a teapot—an upside-down teapot!—when in reality it was an elephant? Damn close, wasn't it? No idea. He had no idea either why he had got into a panic when old Barfield pressed him as to what he was seeing in the yard, that car. He had suddenly become, well, apprehensive, and called it a day out of sheer fright. It was too damn real. What was going on? We should press old Barfield for an answer to that. He would like to know what was happening to him.

I liked "old Barfield"—considering that the professor was twenty years younger than any of us. It all began to fall into place; we had, tentatively, reached the island.

It did away with the picture we had of ourselves as scared old men lured out of hiding to be exploited by a group of faceless men. Our collective mood changed, except for Pjotr—he was at a loss as to what all this was about. He was prepared to wait until he got his orders, but he had given up trying to understand anything in which he was not personally called upon to do something. He looked lost; maybe because of his hat. The bosun was the only one who could communicate with him on his level; while we were arguing back and forth in a state of excitement, the bosun went away for a moment and came back with a candy bar—a Baby Ruth—which he gave to Pjotr, who couldn't have been happier. To sit there munching chocolate seemed, to him, to give the whole thing some meaning.

Miss Bastiaans did not take part in the discussion, she just listened. When it was all over and we had polished off our spare-ribs and arrived at the coffee, she suggested that we take a walk, she and I. It seemed an outlandish suggestion, as I had difficulty walking any distance. Nevertheless, I joined her and we walked past the travel agency, the pharmacy, the books and blooms, to sit down on a bench intended for tired pedestrians.

"Well," she said, "what did you think of it?"

"A good beginning. Everybody seems to have gained confidence and a sense of direction. I think old—I mean, Barfield managed to make the whole thing real for us."

"You do realize that Tex was wrong. It is not just that you concentrate your mind on something and forget about your body. Eventually there will be a separation."

"Well, we'll have to see."

"It may be alarming, especially the first time. I wonder if you could prepare them for this."

"Miss Bastiaans, with the exception of Pjotr who is just waiting around, they are all highly intelligent, experienced men. My warning them that things might be getting alarming would have an adverse effect. It is the alarming part that will turn them on, if you ask me."

She thought it over, arms spread across the back of the bench, knees crossed. The scene seemed a fantasy on my part: sitting on a bench in a Texas town, by the side of a beautiful woman who belonged there as little as I did, which made for a sense of closeness between us. Ah, if only it could have been Sylvia!

Out of the blue, she said, "You know, I almost had second thoughts this morning."

"Why?"

"The sight of Tex, lying there so wrinkled, so flabby, so helpless. Hearing him get excited about a teapot. For the first time I fully realized what the consequences were when I accepted this assignment."

"You'll have to explain. I thought this morning's stuff went very well indeed."

"I don't know why. I surprised myself. A sudden—well, I suppose the word is *weakness.*"

"It isn't," I said.

She gave me a cool, considering look. Deep thought became her. My sense of this being a fantasy deepened, the old man's fourth dimension: the marshes of Hades' Approaches, the land between dream and memory. Had I sat like this before? Somewhere? Sometime?

"Mind you, I'm just thinking aloud. I don't want to alarm the others, or you, by turning sentimental. But the sight of that wrinkled old man, naked, helpless . . . Sorry. Sentimental nonsense. Don't tell them."

I wanted to ask her how long ago it was that she last saw a wrinkled old man naked on a couch, but it was none of my business. Interesting, to discern for the first time a crack in her armor. Chances were that it was not a crack, just part of the usual brilliant manipulation.

"Miss Bastiaans," I said, "I think you and I need a drink."

She smiled. "Not at this hour, Commodore. That's evening stuff. You should go and have your nap now."

"Oh, please!"

"Don't join them in the illusion that the island is real," she warned. "Remember Exeter."

"All right," I said. "If you don't want to join me for a glass, I'll be meek and lie down for my nap. God help me."

So I did, with the vague feeling that I had missed something, some connection, some unexpected access to a world behind the present. I could write it on a strip of paper, roll it into a little ball, and put it in the cookie tin. "Thoughts While Sitting on a Bench in Big Owl, Texas." "With a Beautiful Woman"? No. Her presence had not brought about the shift, however brief, into the other dimension. Something else had. I wondered what it was.

37

THERE FOLLOWED A WEEK of our getting used to the procedure, each one of us in turn having glimpses of what the crotch-scratching Professor Barfield called distant viewing, with unusual results. I must confess that I myself had not expected to repeat Tex's experience; I thought it must have been hypnosis or heaven knows what; I could not imagine my seeing a teapot or an aardvark or whatever when Barfield had a picture of an elephant in his hands. But, I don't know what it was—the unfamiliar routine of the waterbed, the electrodes glued to my head, fingers, and chest, the microphone dangling above my face, the earphones with the dream music supposed to put me into the alpha state—when the professor's disembodied voice asked me to tell him what he was looking at, followed by a yawn, it worked.

The first time, I tried to empty my mind of images and words to pick up the first image appearing in the void. It was a most unusual image: a bird pecking seeds off some hard surface. A sparrow? Pecking at what? Seeds on a road, a windowsill? For some reason: a windowsill.

"A bird on a windowsill."

"Pretty good," he said. "Have another look at the bird, though."

I tried to imagine the pecking bird again, but this time wasn't too successful, maybe because of the doubt he had sown in my mind. What else? Windowsill all right, bird wrong.

"A vase of flowers?"

I couldn't think of anything else on a windowsill; it was not an image so much as a speculation.

"Look, friend, don't think. Don't run down a list of things you might find on a windowsill, that's not how it works. Forget about words, conclusions, associations. Just try to visualize what it might be in connection with that window."

I tried to visualize it again. This time, surprisingly, it evoked a memory. My father had brought home a little Buddha statue from one of his voyages. My mother had not been sure she liked it because it was "pagan," and she did not want any idols in her house. "A little statue of some kind?" I suggested.

"Like what?"

"Mind you, this is not an image, but a memory. A little Buddha?"

"Spot on! You see, if only you try, it comes."

"But this wasn't something I *saw*, Barfield! This was a memory of a present my father brought home for my mother seventy years ago."

"It doesn't matter how it presents itself to you, friend. It's the image that counts. You came up with the image of a little statue of Buddha on a windowsill. Okay, that's what it is. Now tell me: Is it a photograph?"

"No idea."

"Try."

"No idea. I think I have given you all I'm able to give at this moment. Let's forget about the rest."

"Okay. For your information, it's the photograph of a painting by a famous woman painter." He tried to remember the name —"It can't be Anita Loos? No, she's a writer. Well, never mind. Come out and have a look yourself. Very good, by the way. You're a good candidate."

"Thank you. Can somebody help me out of this rig?"

Young Dr. Wildeman opened the door to the booth and helped me get rid of the tabs. I dressed and shuffled back to the control room; when I got there I saw, on the television screen, that Pjotr had taken my place on the couch. By the time he was rigged up, he had fallen asleep. Barfield tried in vain to wake him, then threw up his hands in defeat. "I honestly don't know if I can use that guy," he said.

I explained to him that Pjotr, given his mental limitations, could only be counted on to perform the task we had tried to groom him for: to take off for the moon, look for the buggy with the crumpled fender, and read the dial on the dosimeter. "He's memorized that procedure, starting with the dark tunnel with a light at the end, the way he used to memorize a commando operation. Think 1944."

"All right," Barfield said. "Would you like to take over? Maybe he'll listen to your voice rather than mine."

"Are you sure? I'm not experienced—"

"Stop it, Harinxma. Just talk to the guy. Get him into the dark tunnel with the light of the moon at the end. Okay? You have rehearsed it often enough, right?"

With great misgivings I took his place at the mike and said, "Pjotr, are you there?" The answer was snores.

Barfield asked, "How does he read, Wildeman?"

Wildeman read the dials on the instrument panel and came up with a series of esoteric numbers. "He's ripe to go, if ever he is."

"Try again, Harinxma," Barfield ordered.

"Okay, Pjotr, here we go. This is the real thing, boy. You are at the beginning of the long, dark tunnel. At the far end of it you see a full moon. Do you read me? Answer, boy. Do you see the moon?"

To my amazement Pjotr's voice came back, sounding very distant. "Not yet, Skip. I—I see a light . . . not bright, not a bright light, I see—a dim light with shadows—a shadow—crossing back and forth—what is that, Skip?"

"No idea, Pjotr. Try to get a little closer. Maybe it is a closeup of the moon's surface. Maybe you're closer than you think. Do you see a buggy?"

"No, it moves. The shadow moves. It's not part of the moon, I don't think. Give me the landmarks again."

Tex, the most methodical of us, had a copy of the detailed assignment in his briefcase. "Here you are, Skipper."

I unfolded the paper. "All right, Pjotr, here you go. Coming in from earth and positioning yourself overhead, as arranged, there is a rock formation at ten o'clock. A cluster of three little hills at three-thirty—"

"Oh, my God!" Pjotr's voice cried from the loudspeaker. "My God, my God!" He sang the last "God" in a tone of delight and surprise.

"Readings!" Barfield snapped.

Wildeman began to read the dials again.

"There she is!" Pjotr cried, ecstatic now. "There she is! Darling, darling, there you are!"

Wildeman called a warning.

"Get him out of there!" Barfield commanded with a sound of urgency. "On with the lights! Get him out, get him out!"

"How wonderful!" Pjotr's voiced cried faintly, much further from the microphone. "Louise, darling! Not so fast!" Then he fell silent.

He looked asleep on the TV screen, his head on one side.

"Hurry!" Barfield shouted.

The bosun was the first to get to the door of the booth. I followed him. He tore it open, turned on the light. I saw Pjotr over his shoulder: naked, some of the tabs torn off his chest, head to one side.

"Let me at him!" Barfield pushed us aside, entered the booth, took out a stethoscope, listened to Pjotr's chest, lifted his eyelids. "Ambulance!" he called. "An ambulance on the double!"

Wildeman muttered something; the professor said, "For God's sake, hurry up, man!" He pushed his way out of the booth and ran to the telephone himself. The bosun took his place and held Pjotr's hand while I said, into his ear, "Pjotr, tell me. This is the skipper. Tell me, how are you? Where are you? Talk to me!"

No reaction. I heard Barfield speaking on the telephone; then he came back. "Let me have another look."

The bosun and I made room for him. He listened to Pjotr's chest again. "Anyone here familiar with mouth-to-mouth resuscitation?"

"I am," Wildeman said. He took Barfield's place and started to apply CPR to Pjotr.

"What the devil happened?" Tex asked in a whisper. I had not noticed the wheelchair's approach.

"It seems Pjotr has lost consciousness."

"Louise was his fish."

We looked at each other.

He said, matter-of-factly, "Not good, is it?"

"No, it isn't."

"Is he dead, Ome?"

"No, Bosun, I don't think so. Just unconscious. He passed out."

The bosun said, "Oh,"

The ambulance arrived within minutes with an emergency physician, a brisk young doctor who said, "Let me have a look at the patient, will you?"

We made room for him. He did not spend much time on Pjotr. After a few seconds he straightened up and said, "Expired. I'll take him."

"Could we have a moment?" Barfield asked, beckoning the doctor into the passage. They walked off a short distance, then talked in low voices. The conversation ended with the doctor saying, "Sorry about that, but I have to follow the rules. I'll notify the coroner's office."

"Why the coroner?" Wildeman asked, with a sound of alarm. "This is a normal event! I mean: these are experiments to do with sleep, the old gentleman just slipped—"

"It's okay, Wildeman," Barfield snapped. "I have fully informed our colleague."

"May we get at him, please?" an ambulance man asked.

The doctor said, at the last moment, "On second thought, I'd rather leave him where he is. Don't touch anything, just leave him. We'll get him later."

"Why?" Barfield asked. "It's a perfectly normal—"

"Sorry," the doctor said on his way out. "Rules."

"Jesus!" Wildeman whispered. "What is he up to?"

"What do you think?" Barfield walked back to the control room. "Let's put our records in order. I want every move written down, every word."

"It's all on tape!" Wildeman cried after him.

"Not enough. If he is up to what I think he is, we'd better get all our ducks in a row." He disappeared into the control room.

Tex realized how I must be feeling. In an unexpected gesture he took my hand, squeezed it, and said, "It's not your fault, Fancy. You did what the man told you to do."

"Yes," I said, still stunned by the shocking development.

"I don't know what they are up to," Tex said, his voice low, "but pull yourself together before they get to you. You bear no responsibility, you did exactly what the expert told you to do. At no time did you make any suggestion yourself."

"Thank you, Tex," I said, "but I'll have to work this out."

He gave me a shrewd look. He was an experienced commander. I had the feeling he was debriefing me after a raid in which there had been casualties. It was well meant, but my guilt was undeniable. Not just for Pjotr's death but for bringing the confused old man all the way from Paris to this Texas town, for his appointment in Samarra.

"You may feel guilty as all hell," Tex persisted, "but that's in your own mind. Realize that. Factually, you have no responsibility for this incident. Is that clear?"

I only half-listened to him. "What are you suggesting?"

"That we are waiting for the police."

"The police? Why?"

"Because this business must smell a mile to a young emergency doctor in a place like Big Owl. As far as he's concerned, this man died under suspicious circumstances."

"Oh, my God . . ."

Ten minutes later the sheriff arrived: a big man in a uniform with a straw ten-gallon hat which he took off, not out of respect for the dead but because the booth was too small. He looked at the scene without comment, then called, "Photographer!"

Pictures were taken. Wildeman, beside himself with stress and frustration, had to be calmed down by the professor, who seemed to take it all in his stride. Finally, Pjotr's body was collected by the stretcher and taken away. We were about to follow when the sheriff put his hat on and held us back. "Hold it, folks! This is now a police investigation. There will be an autopsy, a coroner's report, that sort of thing, and one heck of a lot of documentation. I'm sorry, but I can't permit y'all to leave town until this has been straightened out. So, go back to Mother Billie's. I'll be contacting y'all presently."

"Can't we go with him to the hospital?" Fons asked.

"Sorry, neighbor," the sheriff said. "Do as I tell you." He said it with an authority that put an end to our protestations. "I'll be questioning y'all before long, don't talk it over among yourselves."

"Can I make a phone call?" I asked.

"Sure, go right ahead. I'll hang around till you're through."

Miss Bastiaans had left a telephone number in San Antonio. I was lucky to find her still there. I told her briefly what the situation was. "All right," she said calmly, "don't worry. Do what the man says. I'll call Rusty."

"Are you through?" the sheriff asked.

"Yes, I am."

"Let's go."

We went back to Mother Billie's; a desolate little group of silent old men herded by the sheriff. At the motel we went to our rooms and stayed put, as ordered. But we communicated with one another via the house phone, which the sheriff had overlooked.

I spoke to Tex first. He said, "It's perfectly clear what happened. Pjotr concentrated on the operation—being propelled to the moon, finding the buggy with the crumpled fender, reading the first dial from the left, memorizing it or reporting it if there was still voice contact with headquarters, then back to base. He wasn't interested in anything else. He sort of hibernated until the action started—*his* action. He knew about the tunnel, but I don't believe he really understood what it meant; he just trusted us."

"That's what gets me," I said. "Barfield pushed it through, but it was us that Pjotr trusted, his old comrades. It was us—*me* —who put him into that tunnel and urged him to head for the light. When he reached the light, instead of finding himself in space or on the moon, he found himself in his underwater world, with his fish waiting for him. He made off with Louise. What a way to go! But that's not the last word. I, myself—"

"Stop flogging yourself, Skipper. All of us let it happen. Go get yourself some rest."

I had barely put down the phone when it rang. The sheriff said in an unforthcoming voice, "For your information: we have just arrested one of your folks, a guy called Booren—*Van* Booren? Is that right?"

"Fons van Buren, yes! What happened?"

"He disobeyed orders and snuck out of his room when no one was looking. We found him at the hospital. Holding the hand of the corpse, for Christ's sake. I arrested him and put him in the slammer. I just want to warn y'all: no more tricks, or all of you will end up in there. This is no joke, sir. This may be homicide." He put the phone down.

There was a knock on my door. I opened. It was the bosun. "Are you all right, Ome?"

"Come in, Bosun, quick. Yes, I'm all right, how are *you*?"

"I don't really understand what happened. Can you tell me, Ome?"

"Pjotr fell asleep on his waterbed," I said, "and died in his sleep. That's really all there is to it."

"They didn't *do* anything to him, did they, Ome?"

"No, just the usual. He had earphones on, he had the mike —you weren't in the control room?"

"No, I was outside. I didn't want to interfere."

I pictured him pacing up and down the hallway, worried. He was the best friend any of us had, the Good Shepherd of the crazies.

I spoke to Tex again on the telephone. About the funeral, if we could all chip in for a headstone. It was like the war: only we didn't have any headstones then, just temporary wooden crosses, which in most cases became permanent. I wondered if on the distant shore we would be watching Pjotr cavorting in the shallows with Louise. An image to protect me from the reality of the dead body, the truth.

During the Nuremberg Trials the excuse "I obeyed orders, I was told to do it" was not accepted.

38

AN HOUR LATER there was another knock on the door; this time, to my surprise, it was Fons.

"Hey, I thought you were in the pokey!"

"He wants us all in the manager's office," he said.

"Who does?"

"The sheriff. He has something to tell us."

"When? Now?"

"Yes."

The six of us convened in the manager's office: Tex, Fons, the professor, Wildeman, the bosun, and myself. The sheriff welcomed us, looking dour. "I have to tell you, gentlemen, that the inquiry has been terminated. There may not even be an inquest. You are free to go whenever you like; I'm through with y'all. You may want to contact the hospital and the funeral parlor, I leave that to you. Have a nice day." It was obvious he was offended by this development.

The manager's office was not private, so the four of us went to the Big Owl Barbecue. The professor and Wildeman disappeared the moment we were set free.

We talked of the surprising development and the sheriff's reaction; it was decided unanimously that I should try to contact the man at home that evening to find out why the inquiry had been so suddenly abandoned. I did not expect him to level with me, but it was worth a try. Tex and Fons went to make arrangements for the funeral. Wearing the straw ten-gallon hat I had bought because the fierce sun was blistering my bald spot, I wandered over to the gas station. I figured they would know, if anyone did, where the sheriff lived. A lanky Texan with "Bert" on his coveralls asked, "Why do you want to know?"

I told him it was none of his business.

"I'm his brother, so you'd better tell me."

"Sorry, Bert, it's private. My name is Commodore Harinxma. I'm part of the scientific research team that's working here in the old high school."

"Ah," he said. His face took on the same expression as that of the officers of the *Atlantic Maiden* to whom we had been known as "the crazies." He took me there in his pickup truck, as I had no transportation.

A large woman with the face of a child opened the door and asked what my business was with her husband. While I was trying to explain, the sheriff loomed behind her and said, "It's okay, Kate. Let the man in."

I put my hat next to an identical one on the hat rack and followed her inside. One wall of the room was taken up by two Barcaloungers facing a large television. I sat down on an ottoman with my back to the screen. I saw several kittens, and a huge male dog stalked me while we were talking. It made me nervous when he suddenly lunged, but he was after one of the kittens hiding between my feet.

"Tell me, Sheriff," I asked, "how come the whole inquiry has been stopped so suddenly?"

He looked at me with a frown. "What is that to you, friend?"

"Let me explain to you what our role is in this thing. The five of us are World War II veterans, Hollanders, with the exception of the man who died, who was a Pole. They drafted us for this experiment, and we want to know what exactly is going on. We want to decide if we'll continue with this experiment or pack it in."

"Would you like a long neck?" the huge woman asked gently.

I had no idea what she was talking about, but decided not to say that I liked my neck as it was. "Thank you," I said, wondering what would turn up.

I don't know what mollified the sheriff; maybe he was not mollified but just so outraged by what had happened that he was dying to tell somebody. His wife returned with a bottle of beer and a dish of pretzels. I took one and gave half of it to the dog. The sheriff said, "Okay, I'll tell you. But you must swear that y'all won't talk about it to anyone else. I don't want to get into trouble, see?"

"Sure." I did not see at all.

"Okay then." He shifted in his Barcalounger. "I was ordered to drop the inquiry by the Pentagon."

"Excuse me?"

"You heard me: the Pentagon. Their representative told me to knock it off. So what could I do? I'm only the law in Big Owl County. But I felt pissed off. Sorry, honey."

"Oh, come on," she said, tired. "Another pretzel, Mr.—I didn't catch your name."

"It's very complicated. You'd better call me by my nick-name, Fancy That."

"Wha—?" I don't think she quite got it. "Well, you gave half of it to the dog, who doesn't deserve it. He snatches what he wants. Have another."

"Thank you, ma'am."

"Not a word to anyone else," the sheriff said. "Deal?"

"Deal. Have you any idea in what way the Pentagon is involved?"

"Don't ask me, friend. Those politicians—well, hell, we all know, we're just suckers. Up in Washington—the Pentagon *is* in Washington, isn't it?"

"I think it's in Virginia."

"Well, wherever, they're all politicians. Obviously, they had a finger in the pie here. What did you say your program was about?"

"It has to do with the future space station. We were asked to perform a few experiments."

"I see." It was obvious he didn't "Well, what have you had to eat other than that pretzel?"

"Excuse me?"

"He means, why don't you stay for dinner?" she said. "I think he'd like to talk to you. He's a veteran himself, not World War II, but Korea."

"Close enough," I said. "Thank you, yes, I'd be happy to."

So I stayed for dinner. It gave him plenty of opportunity to air his grievances against the bullfrogs in Washington. "You know, we ex-military, we don't hold with that kind of crap. When you say 'Pentagon' to us, we think it has something to do with real life, don't we? No, sir, it's full of bureaucrats just like the Capitol, where all they do is play games among themselves. You and me—we're just—what do you call them? Pawns. Take this county . . ."

I had never been subject to southern hospitality before; I must confess, it was wonderful. I became a little woozy after the one long neck became four. I had a delicious meal which I cannot remember, but in the back of my mind was that mysterious keyword: Pentagon. Miss Bastiaans a tool of the Pentagon? Ludicrous! But then, what was it to her? As a headhunter, she'd hunt heads anywhere for the collector ready to hire her. Yet . . .

I balked at the ultimate conclusion.

The sheriff, however, had no such inhibitions. "All right," he said, "let's start at the beginning. How old are you?"

"Eighty-two."

"And the others?"

"Same age, more or less, all from the same war."

"You're all aliens, that right?"

"Yes."

"Who hired you in the first place?"

"A man called Colonel Fumduck, or something. I'm sorry, I've lost his name for a moment—Buckram."

"Y'all are without—y'all don't have any *real* next of kin, do you?"

"Sorry, I don't understand."

"It sounds to me like the Pentagon—or some gungho bubba in it acting on his own—came up with the idea of an experiment to catch up with the Russians, or the A-rabs, or whoever—something that might result in casualties. What would have happened if the man who died this morning had been an American, with a granddaughter, or even neighbors, to cause a stink? That situation had to be avoided, so whoever-it-was got himself a bunch of elderly aliens without next of kin."

"I have a daughter in England."

"Would she raise a stink if you kicked the bucket here?"

"I—I don't know, really."

"Well, the guy from the Pentagon must sure as hell have doubted it, otherwise he wouldn't have picked you. What about the others? The man who died this morning? Does he have any relatives?"

"None."

"And the other old men, apart from yourself?"

"Not really. Their relatives would be dismayed, but I don't think they would know how to make waves in the United States."

"Well, there you go. The guy picked y'all because, if he lost one, who the hell cared? Not that they are bad or cruel or underhand or whatever, just that they have a bright light they're heading for. Some old geezer pining away in a nursing home overseas is given the chance to do something exciting. What's wrong with that? So he croaks? He had a good run for his money and an exciting adventure at the end of it. That's how they reason, I know them. I've dealt with them. No, honey, no more beer, thank you. But maybe our friend?"

"No, thank you," I said, "I'm quite happy." Happy was not the word.

"I'm sure that's how it came about. Who found you, by the way? The Pentagon wouldn't just wade in and pick you out, somebody else must have. Who?"

It was the question I had tried to avoid. "A headhunter," I said lamely.

"A good name." He laughed.

I felt sick. I was sure that Miss Bastiaans had not—or not knowingly.

"Whoever the guy was," the sheriff said, trying to scratch his back by squirming in his Barcalounger, "he had the conscience of a bobcat."

There was no way around it: dear old Bastiaans. Fellow survivor of Holland's Glory. Friend of many years.

"If I were you," the sheriff said, "I'd go home now, wherever it is, Holland, and take it easy. Have the guts to be your age, man! See what I mean?"

Mrs. Sheriff smiled at me with the motherly love of the very heavy. "Holland? Isn't that where the little boy put his finger in the dike?"

"Yes," I said. "But that was in a book."

She agreed wholeheartedly. "I read it as a little girl. There was this little boy and there was a storm and he heard the dike squeak, and—"

It must have been the long necks, but it all seemed to come together in one conclusion: Bastiaans could not possibly have done it.

"He had a little dog called Pip," Mrs. Sheriff said, moved by the memory.

"I'm not surprised," I said idiotically.

When I took my straw hat off the stand in the hall, I noticed a card stuck behind the sweatband that said: "LIKE HELL IT'S YOURS! This hat belongs to Sheriff John (Squatty) Williams."

I exchanged it for mine.

39

THE SHERIFF was kind enough to drive me back to the motel, where I found the others all gathered in my room: Tex belligerent, Fons looking earnest, the bosun upset, as if he foresaw that this was the end.

"Well?" Tex asked. "Let's have it."

I told them, despite my promise to the sheriff that I would not share the Pentagon information with others. I could not keep it from them, for this was the real issue, not whether Miss Basti-aans had sold us down the river.

"Well, this is the limit!" Tex said. "I gave my legs to the war effort, now they want my soul as well? The hell with them! You were right, Fancy, that day you came to see me: I *have* become a pacifist at heart. I'm not about to go to the moon just so some colonel can find out how to plant invisible spies in Russia, or whoever the enemy is nowadays. The hell with them! I'm going home. How about you, Fons?"

Fons looked at me with the patience of a man used to having his fate decided by others. "Well, if Tex is leaving and you're leaving, I can't hang around here by myself. Will they pay for our return trip if we leave early?"

"You bet!" Tex said, ready for all comers. "After they've killed one of us, they won't want the others to line up, hollering 'Hey, wait a minute!' If you ask me, something went wrong. I've been thinking about it, their whole scheme. They chose male aliens over eighty, supposedly without next of kin to make trouble. So they lost one? Back to the old drawing board! But *why* did they lose one? That's where the rub is. They made a basic mistake: not realizing that by stimulating an out-of-body experience in the over-eighty they were, in effect, stimulating the near-death syndrome. And *because* we are old, *because* we have no next of kin other than two nagging women, life has nothing in store for us. The essence of the near-death experiences that people report, about arriving at the end of the tunnel, meeting a being of Light, or something of light, is so much like the out-of-body experience. Except they're told, 'Not yet, not yet! You must go back because—' For all sorts of reasons: babies, obligations, you name it. But we never hear from the ones who were *not* persuaded to go back: *they* just kept going! They died! They put Pjotr through a near-death experience, but instead of a creature of light saying 'Not yet, Pjotr, not yet,' he met his fish. He cried 'Louise!' and made off with her. No wonder, for what was the alternative? Being shipped back to that foul home for old men in France?"

"Makes sense," I said.

"Of course it does. The people who were put through the same experience by Monroe and the others came back because, to them, it was the experience itself that counted. That's where the Pentagon, with all its money and its brains, tripped up. It was a technical error: they put him through a near-death experience instead of an OOBE, and he grabbed his chance to escape from a miserable life. If they had put *me* in that position . . . well, never mind. I'm going home. And so, I suppose, are all of us." He looked about him, and singled out the bosun. "How about you?"

It was an unfair question; the poor man had no choice.

"Well, I sort of liked—I'll miss you. All of you."

"I'll sure miss you," Tex said gruffly. "Nobody will ever drive my wheelchair at that speed again. But I'll be damned if I go on with this game. Use my soul for warfare? I'll choose hell first. And you, Fancy? What's your decision?"

"Well—"

"Don't tell me you want to hang in here with your tooth fairy? She's the one who cooked this up!"

"Now, don't let's rush to conclusions. Let's decide first—"

"She was the one who got us into this and, by God, she must have known! If anyone knew what Colonel Rusty represented, it must have been she! And she calmly—"

"I think we are running ahead of things. First let's decide—"

"We *have* decided, haven't we? We want to go back! I don't even consider the possibility that one of us might not."

"He's right, Fancy," Fons said, tired. "I can't take any more of this. Let's leave—after the funeral . . ."

"All right," I said. "If that's the unanimous decision."

"Of course it is," Tex snapped. "Now, who is going to tell Miss Broomstick? You?"

Sick at heart, I said, "I will."

40

SHE ARRIVED that night at eleven. I suggested we meet in her room, but she was not staying in Mother Billie's, so we met in my room.

When she knocked and opened the door, she looked exactly the way she had when I had first seen her in the South of France: smiling, radiant despite all her sins.

"Come in," I said.

She did; she sat down in the solitary easy chair and crossed her legs, something she did well. "What seems to be the trouble?" she asked.

"I have seen the sheriff. He told me under oath of secrecy that this experiment was organized by the Pentagon. There is only one conclusion: you were a representative of the Pentagon. What you did, in effect, my dear, was sell the lot of us to the glue factory."

She frowned. "Have you been drinking while waiting?"

"I trusted you. I loved you. I've loved you for a long time. But then, I'm not the only one. All of us suckers loved you. Old Kwel was a scoundrel, an ogre, but you—well, be that as it may, old Pjotr was killed by you, don't let there be any doubt about it. You knew what was going to happen, you knew what was awaiting us, you collected five old aliens for your little colonel to do with as he pleased. If he lost a few, who would care? Well, he lost one, and now I'm ready to throw you overboard. You foul, miserable traitor! You have no soul, no heart, no conscience, you are just a walking piggy bank, that's all."

"Do you want me to answer all this or shall we wait until you're sober?"

"I have never been more sober than I am now, old girl. You are a swine. A cold-hearted, soulless swine. You killed a man this morning. Can't I get that through the cotton wool in your glorious ears? *You killed a man*—period. Why don't you go back to whatever it was you were doing before you entered the betrayal business?"

"I've heard you better, Commodore," she said. "I've always enjoyed your harangues, but this time you're overdoing it."

"Am I? Well, then let me tell you—"

"I was asked by a client, Colonel Buckram, to select four elderly navigators for an experiment in time which sounded interesting and exciting. I thought of you, because I often think of you—"

"For God's sake, cut the shit! You make me vomit."

She smiled. "Let me continue, please. I thought of you and decided to give you the task to collect the others, which you did. I had no idea that your lives would be in danger. Nobody imagined that. I thought it was a fascinating experiment that would interest you. I thought it would be one way of liberating you from the usual old-age syndrome. And it did. You may be furious now, but it did. Look at you! Just look at you now!"

I don't know what I was about to say; the way she looked at me stopped me. All that nonsense about whatever his name is—Seneca?—escaping from the clutches of the raving lunatic, forget it. At the age of eighty-two I was helpless in the hands of this shop stewardess of the oldest trade union in the world.

"Come," she said, "let's take this a little less theatrically. I'm very sorry that Pjotr expired. I did not foresee it, I don't think anybody did. I don't want to go in for speculations what the rest of his life would have looked like in that institution in Clamart. The fact remains, he died. To say that I'm guilty of it—are you sure you don't feel guilty yourself and are trying to get rid of some of it?"

"That's not the point. The point is: Did you or did you not know that your employer was the Pentagon? That the experiment was part of psychic warfare?"

"Why should that be the point?"

"To us, whose lives are marked by war, it is. Or rather, it turned out to be, once we discovered what the purpose of our training was. You should have asked us: 'Are you prepared to contribute to the war effort?' All of us would have said no. Can't you see how important that was to us?"

Her face expressed patience. "Be that as it may, I did *not* know. I fell for the cover story of the dosimeter on the moon. Rusty did not see fit to enlighten me—for good reasons, it now turns out. So let's wait until the fuss is over, then we'll talk."

"What fuss?"

"I have to supervise Pjotr's funeral, book passages for those who wish to leave—"

"We *all* want to leave. We—"

She suddenly moved in and kissed me. "Time for bed." She turned away and opened the door. Before disappearing, she added, "Sorry to leave you holding the bag."

I was left to work out what the devil she meant. Bag? What bag? God, give me a crew of pirates any time! I wouldn't have a moment's problem; but give me one woman like Bastiaans—well, work it out for yourself.

41

PJOTR'S FUNERAL was a sad affair, at nine o'clock in the morning after a night in which each of us had lain awake wrestling with his own thoughts.

He was displayed in an open coffin in the viewing room of the funeral parlor. An elaborate coffin; obviously, the Pentagon had paid for it. Because of the price of the coffin, the funeral director had given him the top-of-the-line treatment. He was smiling, with rouged cheeks and a bee-sting mouth, the way he had looked when he came out of Miss Bastiaans' bedroom in her suite in the hotel in Paris. Tex muttered, "He should be wearing his toque." I thought of putting it in, but the bosun had packed it, together with the rest of the women's clothes, to be returned to the rightful owner.

The rightful owner looked gorgeous in black. The funeral director, despite his professional look of gloom, could not control his roving eyes. She became positively disturbing when we were all standing by the graveside; the wind played with her summer dress as if a ghostly sculptor with caressing hands were giving the final touches to a nude statue. We had had a brief discussion as to which religious service Pjotr should receive; as the fish was a symbol of early Christianity, we decided that a Roman Catholic priest would be the most suitable. The priest, despite his vows of celibacy, endured a distracted ten minutes while reading the prayers for the dead, glancing simultaneously over the edge of his prayer book at the wind's work on Miss Bastiaans.

Ashes to ashes, dust to dust; the priest, aware of the fact that his client was a deep-sea diver and a hero of World War II, talked in terms of "triumphant entry" into the hereafter. It sounded Roman.

When the ornate coffin was lowered into the grave, each of us in turn threw some earth on it, which seemed to be the practice there, then walked away, aware for the first time of our surroundings. Small gravestones with ancient dates; a few ornate ones which would not have looked out of place in Père Lachaise in Paris, except for their inscriptions. *He Roped His Last Bull Calf.* And *Mourned by Many Wives, Including His Own.* Obviously, a graveyard was not necessarily a gloomy place in Texas.

I was packing in the hotel and trying to telephone Helen to announce my imminent arrival, when there was a knock on my door. There stood Miss Bastiaans, no longer in black, but in something flimsy and even more revealing; the temperature was approaching a hundred out there.

"I suggest we have a meal together tonight, Commodore," she said. "I have something to discuss with you. Something concerning yourself. It is urgent."

"I counted on leaving in an hour or two with the others . . ."

She gave me a look that would have been improved by tenderness; then she said, "All right, let me give it to you straight. I did not tell you at the time, as we all were busy and it was not an urgent matter. You remember the physical you were given before your departure?"

"Of course. Why?"

"It now seems that one of your test results was dangerously high."

"What might that be?"

"The test that shows the possibility of cancer of the prostate. It's a fairly recent discovery; it's helped a lot of men because it offers early detection. I suggest you visit a urologist and have it investigated."

I felt like asking why she had kept this to herself all this time, but it was obvious why: she had not wanted me to leave until the job was done.

"All right, I'll have it seen to the moment I arrive in Europe. Thank you."

"I think you should have it seen to now, Commodore. You're in Texas, a stone's throw from Houston and the best cancer center in the southern United States. I'll make the arrangements, take you there, stay with you until the results are known. Then we'll see what the next step should be; if there has to be surgery, you should have it done here in America. It will be paid for by your employers. The moment you leave this country you would miss that financial help."

I looked at her for a moment in silence; then I said, "Let's have dinner together and talk it over. I'll telephone my daughter to say there has been a holdup."

"That seems a sensible idea." She opened the door. "I know how you feel. I know what you're thinking. I did not fool you, but we had that out, didn't we?"

"If you say so."

"For God's sake, Harinxma! Stop posturing, it's ridiculous! God dammit, we're of the same profession, sole survivors of the lot! Go, call your daughter, and let's whoop it up a bit."

"In memory of Pjotr?"

"The hell with Pjotr," she said, and slammed herself out.

So I had cancer of the prostate. I had often asked myself in the past how men must feel when they were given what might be a death sentence. To my amazement, it did not make much of an impression on me. I had received so many death sentences in the past that this one triggered the conditioned reflex: *Death, where is thy stingalingaling?* I would worry about it when my number came up. Maybe my number *was* up. Well, I had had a good run for my money; most members of my class were dead.

I had better tell Helen that I had a not terribly serious, but not totally gratuitous, health problem and that I would come home via Houston at a future date.

When I finally got through, a child's voice said, "Yes!"

I said, "This is your granddad."

"You're not!" the child said. "My granddad lives next door."

"Well, would you mind giving me Mrs.—er—whatever her name is, your aunt, neighbor—the lady of the house."

"The lady of the house had a naughty little mouse," the child's voice recited, at five bucks per second. It was like making the dog in France bark into the telephone when you were in Punta Arenas.

"Listen," I said. "You lay off that telephone and call the lady who lives there."

"That's my Mum."

"Well, call your Mum, for God's sake! Call *somebody!*"

Unwise to speak to little children in such tones. There was the sound of a strangled sob; a woman asked, "What *are* you doing to my daughter, whoever you are?"

"Sorry, wrong number." I should have come to that conclusion sooner.

I asked for the number again; this time, after a couple of rings, Helen's voice answered, "Yep! Who is this for?"

"For you," I said.

"Dad!" The joy in her voice was touching. "Where are you? Still in Big Owl?"

"I am, love, but my departure has been postponed. I thought I'd let you know."

"Why? Has the flight been canceled?"

"No. I had a medical before we sailed and it now turns out there is something that should be looked at."

"What?"

"Well—er—" Impossible to call a spade a spade in front of your daughter, who, after all—well—that was the way she had come into the world. "A male complaint."

"Your prostate, Dad?"

"Yes . . ."

"How come you only hear that now?"

"The tests had to be worked up, it seems, and the result only caught up with me now."

"And who was the happy messenger, may I ask? Miss Bastiaans?"

"What the hell does that matter?"

"She had the only valid reason I can think of to keep it a secret from you until this job was over. She wouldn't let one of her team of dogs go to the vet while still lugging loads for her."

"Love, do me a favor. I know you and Miss Bastiaans have congenital differences . . ."

"Congenital differences? Hell! She's a bitch! A heartless, soulless—"

"Helen, I did not call you at considerable cost to witness a slugfest between you and—"

"Okay, okay, sorry. So, when are you coming?"

"I don't know. I have to go to Houston, consult a specialist, and take it from there."

"Are you going to be hospitalized, Dad?"

"I have no idea."

"If you do, make sure you tell me and I'll come right over. Do you hear me, Dad? I'll come right over, I'm not going to have you in hospital in Texas all on your own. Promise?"

"Promise," I said. The courage failed me to tell her that someone else had already booked a ringside seat.

"I see," she said suddenly, with one of those dead voices

women use when they are struck by extrasensory perception. "I suppose *she* will be there."

"All right, dear love. Good-bye." I put the damn phone down. Enough is enough: my prostate and I were going to have a drink with Miss Bastiaans of the loveless eyes. Well, never mind the eyes.

42

WE HAD A MEAL in a Turkish restaurant, the existence of which I had not expected in a place like Big Owl. Maybe it was attached to a Turkish bath.

It was pitch-dark inside, darker than the bar in the Réserve had been when I sealed my fate. It was full of large men and large women in various positions of intimacy, the details obscured by the gloom. I put my hat on a stand full of identical hats, and regretted not having a card inside saying "LIKE HELL IT'S YOURS! This hat belongs to Commodore (Fancy That) Harinxma."

As we were being seated, a beehive-coiffed country songstress was belting out the standard country grief; by the time we had been given a table and ordered vodka on the rocks, the music changed. To an oriental tune of nasal instruments, a belly dancer appeared on the floor. She was huge, and had the most mobile abdomen I ever observed. She went from table to table churning her navel over the predinner peanuts; my fascination was terminated by Miss Bastiaans saying, "Commodore, here's looking at you." She raised her glass, took a hearty swallow, and said, "I had a telephone call from Holland. The nursing home. My father smashed the furniture again, so they had to restrain him. I persuaded them to buy new furniture on my account and keep him, rather than send him to a mental home."

It took me a moment to digest all this, then I said, "I had the impression that both your parents were gone."

She took another swig. The belly dancer and her *omphalos* advanced in our direction.

"My mother died when I was eight. My father never remarried."

"Ah."

"He did not need to."

"Ah?"

"He had *me*."

The belly dancer started to churn her navel over our peanuts. Her belt was full of dollar bills, tucked there by customers. I groped for my wallet; Miss Bastiaans opened her purse, took out a five-dollar bill, tucked it in the woman's belt, and took four dollars in change. It seemed typical: this was how she had become rich.

"Within a month after my mother's death he started to sleep with me," she continued after the woman was gone. "I became 'his little wife.' We kept that up for ten years, then he fell ill with Alzheimer's. He has been in a care facility ever since, to everyone's amazement. Naturally, the disease is terminal. I visit him whenever I can." She polished off her drink and held up the empty glass for the waiter to see.

I wondered—why this sudden confession? There must be a reason for it; there was a reason for everything she did. She was the most controlled person I knew. What was she up to?

"Of late," she continued, "my visits have become embarrassing. The obscenities, you know. I bring about more and more of those of late when I go to see him. Things like 'Show me your lovely little tits,' or 'How about one of our long, slow fucks?' I visit him now only in the company of an orderly or a nurse. I feel guilty for abandoning him, but—well, it's been a long time, all my adult life. He won't die, and he's older than you are."

"I'm sorry," I said. I was indeed sorry for her, but in an abstract sense. I had just heard I had cancer of the prostate, which brought about a certain compassion fatigue.

"I know I should hand him over to—well, there are institutions where they take care of these patients until they die. But I can't do it. I still love him. Isn't it odd? I've always loved him. I had no idea, when I was eight, that what we were doing was wrong. It was our little secret. But he turned me into a freak for the rest of my life. Now I'm only turned on by old men." She smiled. "I know you wondered about that."

The waiter came back with another round of drinks for us. I did not quite know how to handle the situation. Tomorrow she might be wanting to shoot herself for telling me. But, no, she was not the spontaneous type.

"I'm not telling you all this because I need a father confessor. I just want you to understand that I am not a pervert. I loved him heart and soul from the age of eight, like a wife. He loved *me*. Now he's insane, lost in a world of demons and devils. And there's nothing I can do for him, other than pay for his care and visit him occasionally. Most of the time he doesn't know me; when he does, all he thinks about is our making love. It's the last hold he has on life: *Little tits. One of our long, slow fucks.* All that in the presence of an orderly looking at his nails. Let me tell you: hell has many forms. Cheers."

"I'm sorry," I said. It was all I could come up with, for the beehive singer of cowboy love had taken over from the churning navel, chanting "Park with your tail to the sun . . ." Worthy of reflection, but not at that moment.

"Old Arnold knew," she went on. "And, of course, the doctors and the nurses, but they're professionals. Arnold was good about it. He held me close, kissed my hair, said, 'It doesn't matter, love is love.' Even so, there was a hint of it turning him on. Does it turn you on?"

If anything it turned me off. The whole business of the Pentagon, Pjotr's funeral, the four dollars change, the bold confession —it all turned me, in a form of flight, into Master after God, listening to a young mate who could not stand it any longer, whose wife had this, whose mother had that, a girl here, a grave there—*"Captain, what do I do next?"*

"I wish I could help," I said.

"Hell, I don't need help!" She slurped her drink. "What I need is love. No, not that kind of love: comradeship. Someone who's shared my past. The ships, the sailing—Gone forever, Harinxma, all to hell. You know KITCO and Van Dalen fused? Three years ago we were still trying to cut each other's throats, now it's one company, called KWEL VAN DALEN, with a fleet of two oceangoing tugs. Two. So, here we are, the last of the Mohicans." She took a swig from her new glass. "The towing business has been my life. I was eighteen when I started in Arnold's office. It has been ships, schedules, tows, chandlers, dry docks, hawsers, pilots, oilers ever since. Only after I accepted Rusty's assignment and became involved with you again did I realize how empty my life had become. Those little pieces you read to me, the first day, the bits about tugboats and cabin boys, it was like waking up to life again. Do you understand? Of course you don't. To you—"

"Don't write my dialogue, Miss Bastiaans."

"Oh, for Chrissakes!" she cried. "I don't mind your going pompous on me, but don't call me Miss Bastiaans, or Miss B. My name is Ellie! Learn to live with it!" She beckoned the waiter again and pointed at our glasses. The belly dancer saw the gesture and thought it was meant for her. The music had changed and off she went, navel churning like the pupil of a huge rolling eye.

When we were alone once more with fresh vodka on the rocks, I said, "It wasn't the job that rejuvenated me, it was you."

"Come on, Harinxma, don't start playing the flute. I hassled the hell out of you, I sent you ricocheting off the walls and made you end up with your feet in the air in—what was the name of the place?—the White Hart, in Exeter."

"You got me out of there. I went in there all by myself."

"So?"

"The giant tugs were my life too," I said. "The straight-line tows halfway around the globe."

"Like the one I nailed you for, the one with the Chinky-tinks and the little man who wanted to scupper the ship for the insurance money?"

"You didn't know about that at the time, did you?"

"Arnold sure did. I must have closed my maidenly eyes to the ugly truth. I wasn't quite at the stage yet where I went the whole hog."

"Meaning what?"

She ignored that question. "I may hate you, Harinxma. And you may hate me, but we are joined at the hip. Siamese twins of a world that is no more. And what a world it was."

"Why the hip?" I asked.

She was onto me like a flash. "Oh no," she said. "I'm not about to louse up our relationship with one of those ding-dongs of May and December. Well, *May* . . . We are not going to be lovers. I may take you in my arms when you fall overboard in icy water, but don't mistake—"

"I did that myself once. A junior mate, willowy as a bride, cold as a fish. We both were stripped naked, I ended up as a block of ice in his embrace, he was so cold. But there was no life left in his young god's body, no light under those long eyelashes. I was too late. I wrote a letter to his fiancée."

"Saying what?"

"Can the foc'sle humor, Bas—sorry—Ellie. It was a sincere letter. I would have loved to revive that boy for her: such grace, such joy, such dreams. And there he was, dead in the hairy embrace of a captain."

She smiled. "Going to be one hell of a lot of people waiting for you on that distant shore, Harinxma. We may lose sight of one another in the crush. I'll have to wear a rose between the teeth, to help you home in."

There came another of those harrowing waves of grief, that hit you out of the blue. Sylvia. My God, Sylvia. All this stuff was a dream, a play. No one who isn't a widower can have any idea of what that means. After she is gone—a living part of you, the one through whose eyes you saw, whose thoughts you thought

—you are left confused, insecure, in a fog of melancholy. She is there, yet not there. You are here, yet not here. You never realized it before that the shared life is the full life . . .

"What about old Kwel?" I asked. "He is sure to be there, waiting for you."

"Hell, that's a thought. Well, let's just sail on for a while, you and I, flying 'LB.' We'll find a reasonable hotel near the Medical Center, I'll hang around until you are ready to go home to your loving daughter. You and she could easily have ended up like my dad and me, if you had found yourselves alone together when she was young. She treats you as if you had, and me as an interloper."

"Can you afford losing all that time—in case I have to go into the hospital?"

"Don't worry," she said. "Houston is full of heads waiting to be hunted. I may even decide to start a branch of the business there."

"What about your London office?"

"I have a partner, young, blond, keen as mustard. His name is Robert Conway Jones. He'll squeal, but he'll live."

"Why are you doing this, Ellie?"

She stared at me in astonishment. "Here I am, after an hour's trying to explain it to you, and still you ask. Haven't you been listening at all?"

"I listened, but I still don't understand."

"Did you understand why you stripped to revive that drowned mate of yours?"

"That was different. He was a shipmate, I was his captain—"

"Well, what am I if not a shipmate? So, shut up. Let's have another one."

It sounded like the curtain of a play. I couldn't think of anything to say other than "How about ordering some food?"

"Aye-aye, sir," she said. "Waiter!"

43

IN HOUSTON, the diagnosis was prostate cancer.

Instead of going to a church, which I should have done, I took a bus and went to the harbor.

At first sight, the Houston ship channel was not the place to go for old sailors saying farewell to life. It was narrow, oily, messy, busy, and yet—and yet . . .

Freighters unloading with the racket of a row of houses collapsing. Shrimpers, with orange nets billowing high from their masts, foaming up the ship channel with names like *Captain Lottie* and *Tram Phu Pong*. How I loved it all! I would have given my left eye, anything, to sail the *Tram Phu Pong* and catch shrimp in the placid waters of the northern Gulf, lie on my back on the foredeck, look at the small flat prairie clouds in the stark blue sky, listen to the caterwauling of alien sailors to whom I felt closer than to the doctors in the Medical Center.

The urologist Miss B. had found for me was expensive and busy; three minutes per patient after an hour and a half's waiting. Quick finger up the ass, some babble about biopsies, and bingo: one hundred and fifty bucks. The hospital was huge, busy as a mall, and had a lobby like a memorial temple for a surgeon who had performed a triple bypass on some king who as a token of his gratitude had donated a fountain, couches, and a bronze bust of the doctor, available for private prayer.

In the waiting room of the Nuclear Medicine Department, where I was directed for a "bone scan," I was the only patient. After three quarters of an hour a man in a white coat appeared, holding a record file. "Are you the prostate?" he asked.

"Well—I suppose I am."

"Is your name"—leafing through the file with a frown—"Mart?"

"Yes, sir. I'm Mart the Prostate."

"That's all right, then," the character said. "Let's get with it."

On a table, stark naked in an Egyptian-mural pose, with a lid the size of a tomb pressing down on me, I was turned into a human sandwich. No questions like "Are you comfortable?" or "Is this okay?" The man was extremely helpful to everyone except the side of beef in his sandwich. "Harry"—or whatever his name was—"could you give us a hand here, please? We have to move this and we're one short."

"Yes, of course, doctor, right away!" There he went, full of good humor and readiness to serve. Then, from another direction: "Harry, would you mind taking these files to the record room? I have my hands full now."

"Yes, of course, doctor! Glad to."

Meanwhile, Mart the Prostate lay moaning under the lid. Dear God, if this is the greatest medical center in the South, I'll take hell.

Later, as I was talking to Ellie in her hotel suite, the telephone rang. The urologist. "Sir, your cancer seems to be confined to the prostate. There are a number of solutions. You're too old for surgery, but there are—No darling, not up there, please! One shelf lower. *One shelf lower,* thank you—there are other solutions: chemotheraphy, radiation, castration—Darling, please! I said *not* the top shelf, it will come crashing down the moment you— Excuse me, where was I?"

"Castration."

"Ah, yes. Well I—I'll be gone this weekend, so call my office and make an appointment with my nurse. I'll see you some time next week and we'll decide what to do. Okay?"

He did not wait for me to say "Okay" or "Thank you"; he put down the phone. This cardinal of the Medical Center Vatican had allowed me to kiss his ring and piss off.

I told Ellie I had had it with the Vatican. She suggested I go for a second opinion to the Cancer Center, which was the original reason for our coming to Houston. I made an appointment and traipsed off to another large hospital, where I found hundreds of people milling about in a huge waiting area. It seemed at first glance the same crowd, yet there was a difference. Many of those waiting for their appointment showed symptoms of the dread disease: some had no noses, others wore wool caps to hide their hairless skulls, or dragged themselves along on crutches. *Abandon all hope ye who enter here.* It was the most awesomely depressing place I had ever been to.

There I sat, alone, overcome by the hopelessness of this crowd of the doomed, wondering what had brought me here, which secret current of fate had caught me long ago and taken hold and carried me along until I ended up in this place for my appointment in Samarra. I don't think I have ever felt as alone in my life as during the hour of waiting for my verdict: Chemotherapy? Radiation? Castration? By chance, I happened to catch a glimpse of an old, cowboy-hatted Texan standing, rigid with fear, in the crowd; next to him, a young black nurse or receptionist in a white coat. He was desperately thin, wore a T-shirt saying DON'T MESS WITH TEXAS, a belt buckle the size of a saucer, blue jeans, and high-heeled boots. While talking to the patient's wife, who was sitting on one of the couches, the young nurse surreptitiously stroked the old man's arm.

For some reason this image changed the whole place for me. So I had cancer? That didn't mean irrevocable death. Here I might be cured for a while, postpone my appointment in Samarra. I have no idea why the small act of kindness I glimpsed made such a difference; no cardinal charging $150 for three minutes of his time would be able to explain it either. The image put me "in the zone," as athletes call it. A long-distance runner on the point of collapse, or a tennis player slowed down by exhaustion, may magically receive a second wind of energy, of revived hope, and win. Whoever that young nurse was, she would, for me, forever embody the essence of our humanity. She saved me from despair.

I was seen by two specialists who were human and took their

time; later, I had it explained to me that the difference was that they worked on a salary instead of a per-patient charge. It was decided I would receive a daily dose of radiation for eight weeks.

Miss Bastiaans took it in her stride. She had made contact with some prospective clients in Houston; after taking me to the hospital and back to the hotel each morning, she was gone for most of the day. I had lunch by myself in the coffee shop, then went upstairs for a snooze, and continued writing my little pieces on life at sea between the wars, as pulled from the cookie tin. They were a joy to do, especially as Miss Bas—sorry: Ellie—loved them. It became routine for me to read her the day's harvest after dinner in the hotel.

She was so enthusiastic about them that I began to write more than one a day, occasionally as many as three. "Boyhood Dreams," "On Packing," "Departures," "Seasickness," "Diaries"—she loved them all. It did not occur to me that she might be helping me keep my spirits up; they were good little pieces. But, in effect, she was doing what the young black nurse had done: stroking a terrified old man's arm.

After three weeks of daily radiation treatments I happened to pull a muscle while climbing onto the chest-high table. I became bothered by pain in my right leg. It began by my needing a stick; then the pain became such that I had to rent a pair of crutches from a drugstore and hobbled around like Long John Silver. My radiologist at the Cancer Center ordered an MRI: half an hour inside a tank reverberating with deafening hammer and riveting noises, like lying in the axle-tunnel of a ship in dry dock while they are replacing a plate. The diagnosis was: a ruptured disk in my spine. I would need surgery, but not while the radiation treatments were going on; I would have to be Long John Silver until further notice. Then my leg became so painful that I needed a wheelchair.

Talk about your feet never touching the ground! Contrary to what I had expected, it was the life of Riley. All doors opened for me. When I wanted to cross a street a policeman stopped traffic. In restaurants I was wheeled to the best table. Blue-rinsed ladies with Chihuahuas came to pat my cheek; I was invited by an unknown fellow traveler to the Wheelchair Olympics.

Ellie took it all in her stride, and on the eve of my surgery she sat me down for a heart-to-heart talk. "Listen, Harinxma: when you come out of the hospital, you'll need some TLC. That means a nurse, unless we rent a furnished apartment and I look after you. As it happens, I came across one that—"

The mere idea spooked me. "Like hell we will! I can make out very well here in the hotel, with room service and the maid of the watch! More important: my daughter. I don't want to send her into spirals of turbulence by—"

"You talk about her as if she were your wife! She's—"

"So I *do*, dammit! I am not about to set up a little love nest with you, or anyone else."

"Except her, right?"

"Right! Daughters are supposed to look after sick old fathers! In fact—"

"Look, Harinxma, don't let's make an issue of this. It was just a suggestion. If you don't want it for reasons of your own, forget it. Should you change your mind—"

"I'll fall straight into your lap. Right?"

"Harinxma, I am not staying because I am in love with you. I just can't let you flummox around by yourself after surgery."

"Why not?"

"Because there's only the two of us left! Give me a break. Okay?"

"Okay," I said.

"All I do is think how I would feel in a wheelchair."

I did not tell her how pleasant it was. Don't ask me why. Nasty old man's stuff; after eighty, one always eats the rose one loves.

44

SO WE STAYED in the hotel. I had surgery, came out after a week, felt terrific, went for a first walk, tripped up on a ridge in the pavement, tried to outrun my forward fall, but came down, arms outstretched, with my right hand in an ornamental flower bed that turned out to contain the bottom of a broken beer bottle. I bled like a pig, my little finger barely hanging on. Off to the emergency room at the Medical Center, where a jolly young doctor put it all back together while telling me about his aunt, who had done the same. I hobbled out with my arm in a sling, and, dammit, the pain in my hip and knee had returned with a vengeance.

So: back into the hammer tank; diagnosis: the rest of the disk in my back, which had been only partially removed, was now intruding into the nerve. Another operation was needed. This time, feeling not only sorry for myself but crashing out of the zone, I let Ellie move my things out of the hotel while I was, once again, in hospital for back surgery.

When I came out, she took me to a tiny apartment in a rental complex, with two bedrooms and a living room as impersonal as the parlor in a whorehouse. I telephoned Helen to advise her of the change of address. "Terrific!" she cheered. "So glad you did it at last! I'll arrange things here at once, expect me to be with you in, oh, a week, at the latest."

When I reacted with embarrassed incomprehension, she asked, "But—haven't you received my letter?"

I had not. Ellie had swiped it, and thereby remained one stroke ahead of little Helen's butterfly net. When I confronted her with it, outraged, she said calmly, "Harinxma, to bring your daughter over to look after you means ultimately: cold storage in Golden Whatsis."

"You swiped her goddamn letter!" I cried, outraged. "You

didn't even give it to me to read! All you did was to lift her idea of an apartment, and—"

"Cool it, Harinxma. The last thing you need in your present condition is a daughter who sees you as a useless old man."

"Well, what else am I?"

"Who knows? Storage is there for you whenever you want it. But it's *you* who must want it, after deciding that your useful days are over."

"But what else is there?" I cried. "Look at me, dammit!"

"I *am* looking at you. I see nothing wrong with you that can't be patched up in a month or two. You're still the same man, Harinxma. Your place is still on the bridge."

"Ellie," I said, "you are nuts. And don't give me that stuff about Arnold Kwel at ninety. Fransen warned me as far back as Kao-hsiung that the old man was no more than a ventriloquist's dummy on your lap."

"You don't know what you're talking about! Arnold—"

"Arnold left you half the fleet and half his shares."

"Now what the hell does that mean? That I nursed him along until he had changed his will and then put a pillow over his face? Balls, Harinxma! He was terrific, he would have gone on screwing the competition if he hadn't been felled by that stroke."

"Ellie, try to understand that I am *not* Arnold Kwel! I am a sailor, my sailing days are over, all I am good for—"

"So we are back in the South of France, are we? I have to start all over again trying to break the spell that you are ripe for Golden Evenings?"

"You mean Helen."

"To her, you are her old, old dad who falls on his face after three snorts, who—"

"Please! By now, you can arrange this litany for the Mormon Tabernacle Choir!"

She beamed at me. "My God, Harinxma," she said, "what am I going to do without you?"

"Find yourself a man worthy of you, who is under—"

"The hell with his age," she said. "Tea?"

45

A COUPLE OF DAYS LATER my body seemed to decide that enough was enough. I was weak, dizzy. When I wanted to go to bed I could not make it, fell on the floor and vomited. This was it. I was capsizing into death, a shabby death, like a dog by the roadside hit by a car.

Then Ellie was there, looking down on me. She did not ask any questions. She opened up the bed, lugged me onto it, took off my shoes and my clothes until I was naked, straightened me out . . .

"Ell—" I said, and vomited again. Suddenly, I felt her lie down beside me, take my dying body in her arms, and put my head on her shoulder. "Not like this, Harinxma," she said. "Not like a dog by the roadside."

"How did you know?"

"You yelled it all over the neighborhood. So shut up and hang on to me. You're going to be all right. This is not it, Harinxma. Not yet." Her sleek body held me tight; I had not realized until then that she was naked too.

"Why?" I asked. "There's nothing left . . ."

"Everything is yet to come, Harinxma. It may have momentarily passed you by, but it's still within sight. Try and catch up with it. Hang in there. Hang on to *me*."

Amazingly, what she exuded as I lay there with my head on her shoulder was peace. She was the last woman I would have expected to envelop me in stillness in a naked embrace. I remember saying, "Yes—yes . . ." Then I must have fallen asleep in the sheltering arms of Holland's Glory.

46

GOD KNOWS how she got me through this one. She should have called an ambulance, had me taken to a hospital, where I would probably have been dead on arrival. Instead, she shared her own energy with me, her very life, reviving me the way I had tried to revive the dead young mate we fished from the Arctic Sea.

She woke me, holding out the telephone. It was daylight, she was fully dressed and looked cool and businessslike.

"You must call your daughter; she'll be worrying about her dad. I'll dial her for you."

"I'm not awake yet . . ."

"Hush! It's ringing."

When Helen heard who it was she cried, "Dad! How *did* you know? You must be psychic! Crosseyes—remember Crosseyes? —had a miscarriage last night. Harry and I and the children were up until dawn in a terrible state, not to mention dear old Crosseyes—"

I covered the mouthpiece with my hand. "Who the hell is Crosseyes?"

"A dog," she said.

"Helen?"

"Yes, Dad. Can you hear me?"

"Who said—who is—tell me what's happening. The line is bad."

"Shall I call you back, Dad?"

"No! No—"

There followed some superficial chat; I did not tell her about myself. After I put down the phone, I asked, "How did you know?"

"What?"

"That it was a dog?"

"You told me."

"When?"

"Some time ago. Their cat is called Cuddles. How about breakfast?"

She looked down on me. Her eyes were like the sky over the Baltic, no horizon, everything flat, a sense of the spirit hovering over the waters.

"How about a fried egg sandwich? Think you can handle that?"

Out of the blue, I asked, "Ellie—are you a lesbian?"

After a moment of stunned silence she grinned. "Harinxma," she said with gruff tenderness, "stop trying to probe your sore tooth. You're wearing dentures."

To escape from the embarrassment of my stupid question, I nattered on: "I was thirty when I lost all my teeth, would you believe that? I was wounded in the Mediterranean, left unattended too long. We docked in Gib and I was taken to a hospital. I was seen by one of those kindergarten doctors who did the best work of their lives during the war: he said I was going to lose my teeth, the lot; all the roots had developed an abscess as a result of infection, due to wounds. 'All of them?' I asked. He said, 'Don't worry, tomorrow morning you'll wake up with a whole new set of pearlies.' I asked, 'Can I choose?' 'Choose what?' 'What kind of teeth, before you yank 'em all out.' He laughed. 'Absolutely. We offer the choice of two: rat or hyena.' "

"So you chose hyena," she said. "Fried egg sandwich coming up."

In the doorway of the kitchen she turned around and added, "Don't worry. You're saddled with me until you sail and I break down on the quayside."

47

B U T   A   W E E K or so later, when I was back on my feet, I began to suspect she was having an affair with someone in town.

There were mysterious whispered telephone calls, after which she hastily dressed, saying, "I'll be gone for lunch. There's a frozen meal in the freezer. Read the directions. Back as soon as I can," and hurried off. When she came back, she brought with her a radiance I had never noticed before. It was not just a happy mood, or the smiling state of lovers who only think about one another. It was as if she, herself, was in the zone.

It did not affect her basic persona. She was as tough, unsentimental, and untiring as before; yet I could not help feeling a pang of jealousy. We were not lovers. I envied her experience which put her in that state. I had never known her so soft, so gentle, so open. Even during those hours she had held me in her arms to save my life she had remained firmly anchored within herself. Now she had left that safe ground and reached out—to whom? Who *was* he?

More telephone calls: *Pringg, pringg, pri*—"Hushat?"—*pzpzpz*—"Howash?"—*pzz*—*pzz*—"Hoosh"—*pzz*—"I'm on my way, Harinxma!" Then the worn record: my meal in the freezer, read the directions, remember to turn the oven off.

I would wait up for her. Occasionally, they whooped it up until well after midnight, and she reeled in, radiant. The late Captain Cho's dog-eared *Rubáiyát of Omar Khayyám* had said it: "Love is like a fountain that shoots upward to one person and rains down on all those around."

My writings drawn from the cookie tin became melancholy; all the subjects I was pulling seemed to ask for a minor key.

"On Going Gray," "On Dreams." "Retirement." "How to Paint a Sunset." Ah, well, as Captain Bosman used to say: it was that time of year.

48

ONE MORNING, shortly thereafter, the doorbell rang. I went to open it.

"Commodore Harinxma?"

"This is he."

A slender young man in a business suit was standing in the hallway. He had about him the unmistakable aura of the military, as had Colonel Rusty. "What can I do for you?" I asked.

"May I come in? It's rather a long story."

"Sure, but who are you?"

"I'm sorry: my name is Dr. Henderson. I work with the National Aeronautics and Space Administration—NASA—at the Johnson Space Center, just outside town. I am one of the physicians looking after the astronauts."

"Ah—I see . . ." I did not see at all, but never mind. "Come in. Sit down."

When we were both seated, he started, "I'm a friend of Colonel Buckram's. We were in the same squadron in the Air Force. He told me about your failed experiment, the OOBE idea, the dosimeter on the Rover of *Apollo 17*. He had asked me, awhile before, casually, if there was anything left behind on the moon after the manned landings that we at NASA would like to have another look at. I asked, 'To be picked up, you mean?' No, he said, just to look at. At the time I thought it was an odd question, but he always was a bit of—well, a fantasist, if you see what I mean. As head of military espionage that's probably a desirable quality."

"How true," I said, to say something.

"So I told him about the dosimeter on the Lunar Rover deposited by *Apollo 17*; he had put tom-fool questions before, without consequence. Three days ago, he called me up and said, 'You have someone visiting Houston who has been trained to get a reading of your precious dosimeter. Why don't you follow up on that?' He told me the story. When I brought it up with the people at NASA, it was laughed off the table. But I, myself—well, let me tell you why I am here."

"That would help," I said.

"I had no idea that they were messing around with this. When he told me, just as a bit of gossip, while we were having a drink together, I became very interested."

"Talking about drinks, can I get you anything? Vodka? I'm afraid that's all we have in the house."

"No, thank you, sir. It's a bit early for me."

"All right. Carry on."

"Well, when I was a student in medical school, I myself and eight other classmates were ordered by a professor to investigate one aspect each of alternative medicine and write a report on it. We were given three months to complete the assignment and it was up to us to choose what our specific subject would be. There were nine different aspects of alternative medicine, so we simply wrote them on slips of paper and pulled one each. I pulled the Monroe Institute in Faber, North Carolina." He smiled engagingly.

"I see." I began to smell a rat.

"I must tell you that I did not have the slightest faith in what they were doing. I thought it was a lot of hooey, and I tried like hell to get out of it. I offered to swap it with one of the others. I was ready to make it worth their while. But no takers, so I ended up in North Carolina. Well, to cut a long story short, I made a study of hemi-sync, his patented procedure of applying different vibrations to the right and left lobes of the brain. Well"—he laughed, somewhat embarrassed—"I'm not advertising this in my present environment, but I fell for it. I ended up not just as a believer, because it's not a matter of faith, I saw it happen in front of my own eyes. I took part in some of the experiments myself and found them most effective in bringing about an OOBE. And there were other applications in medicine which I found equally fascinating—in psychiatry, particularly. Then I heard what Rusty had been up to, the unfortunate outcome of his experiment, and I thought I might have a talk with you, in a general sense."

Aha! Ellie at work. I wondered why she had not brought it up herself; this was a cruder maneuver than I had come to expect from her. "Before we go any further: when did you meet Miss Bastiaans?"

He frowned. "Miss who?"

"Well, surely she is behind all this. It has her name all over it, in big letters."

He acted bewildered. "I'm sorry, sir, but I don't quite understand. Who is this Miss—what was her name?" It was a clumsy effort that wouldn't have fooled a child.

"Are you trying to tell me that what you are obviously proposing has nothing to with Miss Bastiaans?"

"I'm sorry if I have disturbed you . . ." He looked about to rise and leave.

"Miss Bastiaans," I said, "was the one who sold me to your friend Rusty in the first place. She runs a headhunting agency in London. The Pentagon hired her to find six World War II veterans, prepared to go through an OOBE. I was supposed to head this group, but I found only four who were prepared to do it; one of them was Pjotr Warszinsky, who bought it as a result of your friend Rusty's experiment. Now, you are sure you don't know her?"

"I assure you, sir, I never even heard of the woman—er, the lady. Should I have?"

"That's all right. I just wanted to make sure. Go on. So you are a believer in Robert Monroe's method. Now, what's the reason for this visit?" As if I didn't know.

I had spooked him; he took a moment to recover the initiative. Finally, though, out it came, just as I had expected—the same old story, a repeat performance of his friend Rusty's. The lunar buggy with the dosimeter, the circumstance that there would not be another manned moon landing in the foreseeable future, the need they had at NASA for the radiation information in view of the space station under construction. He had discussed it with his immediate colleagues at NASA and they were interested. "But," he said, "we cannot make it an official program, in view of the fact that right now the funding of the space station is under discussion in the House, and later in the Senate. If it became known that NASA was now dabbling in the occult, which is what it would look like on the Hill, it would definitely not help. But we *do* want to do it, on our own initiative, on our own time. So—"

"So you thought of me."

"The reason being that you went through the entire training and know exactly what it's all about. You could just pick up where you left off, after—well—the unfortunate incident."

"Thank you for the suggestion, Doctor, but as you can see, I am not in top condition. I've had eight weeks of radiation, two operations—no, three—I'm still pretty shaky. And, quite frankly, I'm not eager to repeat my friend Pjotr's experience."

He looked bashful. I still could not believe that Ellie was not behind this. It smelled of her, it tasted of her. But then, maybe I had plotting on the brain.

"Would it be possible, sir, for you to just come and visit us at the Space Center, to get to know my colleagues? I'd come and pick you up if you needed transportation. It would be most helpful; and the matter is serious. We really need that information; any way of getting it should be explored, and, if possible, exploited. What do you say?"

He sounded so eager, so serious. He lived in another world. Or had I withdrawn into mine? Should I venture out from this dark corner of the forest and join the human race?

"I'll think it over, Doctor. Let me have your telephone number. I'll give you a call tomorrow. How's that?"

"That would be wonderful, sir." He took out his wallet and handed me a card before taking his leave.

This called for a snort. While pouring a stiff one from the icebox, I took my bearings. Here I was, a recluse in a little apartment in a town called Houston, manufacturing my little cultured pearls about life at sea between the wars. Out there was the space station, the promise of travel to the stars. Here was a chance to become familiar with the world of the future, rather than meow about the past, old tomcat on the roof . . .

I took my drink to my chair. Face it, Harinxma: What's all this about? Are you interested in exploration, or just in getting out?

Out of what, exactly? Not the confinement of these three rooms, but Ellie's orbit?

If she had not started a love affair that made her radiant in smiling absentmindedness, I concluded, I would not have considered being carted off to a space station, where to climb stairs, slog down corridors, meet fascinating men who failed to fascinate me, and start toying with out-of-body experiments again. No. Writing about the past was more interesting than exploring the future with virile men in the prime of life, eager to explain the latest evolution of Singer's Automatic Sewing Machine—

The telephone rang; I went to pick it up. "Yes?"

"Is Ellie there?" a male voice asked.

"Ellie who?"

"Ellie—what's her name?—it's Dutch. Bastiaans."

"Ah. No, she's not here. Can I take a message?"

"Ask her to call Jack Frolick, as soon as she comes in. She knows the number."

Aha! The secret lover, out of the bushes at last! Jack Frolick, for Christ's sake. Sounded like a character from Dickens: Uriah Heep with a Texas twang.

Somebody kicked the front door. I opened up, ready to speak my piece to whoever it was. There she stood, breathless, her hat on one ear, hugging two paper bags full of shopping. "Creeps!" she said. "At this hour it's like a zoo out there! Have you made tea for yourself?"

"No," I said, taking one of the bags from her; it weighed a ton. "I made vodka." I took it to the kitchenette and started to unpack the contents on the counter.

"Have you talked to your daughter?" She was still out of breath.

"I thought of it too late, I'll do it tomorrow. What kind of day did you have, apart from the zoo?"

"Oh," she said, putting the milk in the fridge, "as usual: busy busy busy. And you? Did you do any writing?"

"I had a visitor," I said. "You know: the young man you sent to see me. Henderson."

"I?" She stopped in mid-motion. "Who are you talking about?"

"I'll tell you, but close the door, or the thing will run full steam for an hour."

For some reason, she kissed my forehead, put the cheese in a drawer, and closed the door of the icebox. She said, "Let's sit down, my feet are killing me."

We sat down and I told her.

She was genuinely baffled. She had never heard of Dr. Henderson. She had not had any contact with Rusty Buckram after Big Owl, and he had never mentioned a Dr. Henderson. "I honestly have nothing to do with this, believe me. If I had set it up, I would have had no reason to keep it from you. I would have told you myself."

I believed her, maybe because of the radiance. "There was a telephone call for you, just before you came in."

"Who from?"

"Believe it or not, a gentleman called Jack Frolick. Unless it's a pen name."

She went to the phone and dialed a number. "Jack, please." She waited.

So did I. Another spot of vodka on the rocks was the answer. I went to the icebox, got the booze, got the ice.

"Jack? Ellie here. What's up?" She listened.

I dropped ice in the glass.

"Oh, *no!* I'm so sorry . . . he seemed fine when I left. I gave him a back rub less than two hours ago."

Back rub? Was she working in a massage parlor? Talk about still waters! I poured the booze onto the ice.

"Oh dear," she said. "So sorry. It always affects you, doesn't it? Do you need me now?"

Need me now? Dammit, I hadn't seen her all day! I fetched a little bowl from the crockery cupboard and filled it with honey-cured peanuts.

She put the phone down.

"I hope all is well?"

"Hm? Oh, yes. Yes—yes, all's well." She seemed absent-minded.

I took a slug, tossed a fistful of peanuts at my tonsils, and nearly choked. Finally, I managed to croak, "Would a brief explanation be in order, maybe?"

She gave me a far-away look. Then she woke, focused on me, and said, "Okay. I'll have a glass of the same."

I poured her a double vodka on the rocks with a sense of regret. Why hadn't I left well alone? Why aggravate the situation by bringing it out into the open? Too late now. I handed her the drink and cut a few slices of the Cheddar cheese she had a passion for, then sat down and said, "I'm sorry, Ellie. It's none of my damn business."

"Well, now you've found out, I might as well confess, mightn't I?"

"All right," I said. "Who is Jack Frolick, and what lucky gentleman received your back rub?"

She gave me a level look. "Harinxma, you are a silly old bugger, aren't you? Cheers! To secret lovers called 'Frolick.' Ha-ha!" She burst into laughter. "Never occurred to me: the perfect name for a Victorian rake, isn't it? Ha-ha-ha!"

I began to feel miffed. "Indeed," I said. "Very funny."

"All right: Jack Frolick is the head nurse of the refuge for children with AIDS, where I work."

"You *what?*"

"I work. As a volunteer."

"Oh."

"Don't look so startled, old friend. Four weeks ago I took a course in the care of the terminally ill. I took it in order to, well, learn the ropes. I wanted to be ready for all eventualities. Don't take it personally; it's just a quirk I have: I like to be prepared at all times. I was surprised by the number of people taking the same course, all kinds of people: male, female, old, young—there was one fat jolly woman called Kitty. I was drawn to her, she was comforting among all those Texans—did you know that in Texas the word 'head' has three syllables, by the way?—well, never mind. One day she asked if I had an hour or so; a colleague of hers had failed to turn up at the refuge for AIDS babies where she volunteered. So I accompanied her to this strange, haunting place; I must show it to you, one day. I went just to help her out that day, but the moment I entered the refuge I—I just caved in."

"Explain that to me."

"I never experienced anything like it before. I have always been Numero Uno myself. Now Numero Uno is—or was—a one-year-old Chinese baby, a little boy: terrified, angry, unapproachable, until I gave him a back rub; then he just melted and started to cry and when I turned him over he reached out to me. And so on, and so on." She emptied her glass and held it out to me. "Let me have another one."

I could not believe it. This tough, hard-bitten woman? There I had been, eulogizing a young black nurse who stroked a frightened old man's arm, while all the time—"I thought you had a lover," I said.

"I know you did. I thought: so he thinks I'm having an affair. I figured it would seem less disturbing to you than the fact that I was taking a course in—you know?"

"But what about Arnold Kwel? You had that experience with him to go by, didn't you?"

"No, he died of a stroke while I wasn't around. He dropped

dead, just like that, at his desk. I never had to look after someone who—who took his time about it. Sorry about all this."

"Don't be silly, I think it's terrific. But, just as a matter of interest: What made you go in for this in the first place? I mean, when did you feel the need to take the course?"

"The night I held you in my arms. You probably never noticed, but I was in a blue funk. I wanted to look after you, care for you, see you through, but I had no idea what to do. I just played it by ear. I lay there wondering: Should I have taken him to a hospital?"

"I'm glad you didn't. That would have been the end of me."

"I went on holding you all night, praying it was the right thing to do. That I was not murdering you by sheer incompetence."

"You're nuts! It was the very thing that kept me from slipping over the edge!"

"I had to be sure. I picked up from the newspaper that the Medical Center was starting a course for the care of—etcetera. So I went. I told you the rest. Now I'm addicted. Never before has my life—well—made such sense. Odd, isn't it? Never before—well, etcetera, etcetera. Where is that drink? Do we have more of this cheese, or did you stuff it all?"

I went to get it for her. So the radiance, the strange joy with which she came home each time—

"And what about you? Are you going to do it?" she asked as I came back from the icebox.

"What are you talking about?"

"Your visit from NASA."

"Ah—that . . ." I had forgotten about NASA. The discovery of what she was doing had wiped out all that. Tough old Bastiaans of the loveless eyes.

I wanted to say, "I have to think it over," but found that, for some reason, there was no longer any need to. I said, "Now that I know what you are up to, I might as well venture out myself, instead of moping around writing somber pieces. You are terrific, know that?"

She gave me a searching look. "I hoped you would understand, but I wasn't sure."

I said, "Well, now you know. Let's drink to that."

She lifted her glass in response. "Godspeed and happy sailing."

It was very moving, but somehow I suddenly knew that, at long last, my number was up.

As we chatted on, I decided that that was nonsense. I even thought of a name for this maudlin phenomenon: the Pjotr Syndrome. It had always happened after casualties: everyone went through a brief episode of thinking their number was up next. Well—some had been right.

49

NASA APPROACHES: abandoned hotels, crumbling shacks. If it is possible to have Tobacco Road leading to space, Houston has it.

The car obeyed a sign that said NASA—ALL VISITORS TURN RIGHT. I was helped out of the machine, hamming it up, an old aristocrat on the way to the guillotine. In the reception office I was asked by a woman behind a counter for my rank.

"Commodore."

"Navy or yacht club?"

Good question. "Neither. Commodore, retired, of a fleet of oceangoing tugboats, deceased."

She looked at me with a twinkle in her eyes. "Name, please?"

I told her and was given an identity tag saying I was an

authorized visitor. She directed me to Building 37, the Physiology Lab, a green shack in a flat world.

As I stood looking at it, something odd occurred: I found myself back in May 1944. There we were, all "W"-tugboats, waiting to start towing the caissons for the two Mulberry Harbors, under enemy fire. The same atmosphere, the same kind of building for our HQ.

I stumbled up the steps to the front door and entered a long hallway lined with doors marked Exercise Physiology Lab, Astronaut Candidate PRS Test, Neuroscience Motion Lab, Micronutrient Analysis Lab, Bone Densitometry Lab, Muscle Physiology Lab—finally the office of the Commanding Officer. I was ushered into the room in which an older man was sitting behind a desk. My guide, Dr. Henderson, introduced me to the Commanding Officer, who wore a baseball cap saying YOUTH BRIGADE and a T-shirt with the legend GET LOST. He was introduced as Colonel—I did not catch the name. It did not matter, it turned out, as everyone referred to him simply as "Turk." Turk took me back to the atmosphere of waiting for the big crossing in May '44. We had worried about towing those caissons, huge, unwieldy monsters, under enemy fire; he was worried about the rumor leaking out that NASA was now into out-of-body experiences. I had to pledge that I would keep this thing under my hat.

I made the pledge. He gave me an appraising look, and said, "Hmm. Let's hear your end of the story."

"Excuse me?"

"How you became involved in this. What you did. What you, yourself, think about this experiment. I have your CV right here, so start with how you were drawn into this spook stuff. Sounds out of your league, not your line of work."

I told him about Miss B.'s visit to the South of France, my meeting Rusty and agreeing to form a crew of old veterans.

"Why *that* old? I haven't found the rationale for that in the report."

"Because it seemed prudent, to whoever dreamt this up, to pick old men, aliens without much in the way of family. In case they lost one."

"So they did. Any consequences?"

"He was an old pensioner without any relatives, gathering dust in government storage."

"I see. You were the funny one on board."

It was time to straighten him out. "Look," I said, "I have been asked to come here and listen to a proposal, not to be grilled like a new recruit. Let's get down to business and skip the display of tail feathers."

He grinned. "What do they call you? This name of yours probably doesn't travel well outside Holland."

"Fancy That."

"Sorry?"

"That's what I was called. 'Fancy' for short."

"I see. Well, Fancy, we are considering picking up the OOBE experiment where the military left off. As you must have realized by now we'll do it as an interdepartmental testing procedure of the viability of the process. There will be no record other than an internal technical one. We do it as a private exercise: three cuckoos whooping it up in someone else's nest. But first, tell us how you feel about the experiment yourself. Do you believe in it?"

If I said "No," that would probably mean the end of it. I discovered, to my surprise, that I was within range of the sirens. Beyond was the biggest ocean of them all. Though at my age it was crazy—

"I do," I said.

He scrutinized me. His eyes were better than a lie detector. "And your sister," he said.

"Excuse me?"

"French: *Et ta soeur.* Meaning, like hell you do. How so?"

"Are you looking for believers or test pilots—if that's the word?"

"You must realize that if we have another casualty, the fat's in the fire."

"You mean my soul?"

"Seriously: Does this thing interest you? Sufficiently to put your neck on the line?"

"What we should avoid," I said, "is dramatization. Pjotr Warszinsky's death was caused by a quirk in his makeup. He was out of touch with reality to begin with, and only chosen because he used to be a deep-sea diver who might feel at home in the out-of-body state. The procedure that was intended to bring about an out-of-body experience resulted, in his case, in the near-death syndrome. To him, Nirvana was the underwater world, and its inhabitants, especially one whom he followed into whatever. His soul swam off with a fish named Louise."

I could guess his ruminations after that little speech—they would be typical of the commanding officer: "What kind of bird is this? Is he competent? Will he give me trouble? Is he a lush, a nut, a liar living in his own world?"

"Okay," he said. "The presumption here is that after a certain procedure, which is Henderson's baby, your consciousness or whatever will be or might be transported to EVA 4, the Rover with the dosimeter. A shaky presumption, but in our line of work we're used to them. Some of our results are the outcome of presumptions that, in civilian life, would have landed us in the loony bin. The procedure itself presents no problem. Either it works or it doesn't; if it doesn't: back to the old drawing board. But the possibility of another casualty worries me. Anyhow: assuming we put this into motion, our first task will be finding the real estate."

"You lost me."

"The proper locale for the experiment. We'll start by looking at the possibilities, and talk as we go along. First, lunch. Okay?"

"Fine with me," I said.

Henderson, Turk, and I went to have lunch in Building 11, the staff canteen. We sat down at a table with some other characters, all involved with problems in a different dimension which they had put briefly on hold, to have a cup of gumbo, a BLT, and coffee. Lots of coffee. I chose "the special," whatever that was. Fifty years had dropped off me. I was back in the Light of Asia, a harbor pub in Dover run by a Pakistani who hated the British and kept the German radio turned as loud as he could, even if it was the BBC in German. There we congregated: tugboat captains, convoy captains, snotty British ASR characters with mustaches that forced them to pass through doors sideways, chief engineers worrying about nipples on bilge pumps, young mates dreaming of a future they would never have. Nobody talked about death or danger or the recklessness of towing concrete monsters the size of a city block across the Channel under fire. I had never been able to describe the atmosphere in that saloon; now, fifty years later, I was back in the same atmosphere of waiting, and the irrational certainty that everyone else might die but you were immortal.

Turk raised his glass and said, "You're on, aren't you?"

"I am," I said.

"Good! When can you start?"

"Any time. Just send a car and I'll be there."

"Bingo," he said.

Without my noticing, the place of the man opposite me had been taken by a cat staring at me with motionless golden eyes.

"That's Henry," Turk said. "If *he* accepts you, you really are accepted as a member of the spearhead of evolution."

By the look of Henry, that would take awhile. But as I looked about me at the men and women of my new world, arguing and expostulating in small groups around their tables, I felt a growing joy, the same hope expressed in the coat of arms of my native province Zeeland, frequently plagued by devastating floods. A lion, up to his hips in stormy waters, holding a bunch of lightning in one paw and supporting with the other a crown, which seems to be his most precious possession and sits awry atop his mane, as if grabbed at the last moment. Its motto: *Ik worstel en ontzwem*—I struggle and swim free.

50

AFTER LUNCH we made the rounds of the Space Center, starting with a visit to Mission Control, a place of absolute quiet. I sat down behind the surgeon's desk in the back. One row farther down sat the astronauts and the flight directors. A huge world map showed the position of a space craft, manned or unmanned, presently circling the planet, in brackets as it had entered darkness. Again it was like Dover: the amphitheater with the VIPs looking down on the chart of the Channel. Lacking were the Wrens with their tricornered hats, their croupier's rakes shoving the ships' models to their new positions between England and France. God bless those glorious girls, who loved and sustained us until our number came up.

On the way, by staff car, to the next location, Turk said, "Well, now you have seen the machinery, which is pretty good. It took a few million years of evolution for us to get here, but what about our goddamn souls?"

It was an odd question; Dover made me take it in my stride. We had worried about our souls too. "Are you expecting an answer from me?"

"Well—you're old enough. You're a sailor. I—hell!" He had glanced at his watch. "I'm supposed to keep an eye on a female astronaut making her first space walk in the pool. Let's go, we can talk while I watch from the window of my control booth."

It was a small, soundproof room in another building. A large window overlooked a swimming pool. He sat down at a desk with a mike and a loudspeaker; the mike connected him with a young woman whom I could see from above. She was in the process of being put into a space suit that gave her the appearance of a deep-sea diver. A crane picked her up, chair and all, and lowered her into the pool. Two scuba divers fitted her out with weights around her waist and ankles until she had achieved weightlessness and moved away clumsily, as she would in space. Her task, I gathered, was to open the door of what looked like a safe underwater. She slowly approached the safe, while Turk went on talking to me. "Here we are, ready for a manned mission to Mars. We will, today or tomorrow—Take it easy, honey, don't force it, just float, you've got all the time in the world.—Let's say we colonize Mars. Terrific. But what are we *doing* there? Huh? What is our business there? Is the process of evolution one of random chance? If not, what is the purpose of our colonizing other planets? Is there a message in what we're doing? If so, what is it?"

I looked at the message on his T-shirt. "Explain that to me," I said.

"What?"

"The message on your chest."

"Huh? Oh—*get lost.* In my position, you are continuously held up with questions from characters too lazy to think for themselves. The message brings about a natural selection. But, seriously: Are we just a tribe of superintelligent rats without soul or conscience? A virus that attacks and ultimately destroys the very body it feeds on—as we are doing to this planet? Once we arrive on other planets, will we have anything else to contribute besides hatred, war, self-destruction? Are we a plague visited upon them, like the Serbian general whose troops rape, massacre children, burn whole families to a crisp, and call it 'ethnic cleansing'? Make no mistake, friend. Forget about Dante, forget Beethoven's Ninth. General Smile-o-vitch and his toys are *us.*—Keep your head down, honey!"

The woman in the space suit tried to obey.

"Give me *your* answer," he continued. "What *is* the message that will justify our landing in alien worlds?"

All I could come up with was the incident of the young black nurse who had stroked the old Texan's arm. This was neither the place nor the time to talk about Ellie's conversion.

But he understood what I was talking about. "Who knows," he said, "maybe compassion is what we need. Let's take one of her sort along for our landing on Mars."

I knew we had many discussions coming, sober and unsober. We were of the same happy breed: old men who ought to be explorers. Crazy men, to whom it was not enough to discover the South Pole or climb Annapurna but who wanted to take a message there, like a flower.

After the underwater test, we returned to his main office, where we joined Dr. Henderson and a few other young men who turned out to have something to do with a committee called Human Research Policy and Procedures.

We discussed the various aspects of stimulating an out-of-body experience for me to read the radiation dial on the Lunar Rover at EVA 4. Then, to no one in particular, Turk said, "Okay, folks. This is the guy we need. His name is Commodore Hazzemetaz, otherwise known as 'Fancy.' Welcome, Fancy."

We shook hands, and that was that.

51

WHEN I CAME HOME I found Ellie waiting for me. Seeing her there brought about a flash of recognition: Sylvia, Dover. *How did it go, darling?*

"Hi," she said. "How did it go?"

God—one of those awful moments when your heart breaks.

"I need a drink." I headed for the kitchenette.

"Easy does it," she said, standing behind me. "If you're into this you should lay off the booze."

"Into what, dear?" Ice plopped into vodka.

"A Colonel Huntzinger called. You'll be picked up by a NASA car at seven-thirty tomorrow morning, and please bring your medical records."

"Okay." I joined her and, because of the full glass, lowered myself cautiously into my chair. "Cheers."

"I gather you have signed on for another round?"

"I have. What was your day like?"

Suddenly, she kneeled beside me, put a hand on my knee, and said, "I know, I'm sorry."

"Know what?"

"You always have the same look in your eyes when you go through one of these. I understand. We never really grieved. We should have, but turned away. Now we get hit at moments like this, and it is sheer hell."

Her insight into men's souls was eerie; old Kwel with bells on. "Forgive me," I said. "I didn't intend to bother you with it."

"Hell," she said. "That's what I stayed around for! Not just as a wet nurse. So tell me. From the beginning."

On impulse, I bent over and kissed her. Not in a twitch of senile lust; out of gratitude and admiration. I hoped she would read all that in my impetuous embrace. Well—embrace: just a peck on the lips.

"Harinxma," she said, "you're a nut. Give me a sip."

I handed her my glass. She drank; I said, "Huntzinger, or Turk, as he is known, called me 'Commodore Hazzemetaz.' He sports a baseball cap with YOUTH BRIGADE on it, and a T-shirt that says GET LOST."

"I see. One of those."

"Of what?"

"A show-off. We had a chief who thought of himself as a great one with the girls. He wore a jersey one of his groupies had embroidered with the flags 'KLT'—*About to lay alongside*. You probably never met him. He was full of gas."

"What was his name?"

"Hangsel, believe it or not. Why did you kiss me?"

"Because I thought you were terrific, but didn't want to sound full of gas."

She smiled, patted my knee, rose, and gave me a fleeting kiss herself. "Pizza tonight?"

"Whatever. I meant it—you *are*. Let's go and have a pizza and I'll tell you all about my day, if you'll tell me about yours."

"You're in the bag, then, I gather?"

"Let's hope it's not a body bag."

"We have been there before, haven't we?"

"Ah, yes, when we were young and gay."

"Now you are old and somber, is that it?"

I looked at her with the odd feeling, once again, of the past sliding along with us like the shadow of an airplane: one of the moments in which she *was* Sylvia.

"Okay, let's go," I said.

52

DURING THE DAYS that followed I was picked up every morning at seven-thirty by a NASA car, and delivered back home at five in the afternoon. It was fascinating, exciting, but soon I was cross-eyed with exhaustion. Ellie was usually home when I came back; if she was held up at the refuge, she left a message on the answering machine.

We had dinner together in the nearby Vietnamese Pizzeria, so expensive that we could freely talk in the always empty restaurant. We debriefed over a bottle of Chianti.

"Tell me what you were up to today, Harinxma."

"Turk, Henderson, and I went looking at real estate for the experiment," I answered. "They don't have an isolation booth like the one in Big Owl, but a number of alternatives. First, Turk suggested sticking me into a space suit and sinking me in the pool. I would be weightless, and to him, that seemed a pretty good solution. Total isolation, no physical stimuli, plus a means of communication inside the helmet. He didn't understand that to me this was a hilarious suggestion. Then Jim Henderson came up with a bizarre contraption: an 'isolation bubble' in which aspiring astronauts are given a taste of the psychological effects of being alone in space."

"What is it?"

"A huge, inflatable—"

"Eatinow?" the Vietnamese waiter who loved us asked.

We loved him too. "No, we'll wait for a moment, thank you. We'll first have our wine, then decide."

"Velly good, velly good! Nice wetha?"

"Yes. Getting a bit hot, but splendid."

"All right now, where were we?"

"Isolation bubble."

"Ah, yes. It's an inflatable ball, the biggest beach ball you ever saw. It has a zip-up entrance, and inside you have to sit in the lotus position or lie on your side in the fetal position. They zip up the balloon with you inside, air is pumped in, and it turns into a womb: warm, quiet, dark, and silent except for the sound of your own breathing and the soft rush of the air as they go on pumping it in. Jim Henderson said that occasionally he has himself zipped up in there for an hour of meditation. He called it the most restful environment in the whole of the Space Center. If I decide to go with that form of sensory deprivation, they'll have to add earphones and a mike."

"Did you try it?"

"It *sounded* splendid, but with my crotchety undercarriage and the lingering pain of the two back surgeries I couldn't get comfortable. I loved the principle, though. Well, cheers."

"Now what?"

"We go on looking. There are other possibilities; we'll try them all. In the end we are sure to come up with something as good as in Big Owl."

"How do you feel about the whole thing now?"

I took a sip of my wine. "Well, I'm ready to roll, I think. But it may be that the setting is the attraction, not the assignment."

"Explain that to me." She looked tired and drawn, but her eyes won out.

"Must we talk about this now? Let's order first."

We ordered the usual, had the usual chat with our Vietnamese friend. Then I asked, "What was *your* day like?"

She took my hand and kissed it, with a tenderness she rarely showed. "Don't worry, you'll be all right. I'll be there."

Behind the counter the owner applauded.

"Let's find another restaurant," I said. "I can't take any more of this."

"It's just his culture."

"I know that East is East and West is West until the twain shall meet—*at God's big judgment feet*, as my old chief engineer used to say—"

"Don't worry, you'll do fine. You are in good shape. And you radiate."

Well, now! "That makes two of us," I said. "The Radiators, high-wire circus acrobats—"

"Maybe we both feel fulfilled by what we are doing?"

"Ellie, be rational. I can accept that you are feeling fulfilled; but I, so far, haven't done a thing to justify any radiance on my part."

"It's not what you do," she said, "it's where you are. You are now back in the world that has been yours ever since you were young. Setting out from the Strait of Magellan to Taiwan can't be much different from sailing into deep space. You are back among your own kind; the way you described the staff canteen made it sound like a bar in a harbor on the shore of the biggest ocean of them all, complete with bar cat called Henry."

Which distant bell did this ring? Ocean, harbor, bar cat? . . . *Bye, love. Godspeed and happy sailing. Don't eat too many sweets—*

Sylvia again. Where would she be now?

I must have absented myself from felicity awhile, for she suddenly said, with that disturbing sixth sense she had, "That's the next question: after the distant shore—then what?"

"Excuse me?"

"After the hugs and embraces with those waiting on the beach, do we all camp together in the dunes, or in some beach community of our own creation? For ever and ever? Or—what else?"

"Let's talk about that some other time," I said, as the food arrived.

53

CHOOSING FROM seven possibilities, Turk, Jim Henderson, and I ultimately agreed on the site for the experiment. After the bubble, I had tried and rejected the Exercise Physiology Lab, the Astronaut Candidate PRS Test, the Neuroscience Motion Lab, and, finally, the Hyperbaric Chamber, which had seemed, for a while, to be the most suitable: a decompression tank for astronauts on their return from outer space. It was monitored and had a series of bunks but no control room sophisticated enough for our purpose. We finally settled for the 50,000-Foot Testing Chamber, which had seats instead of bunks but a fully instrumental control room from which the inside of the tank could be observed.

Turk and I had become like shipmates. Our main tie was the shared awareness of the limitations of the "spearhead of human evolution." Materially we could now do almost anything we wanted: fly to the moon, send explorers to Mars and ultimately to other islands in the ocean of space. But once we achieved manned landings, the old question would arise: Was it General Smile-o-vitch and his toys that represented the true nature of man, or the black nurse? Our discussions must have been like those between a Roman general and his centurions marching at the head of a column, to while away the endless boring hours. They too must have asked themselves: What are we doing here? What is our gift to these whooping barbarians with their painted bodies, their women disfigured by tattoos to mark them as personal chattel, their human sacrifices? Our lunchtime discussions in the staff canteen attracted a permanent audience, as had the mess-room debates on board the late oceangoing tugs. During those long voyages we had had lengthy daily discussions that always led to a debate on the nature of God, a subject guaranteed to last until the end of the voyage. After a number of lunches of gumbo, BLTs, and coffee, Turk's conclusion was: God is like the x in an algebraic equation. You cannot solve an equation without introducing x the unknown, and the answer only comes when you ultimately eliminate x. The same goes for God. We can't solve any problem in our lives without assuming the presence of God, but once all the questions have been solved, we'll find we have eliminated him. We went on to tackle other eternal questions, the way we had done on shipboard, the way it must have been on board Ulysses' trireme.

One day Turk turned up with a little book he had picked up somewhere called *Definitions of the Nature of God*. "Hey, Fancy," he said, "you'll love this. Boy, the arguments we can steal from this book! It's a must for astronauts. We'll have to force it on the arrogant bastards."

No astronaut ever objected being called an arrogant bastard if Turk did the calling. They loved him for the same reasons, I suppose, that in the distant past I was loved, if I could believe the bosun.

I took the little book home. My nights consisted of long periods of reading interspersed with brief periods of sleep; this one I read in one sitting. Fascinating how wise men, gurus, prophets, apostles, pompous idiots, and philosophers over the ages defined the eternal presence in our lives referred to as "God." Some of the definitions were thought-provoking; others of a pomposity not to be believed. Most of them ultimately led to variations on the word *I*; but then there was the seventeenth-century philosopher who described God as "an infinite ocean of light and love."

The definition struck me as meaningful in connection with Ellie coming home from the refuge with that indefinable aura of exhaustion and joy. I had tried to define it without success: here I found a definition of sorts: if God was an infinite ocean of light and love, then Ellie, after a day at the refuge, came home from the beach.

I was so pleased with that definition that I told her. She looked at me with a trace of exasperation. "Harinxma, it's dear of you to glorify my present activity, but don't take off into the great blue yonder. I'm no Mother Teresa. So, please, take my halo and put it back on the hat stand. Tea?"

"No," I said, "this calls for a snort."

She headed for the icebox. I wondered about Mother Teresa doing the same. Not likely. Snorts were strictly for pilots after the job was done and the ship approached the outer buoy, where the skipper's job began.

I liked my definition of her as a pilot. It was always a great feeling to hand over the command to a competent expert of the estuary leading to the ocean. She must have been one of the best; she was in my case. I had to return to the cancer hospital every so often for a checkup; of late they had become carried away and subjected me to painful tests, like ramming a periscope up my nether world and forcing tubes down my esophagus. I was getting tired of it, I wanted to concentrate on the fascinating world of the space center, so I asked Ellie to take over and act as my pilot. It was she henceforth who suffered through the aftermath of medical analyses and conferences, while I showered in Building 37, put on a track suit, and flip-flopped in my sandals to the 50,000-Foot Testing Chamber, which Turk referred to as "the Snoozería." There I lay down on a waterbed installed for the occasion and was outfitted with stickers, leads, a wired suppository to register my body temperature, and, ultimately, a set of headphones. A mike was lowered to a hand's width from my nose; then Turk's voice, snappy as a turtle's, would ask, "All set for cuckoo-land?"

"Aye-aye."

"All right, here goes. Listen to the birdie and tell me when it splits into two."

"Now."

"Which ear has the highest vibration?"

"Port."

"And now?"

"Starboard."

"Now?"

"Both gone, seemingly."

"Good. You relax and think of pleasant things like necking in the hay."

"Too hectic, at my age."

"Snoring in the hay."

"Okay."

"But don't drop off! There's work to do. Stay with it."

"Roger."

"Ready to strike out for the moon?"

"I'll give it a try."

"Okeydoke. Here goes. Ready for takeoff?"

"Ready . . . But no cigar."

"I'll change the vibrations. How about this?"

"Uh-uh,."

"This?"

"Sorry."

"This?"

"Nope."

"You sound dreamy. Where are you? Snoring in the hay?"

"In a Roman courtroom. Three judges."

"Harinxma, wake up! You're supposed to concentrate on the moon, dammit, not get lost in a library!"

"I like the presiding judge. No one is going to hoodwink that one."

"Will you listen to this, folks? The man's mind is supposed to take off for the moon at great cost to the company, and what does he do? Harinxma! Wake up!"

"I am awake, dammit, but no moon. My mind, left on its own, takes off for ancient Rome."

"Enough fun and games! The word is *Lunar Rover*. Visualize the Lunar Rover. Now."

"Hmm."

"What does that mean?"

"Don't know enough about it, I find."

"You *find*! After how many weeks of study? What *can* you visualize? A chariot with Ben Hur?"

"In the alpha state I cannot 'visualize' objects as I would when—well—as I would where you are. I visualize, or try to, the spirit of the thing . . ."

"Dear God and little green apples! Will anyone here describe to me the *spirit* of a moon buggy?"

Somebody mumbled something, somewhere, while the judge gazed at me with old Kwel's eyes and said, "A fascinating judicial conundrum but I cannot arrive at a decision without having heard a representative of the grass."

"Grass? He's hallucinating about grass now! Harinxma, have you been smoking pot?"

"Wonder what all this is about. Why—"

"All right, let's turn off the footlights and get him out of *Quo Vadis*. Anyone know where Taxi is?"

Somebody mumbled. *Click*, no more sound. Lights on. "*Whoof!*—I'll need a moment."

"Like hell you do. Get off your butt, let the chief take his bugs off you, and join us for the postmortem."

So I joined them in the control room: Turk, Jim, and Jeanie, the recorder.

"Are you with *us* now, judge?"

"Still a bit groggy."

"Well, we've discussed it among ourselves. There's only one man alive who can acquaint you with the spirit of the Lunar Rover, and that's Taxi himself."

"Taxi?"

"The man who designed and manufactured all of them. He happens to be around today. So, put some clothes on and let him take you to the peepshow. They have one, sitting right there, in a decor of the lunar landscape."

"Where's that?"

"The exhibit for tourists. I'll give him a call, if they can trace him, and tell him to pick you up here for a visit to his baby and its spirit. Okay?"

"Fine with me. Sorry about—"

"Never mind, we'll get there in the end. Why the Roman stuff? Any idea?"

"I studied Roman history as a hobby for years. Especially the reconquest of Britain in the fourth century A.D., after the barbarian uprising."

"Sounds classy. How come?"

"The transport of the invading legion was effected by barges, towed by triremes. Which makes it the first recorded deep-sea towing job in history. I wanted to find out who the guy was who came up with the idea. It turned out to be a general named Theodosius, father of the future emperor Theodosius the Great."

"So?"

"So I became addicted to Roman history, to the point where I identified with a Roman."

"The general?"

"No, a centurion. A Roman John Doe who left no trace in history. He became what Joseph Conrad would have called my 'secret sharer.' He has stayed with me ever since; I experience more and more Roman episodes as I grew older."

"Meaning what?"

"Brief flashes of fantasy, shards of a dream world. At the most unlikely moments and places."

"Hmm. So you're finally out of the closet: you're a nut."

"That's right."

"Might as well meet another one. I'll call him right now. Jeanie, try Taxi again."

Jeanie the recorder gave me a reassuring smile and picked up the telephone. I needed no reassurance; I knew Turk like a brother. It was a bore, but I simply could not achieve takeoff. We had gone through the prelims several times, applied the proper mechanical impulses, induced an alpha state approaching weightlessness, but I simply could not detach my whatever-it-was from my body. I was ready to do so, I knew exactly where the moon buggy was, had discussed it at lunch with the astronauts who had left it behind, heard the story of the left-rear fender half a dozen times—there was no question of my making a mistake or finding myself at a loss once I got there. Each time I settled in my seat, Turk "lit the burners," but I simply could not achieve liftoff, sliding sideways or backwards, into stuff like the Roman courtroom with the judge who could not pass judgment before hearing a representative of the grass. I wondered what episode that was; I must have come across it years ago in my research. Judea? Rabbis? . . .

"He's on his way," Turk said. "I'm going to leave you to it. If I come along it might scare the spirit of the buggy."

"I don't mean 'spirit' literally, Turk. I—"

"Don't worry—I read you. The other day the Dalai Lama was asked if he would like to be reincarnated as someone else next time around; his answer was that next time he would like to be reincarnated as a bridge."

A tweeter beeped. "For you, Colonel," Jeanie said, holding the horn out to him.

"Must be the Dalai Lama," Turk said. "Taxi? Hi, Turk here. I have with me—"

Jeanie closed her eyes with fatigue.

54

HE WAS AN AMIABLE, balding man, middle-aged, in a blue business suit. He listened with benevolent equanimity to Turk's introduction of a man in his eighties, ex-tugdriver, trained to undergo an out-of-body experience during which he would try to visit EVA 4, locate the Rover with the crumpled fender, and read the dosimeter on its dashboard. "Now he wants to meet its spirit before takeoff."

Instead of laughing or even frowning, the man gazed at me with benevolent interest and said, "Nice to meet you. Ready when you are. Your car or mine?"

"You'd better take him there, Taxi," Turk said. "And hang on to him going down stairs, he's likely to take a swan dive."

Taxi and I contemplated one another with unabashed curiosity. I had worked with men all my life, but never met anyone before with such stillness at the center. I was struck above all by his quietude; we all walk around filled with some sort of turmoil, however innocuous; he looked totally at peace. Not the peace of superiority; what he radiated was modesty. Fascinating.

As he drove, we chatted in a casual way. He shied away from being called "designer of the Lunar Rover." All he had done, he insisted, was coordinate other people's ideas. Like Einstein, who said his ideas had been floating around forever, all he had done was pull them together.

He parked the car near the entrance of the exhibit building. We got out and joined the queue of visitors at the box office. When our turn came, to my astonishment, he paid for his own ticket. Mine was cheaper because of the senior citizen discount. Intriguing, that the father of the Lunar Rover should pay to visit his own creation. It must be saintly modesty, or the overriding desire for anonymity.

We joined the crowd shuffling past a row of large dioramas of the lunar surface. The Lunar Rover was parked in a desert setting surrounded by dreamlike mountains. He stepped over the barrier meant to keep the crowd away from the display and helped me do the same.

A security guard was on him in a flash. "Hey, Mister—!" He was shown a badge, or an identity card, and backed off after an apology.

"Well, this is she," Taxi said as we stood beside the other-worldly machine. The fact that he called her "she" gave him away: this was his true love, the way a painting is to its artist.

She was indeed a work of art. My study of the plans had not evoked her reality for me, because to a mere mortal she was unimaginable. At first glance she was no more than a small electric conveyance on wheels, like a golf cart; her otherworldliness came from the equipment. She bristled with antennae, disks, sensors— in a way, she was what the *Isabel Kwel* had been to her designers: a paradise tree full of esoteric electronic equipment, the ship of the future. But the *Isabel*, as dreamed, was an instrument of human compassison, built to locate ships in distress, men on rafts, desperate castaways lost at sea. This miracle contraption, true spearhead of human evolution, was the ultimate instrument of man's insatiable curiosity. Rolling slowly on the virgin desert of the moon's surface, she could see, hear, explore, report, listen. Her driver seemed subordinate to the individuality of his machine, to her spirit standing beside me.

"Incredible," I said.

He shrugged his shoulders. "When you get down to it, she's no more than a combination of nuts and bolts."

"That's like Rembrandt saying about his *Night Watch* that it is no more than a piece of cloth and a bunch of paint."

"Well, that's what it is, isn't it?"

"Partly. The whole is cloth, paint, and Rembrandt."

"So this is a bunch of nuts and bolts and fifteen brilliant minds."

"Okay," I said. "I give up. But I mean it: this is in the same class as *The Night Watch*—she is a work of art. Maybe that's what art is today."

He smiled. "You're very kind to say so, but look at her without romanticism. Ultimately, she is just a tool, like the first stone club, only more sophisticated, as we ourselves are."

"What about her spirit? Is that you?"

"Most definitely not. If she has any spirit, it is her own, not mine or anyone else's. It's possible she has. According to Paracelsus, 'Every form has spirit, but there is spirit without form.' Whatever her spirit may be, you'll have to communicate with it on a one-to-one basis."

"But where did she come from? Whose brain, whose soul? Who is her father, her creator?"

"I suppose that is why we had to invent the word *God*."

"You think we invented God, not the other way around?"

He smiled. Curious visitors had gathered in a little group behind the barrier, waiting for something to happen, trying to pick up what was being said. They must feel sure they had heard wrong—"God?"

"Sounds like we're back at the lunch table," Taxi said. "Maybe that's where we should continue this discussion. Shall we?"

"Fine with me," I said.

The little crowd made way when we stepped over the barrier, back into the everyday world. They did so respectfully; they must have reached the conclusion that we were some kind of priests.

Maybe we were.

55

EVEN MY ENCOUNTER with the Lunar Rover and Taxi, its creator, could not make me reach the point where my body released my consciousness. I remained stolidly curled up inside the cocoon of my body.

One effect of the encounter, though, was that it helped me articulate to what extent the world of the Space Center was part of another dimension. I had always had the feeling that the moment I entered the gate I crossed the frontier of a separate reality, but I had never been able to put into words for Ellie what exactly the process was. Was it a change from one world to another, or an enrichment of the one in which we lived? For some reason, meeting Taxi and standing beside him as we contemplated his otherworldly creation, a veritable fleet of which was now parked on the moon, made clear to me what exactly the Space Center represented. It was not a different world. The different world was out there, in the ocean of deep space; the Space Center acted as an airlock between the two, the transition chamber for mortals wanting to pass from one world into the other. It sounds like nitpicking, this persistent and sometimes boring search for the right definition, but it was essential to the process of my planned transition that I acquire an articulate concept of what exactly was involved.

I must say that I flourished in the transition chamber, amid its highly original crew. My body was a shambles; I shuffled and stumbled, beset by aches and pains in muscles and joints; my mind was a sieve as far as memories went, or words, anything that was not directly connected with the experiment and the heated philosophical discussions in the staff canteen. To get up in the morning was an exhausting heave, the drive to NASA a mind-numbing kangaroo ride in rush-hour traffic. On arrival, I was a moody wreck, a cantankerous old man wondering what the hell he was doing here, why didn't he stay home with his cookie tin and scribble memorabilia, but the moment I opened the door to Building 37 and slogged down the endless corridor, past the Exercise Physiology Lab, the Astronaut Candidate PRS Test, the Neuroscience Motion Lab, I became conscious of the fact that I had entered the air lock. New life seemed to freshen my dusty old mind. Even the old donkey of my body pricked up its ears and quickened its clip-clop gait at the thought of the carrot of the isolation booth, the waterbed, the sheer physical excitement of being readied for takeoff—wings, ailerons—a rose for Icarus.

In actual fact, however, the OOBE process was at a standstill, but that did not diminish the process of rejuvenation. We had been at it for two weeks of daily efforts, trying to achieve takeoff. In the end Turk called a meeting of crew and support group and summed it up. "Folks, this obviously is not going to work. Everybody here has done what they could, I appreciate that, but the commodore remains cemented to his bed, while his consciousness frolics among Romans and private jokes that make him shake with laughter while we sit glumly by. All the intricate machinery of the twenty-first century has proved of no avail; something is needed to move this experiment off dead center. I have given it all the thought I can and drawn a blank. I am open to suggestions. Has anyone here any fresh ideas for the next move?" He looked around the table expectantly.

It took awhile before anyone spoke up. The one who set the ball rolling was, surprisingly, Jeanie, the recorder, whose function was to keep the tape rolling and later type up the results.

"Sorry," she said, "this is probably stupid, but I get—or got—the feeling that the commodore and all of us are waiting for—I know this sounds stupid—a bus."

"A bus," Turk repeated.

"Very good!" Jim Henderson cried. "That's exactly right! Not a bus, maybe, but *some* conveyance that will get the subject moving."

"The subject being me?" I asked.

"Sorry, yes. Of course. I mean, I too have thought about this a great deal. I started by formulating for myself exactly what 'departure mode' means to *me*. To me it means: opening the garage door. Getting into my car. Pressing the button of the automatic door closer once out in the yard, then driving off to—well, my destination is secondary. But the process of leaving, in my case, does involve a conveyance, namely a car. In Jeanie's case: a bus."

We all thought this over. Jim Henderson asked, "What you're saying is: let the subject formulate his personal mode of departure and take it from there?"

"Right."

"Okay, Commodore?" Turk asked. "What's your mode of departure? When you think of leaving, what conveyance comes to mind?"

"A ship."

"Bingo!" Jim cried, and slapped my shoulder.

"Let's try and keep this discussion adult," Turk admonished. "Okay, describe your personal mode of departure."

"I don't understand what you're after," I confessed.

"We're trying to analyze," Jim said, "the mode of departure familiar to you on a subconscious level. The myth of leaving, if you will. In your case it is *not* stepping outside and catching a bus, or taking your car out of a garage. When we asked you what 'departure" evokes for you, which conveyance, you answered: a ship. All right, a ship. The ship leaves. Describe how, in detail."

"Well, it casts off. Leaves."

"Come on, Fancy," Turk urged, "be specific. You have left harbor with a ship hundreds of times, that must involve a routine, a sequence of events, steps. Tell us what they are."

"Look, a ship is not a rowboat. This doesn't involve only myself; it takes a whole crowd of people."

"Such as?" Jim asked.

"Well, a whole crew!"

"Surely you don't have the crew with you on the bridge? Who's there with you when the ship leaves?"

"My first mate. The helmsman. The pilot."

"Pilot!" Turk cried, as if that were the solution. "You need a pilot."

"To do what?"

"To trigger the sequence of conditioned reflexes called 'departure mode.' "

These men were no fools. Still, I needed to get a clear idea of what they had in mind before I left them to it. I said, with what may have been audible impatience, "Will somebody have the kindness to explain this to me? Why the hell do I need a pilot to get off the waterbed on my way to the moon?"

" 'Pilot' means someone familiar with the procedure. A colleague, a pro, who can talk you through it," Dick explained.

"Talk me through what?"

Turk said, "Like talking down a plane when the pilot has lost his bearings in a fog. Someone in the tower who has voice contact with the pilot says, for starters, 'Okay, Popsy, relax. We'll talk you down real easy. Relax. Start by leveling out, okay? Level out. That's right. Now, are you relaxed?' The pilot says, 'Sort of. Go on.' The tower asks, 'What's your altitude?' The pilot answers, 'No idea. My instruments are on the blink.' The tower says, 'Never mind, we've got a reading right here on the screen. Compass out too?' 'Positive.' 'Okay, no sweat. Let's start by giving starboard rudder. Six points. Do you read?' 'Roger.' 'Good. Now—' and so on and so on. The tower talks the kite down like a midwife assisting at a birth. That's what we need for you: a voice, like the tower, to talk you off the bed, and to go on talking until you're airborne—I mean, on your way, with the goal in sight."

"The goal being the moon?"

"Correct."

I thought it over. It seemed a far-out idea. But then, we'd tried everything else. "I wouldn't know where to find an expert familiar with tugboats."

"A harbor pilot? We can get one for you."

"No, this needs someone with an intimate knowledge of oceangoing tugs. The sequence of events as seen from the bridge."

"Well, plenty of tugboat captains around. We'll rassle one up for you."

"Sorry—I don't want to seem difficult, but a young skipper off a modern tug wouldn't know what I was talking about. It needs someone my age, familiar with the old equipment, accustomed to the terminology of, say, the sixties."

Turk said lightly, "Okay, we'll call the Smithsonian."

I laughed.

"Look, Commodore," Jim picked up peaceably, "before we end this meeting, we're going to have to state once again in simple terms what exactly we are trying to achieve, and how. We have decided to cease our efforts to make you, alone, under your own steam, achieve separation of your consciousness from your body. We want to give you some assistance in the alpha state by having an expert go through the motions of leaving port with a ship of your vintage. To that end, we need a knowledgeable spokesman in the tower able to talk you through the process of departure in the terminology you are accustomed to. We'll all think this over, and try to find an expert who fills the bill, starting with your home company in Holland. How's that sound?"

"I'm afraid my home company no longer exists. There are no oceangoing tugboats worth speaking of any more. The men who sailed them are either dead, or lost to the world."

"Well, let's try and find an oldtimer who—"

"No, don't. Let me think this through first. See you all to-morrow, if that's convenient. Turk?"

"Okay," Turk said. "Anyone else? No? Very well. Meeting adjourned."

Chairs rumbled; the chatting started. As people moved to the door, Turk hugged Jeanie and said, "You're the one who got us moving. Thanks."

She blushed. "I—I just thought of a bus . . ."

"That's right. Newton just thought of an apple." Turk spotted me. "Don't worry, Fancy, we'll get you to the moon."

"And back?" I joked.

"Who cares?" Turk slapped my shoulder. "Sooner or later we'll all join you, wherever you may be. There must be *some* place. That's what we need: hope."

"Let's talk over lunch," I said. "Before I have my nap in the 50,000-foot tank."

"I never knew it was a nap. I thought you were practicing."

In Building 11 I sat down opposite Henry, who stared at me across the table with his golden eyes.

"A thought," said Jim, pulling out his chair. "Take Henry with you to the moon. How's that?"

"Sorry," I replied. "No passengers on a tugboat. Just the usual rabble, as independent and ornery as they come."

Turk asked, "What do you say on board an ocean tug, Fancy? *Bon appétit?*"

"We say *Mahlzeit.*"

"That's German, isn't it?"

"Yes."

"Why German?"

"Don't know. That was just the way it was."

"See?" Jim commented. "This is how it works: find someone who says '*Mahlzeit*' in German and a Dutch tug driver is back at his mess-room table, thirty years ago. We need the keyword to get you back on the bridge."

I laughed. *"Harinxma, get back on the bridge!"*

"What's funny about that?" Jim asked.

"It's a long story. Okay, Henry: come and get it."

The harbor cat was beside me in a flash to snatch his bit of bacon. Somewhere outside, a ship's horn would boom. *All passengers leave.* The door of the saloon would be ripped open: "Anyone here off the *Taurus*? You've got three minutes!" Slam. It had always frightened the cat.

"Got the idea, Fancy?" Turk asked.

"I think so," I said. "Or beginning to."

Henry licked my fingers. The suggestion of this being a harbor pub on the shore of an ocean was very strong.

---

5 6

ELLIE'S CAR was in the shop, I asked the driver from NASA to pass by the refuge so we could pick her up.

I had never been there before. What I expected was a hospital-like edifice; in its stead I found a row of dilapidated villas with tricycles and swings in their front gardens. I rang the bell of the first one; a black girl of about three opened the door, stuck out her tongue, gave me a raspberry, and closed the door again. I was about to try the next house when, behind the closed door, I heard a familiar voice sounding as if she had caught a stoker urinating in a corner behind a ventilator. "Woof! Waf! Vroom!" The door swung open. "Hi there, Harinxma. Kind of you to come. Just a sec." She had her hair piled up and tied together with a rubber band, and she wore an apron with wet and brown patches. So that was what she smelled of when she came home. She was carrying a little ape-man with staring eyes seeing nothing. "Care to come in?"

I am, by nature, a hypochondriac; to enter a house full of

AIDS babies with colds was not my idea of a casual visit. But it was her world, and it was time I had a look at it, however briefly. "I'd love to," I said and she laughed. Before she was able to say anything, her skirt was lifted from the inside and the same little black girl peered out from between her legs to give me her raspberry. She too copped it, like the stoker, but it must have sounded less terrifying under a set of skirts than in the open. Mother Teresa grabbed under her skirt and produced the little girl, pulled by a braid. "I was changing Benjamin Franklin," she said. "Atchafalaya here was helping me."

"Atcha—who?"

"This one." She still held on to the braid. The little ape-man on her arm blew a snot bubble.

I followed her into the dusk and the stench. Even a saint would have faltered, but a woman came through a door to welcome me in a jolly manner,. "This is Kitty," Ellie said, "and this is my friend and countryman Martinus Harinxma, also known as 'Fancy.' "

"Hiya, Fancy," the woman said, shaking my hand as if to loosen the card up my sleeve. "How are ya doing today?"

I told her, and put the same question, and she told me, but I was not paying attention, for a child had turned up with a doll's pram and I had just realized that the doll was alive.

"This is Annie," said the woman. I said, "Hiya, Annie? How are ya doing today?" The doll choked, coughed, and seemed to die.

Well—etcetera, etcetera; there was more of the same as we penetrated the gloom of the refuge. When Ellie finally put Benjamin Franklin on a changing table and started to take off his underwear, she herself thought I had seen enough.

"I'll be through here in a jiffy," she said. "Why don't you go ahead and wait in the car?"

I obeyed, shuffled to the car, collapsed on the back seat, yawned, and returned, with a sigh of relief, to my role as old man with arthritis looking for the glasses that were sitting on his head.

I must have fallen asleep, for suddenly she was sitting beside me. "Sorry I was held up—you arrived just at potty time." She had changed, but still carried the smell of the refuge.

"Okay. Home, George."

"Yes, Commodore, sir."

"Boy," she said, in Dutch. "You're addressed by your full title at NASA?"

"Yes."

"Why?"

"Because 'Ome' is hard to pronounce, for Americans."

"I see. And what have you been up to today?"

I told her, ending with Turk's suggestion.

"Hmmm. What he means is that, lying there bristling with earphones, chest tabs, and so on, your mind casts off and sails a ship to the moon?"

"That's about it. I can't do it on my own. I've tried, it won't work."

"You must try to call up a harbor in your mind, and a ship, but you can't make that real enough by yourself, is that it?"

"That's why he came up with the idea of a pilot to talk me through the successive stages of the departure."

"Meaning *me*."

"You?"

"I have left harbor on our ships enough times to know the procedure by heart, starting with the long blast of the ship's horn. I can talk you through it up to the point where the pilot leaves. Is that the idea?"

"Well, if you're prepared to do it . . ."

"We should go over the various stages together first, and put them down on paper. Or would that spoil the spontaneity?"

"I don't know. Off the top of my head I'd say: let's talk it through in detail without writing anything down as yet."

The car arrived in front of our apartment complex.

"Okay," she said. "A couple of snorts, and let's get with it."

"But how about your day?" I asked, as we walked into the apartment.

"Oh, we'll get to that later." She opened the icebox, took out bottle, glasses, and cheese, shook crackers into a bowl, carried the tray to the coffee table, poured the glasses, and handed me mine.

"Here goes: prosit!" She knocked hers back, one pinkie in the air. "All right. Your ship is preparing to leave port. First question: Which ship?"

I'd thought that over. "I'll read it to you." I brought out a little piece I had written on "The Ship I Loved Most."

"Lovely," she said, "but that's a dream ship. That was how the *Isabel* existed only in the minds of the architects. Arnold nixed all the 'new age' equipment."

"Well, this whole procedure is happening in a dream state anyhow."

She frowned. "Are you sure about this?"

"Why? What's wrong with it?"

"The ship you write about leaves on a mission of mercy, in total darkness, responding to radar echoes from men lost at sea. But if that's the one you want, fine. Next question: Which port?"

"Doesn't matter, any old where."

"I think it does. You're supposed to travel down a long narrow tunnel with a light at the end."

"Like Pjotr."

"Like everyone else who attempts an out-of-body experience. Adapt your departure to that concept."

"How?"

"Think of a long, narrow canal, in the dark. Pierheads, the sea, then head for the moon. Isn't that the idea?"

"A canal ends in a lock, ablaze with lights if it's still dark. And that's no good: the light at the end of the tunnel should be the moon."

"How about a narrow river? A channel running between islands? Surely you remember a setup like that?"

"It doesn't have to be realistic, does it? I don't need the

memory of an exact location. God knows I've done it often enough. Just a summing up of the standard procedure I've lived through numerous times."

"All right. Where do we start? When I come on board? Where?"

"The pilot comes on board just before sailing, normally with the skippers of the harbor tugs. Then they have the predeparture discussion."

"What state is the ship in at that time?"

"A madhouse. Relatives of the crew. Snarling little dogs. Whining children. Candy wrappers everywhere."

"Then the long blast, right?"

"Right. Once everybody is off the ship, you are on the bridge. The captains of the harbor tugs are back on their own ships, waiting for orders. I start by putting the engine-room telegraph on *Stand by engines*."

"I remember that," she said. Even so, she took out a writing pad and a pencil and made a note. "What's next?"

"I tell my first mate, who's on the bridge with me, to cast off, stern first."

"The pilot doesn't?"

"No, captains of oceangoing tugs get free of the shore themselves. You take over when the harbor tugs do."

"Okay." She wrote. "Next?"

"I order the shore-side spring on number-three bollard to be belayed and post two men there. The mate yells the order. I give it, he does the yelling."

"Right. Why the spring?"

"If the ship has no thrusters—and mine didn't at the time—and if we're moored on the port side, I order *Hard port* after the moorings are in and give a brief burst of *Dead slow ahead* to swing the stern out. I can only do that if the ship is restrained by a spring on bollard three."

"Then?"

"Once the stern has swung free I order midships rudder, take in the spring, then back into the open, dead slow. That's where you come in."

She wrote it all down. "What do I do?"

"You tell the skippers of the harbor tugs what to do by walkie-talkie."

"What *do* they do?"

"They take the ship out into the channel, that tunnel you mentioned, whatever it is; they put me on course, cast off, and then let us carry on under our own power."

"When do I leave?"

"Just before the outer buoy. There'll be the pilot-launch, we'll say good-bye, you take the rope ladder down to the launch, I give you three blasts of the horn for 'Thank you.' The launch responds, and that's that. Then she's all mine, I pass the outer buoy and head for the open."

She finished her notes. "Okay. Right." She put them aside. "Anything else?"

"We should be talking about *you* now. What was your day like?"

"Not tonight. I mean, I have adjusted already. There was something else you wanted us to do. I forget now what it was. You mentioned it, I think, yesterday."

"Oh yes, the initials. I forgot about those. Would you test me on those damn things? The whole topography of NASA is in initials, and I really need—well, let's start with page one, okay?"

"Okay."

I went to find the list: *NASA, Johnson Space Center, Flight Rules—Appendix A: Acronyms and Abbreviations.* I handed it to her.

"Start from the top?"

"Yes, please."

"Okay, here goes. AG."

"Air to ground."

"AGS."

"Acquisition of signal."

"FCR."

"Flight control."

"FD."

"Flight director. I presume that will be you, in this case. Won't it?"

"I have no idea. As I understand it, I'm the pilot, involved only in the departure mode. The code for pilot, by the way, is PLT."

"I know."

"Here's a tough one: HRPPC. Take your time."

"I needn't, I know that one: Human Research Policy and Procedures Committee."

"LCC."

"Launch Control Center."

"It may also stand for Launch Commit Criteria, but in order to find out which you have to consult Document NSTS 16007."

"Terrific."

"Next: LO."

"Let's have dinner."

"You don't want to carry on with this? Three more pages."

"I'm tired."

"Okay."

She went to the bathroom, came back, picked up her purse, and said, "All set. LO—liftoff."

As we stood waiting for the elevator, I asked casually, "By the way, did the hospital call in the results of my latest work-up?"

"They did. Rather, he did, the doctor. I'm seeing him to-morrow for the whole story."

"Why you?"

"Well, I'll be in the same building. We'll meet for coffee and a Danish at eleven. I'll give you a full report."

The elevator arrived. I did not ask any more questions; but again, I had that feeling my number was up.

57

AFTER THE WELCOMING "Ha-hoo! Hottie today, woof!" on the part of the Vietnamese owner, we settled at our usual table in the empty pizzeria. Their main trade was take-outs, we seemed to be the only ones who liked the ambiance of tiled floor, scraping chairs, and the ha-hoo hoots of friendship.

We ordered the usual, ate the first bites; then I said with a casualness that did not quite come off, "Not so good, I gather."

"Hm?"

"The results."

"For an eighty-two-year-old man after three operations and eight weeks of radiation, they are exceptional. Look at what you are up to every day. If the results had been bad you'd have been in locker six."

I smiled at the tugboat slang for "laid up in bed." Odd thought; no one in the whole wide world talked in those terms any more. Not only the ships and the men, but the entire culture of Holland's Glory had gone from the earth unrecorded. Talk about Mohicans. "You had better own up," I said. "I can take it."

She put down her fork and took a sip of iced tea. Then she looked at me with the eyes that, somehow, were part of the lost world of the oceangoing tugs and said, "Why don't you trust me?"

"Ha!"

"I mean it. I admire you, I think you are terrific. I would never do or say anything that might knock you off your pins."

"Then, it *would*, if you told me?"

She sighed. "Like all men, young and old, you are a hypochondriac, one of the worst I have known. After talking to someone on the phone who has a cold you take vitamin C."

Shaken by a gust of fear, I wanted to kiss her, embrace her, make love to her, hide in her arms from the presence in the doorway with the light behind it. I thought of putting my hand on hers. I did nothing. "Good stuff," I said, chewing on another bite of the garlic pizza.

"Harinxma," she said, "give the Mimi act a rest."

"Excuse me?"

"You're sound as a bell, or you wouldn't be cavorting around NASA every day, eager to hop onto the slab and lunch with the boys."

"But I—"

"You have not been observing yourself over the past month the way I have. The moment you became part of NASA, your age ceased to matter, your physical condition lost importance, you were IDM waiting for LO, and now you're at the point where you are ready to sail, if you can get free of the shore."

"Look, all I meant to say—"

"Now you have hired me as your pilot, and as pilot I say: stop hamming it up. You are not at death's door. You're an eighty-two-year-old etcetera who by a miracle has slipped into IDM after he became part of the incredible place called LBJSC. I learned the damn initials by listening to you. Time you did yourself."

"What's IDM?"

"In departure mode."

"Am I?"

"I should damn well hope so." She sounded tough, but nothing could hide the concern in her once-loveless eyes. Maybe I was imagining things.

She put her hand on mine. I had not been imagining things.

"What's LBJSC?" I asked.

"Lyndon B. Johnson Space Center. As if you didn't know."

"I'm scared," I said.

"I know you are. You know what we used to say? It's all part of the deal."

"Yeah."

"I'm here with you, right up to—"

"I know," I said.

"Hoo-hallo, hip?" The owner of the restaurant stood, smiling, by my side.

"Delicious," I said, "as always. This is a good place."

"Ha!" he cried, pleased. "Hoom cookie."

"Excuse me?"

"Home cooking," she translated. God, if only I could die in her arms.

"Harinxma," she warned.

"Huh?"

She hummed Mimi's farewell aria.

"Sorry," I said, laughing.

"Hoo!" the Vietnamese cried. "Bandy?"

"You're not kidding," I said.

She smiled at him. "A glass of brandy would be terrific, thank you." Then she looked at me sternly.

"Roger," I said, "I read you. Brandy it is."

58

THE NIGHT BEFORE the moon flight I could not sleep. I tossed and turned in the dark, awake with superficial concerns. Where had I put my briefcase? We must go over the list of abbreviations again. Funny joke, that one of Turk's about the —whatever. Hot tonight. Houston *was* hot, hot as hell.

Hell. What would hell be like in my case? Not Hieronymus Bosch's nightmare vision of bat-eared ghouls tunneling up some poor soul's rectum. Nothing to do with past sins, but with the loss of present delights. Like NASA. Turk: "Keep your head down, honey." And, "Look here, Harinxma, your objective is—"

Ellie. Who would have thought, when she appeared in the doorway of my dayroom on board the *Isabel* all those years ago, that we would end up sharing an apartment in Texas where I would be training for an out-of-body mission to the moon and she take up the care of dying AIDS babies? Frankly, I was scared. My number was up. She made an effort at trying to hide it, but the tests were positive. So I had better answer the question: What will hell be like in my case? Pain? Physical disintegration? In semidarkness? A deathbed lasting God knows how long? Maybe months?

Well, let's stay with NASA, the magical transition from breathless old man into future astronaut. The earphones in place, the soundproof door closed, the voice of Control saying, "Okay, Pops, give us a voice reading."

"Gorgeous Fanny had an Annie—"

"No spoonerisms, Harinxma. Quote something from the Kamasutra."

"With A. dangling from the chandelier, B. mounts the tea table and cries: '*Simii scandentis partes posteriores nudae videntur.*' "

"Roger, got it. Here goes: In which ear does the birdie sing highest?"

"Port."

"And now—"

"Harinxma?"

I had not heard the door open. There she stood, the hall light behind her. I asked, "What's up?"

"I had the feeling you were in trouble."

"Me? In what way?"

"Make room, I'll join you."

I hesitated, then pulled back the sheet for her. She climbed in and lay down beside me, taking my head on her shoulder, the way she had that night of the dress rehearsal.

"Don't be afraid," she whispered, close to my ear. "I'll be there. I promise."

"Why, Ellie?"

"Well, this is the way it worked out in the end. Didn't it?"

It did. The vision in Kao-hsiung; the silhouette in the doorway had been of the Angel of Death.

"How did you know I was in trouble?" I asked.

"I put myself in your situation, and—well, here I am. And I will be when you come back. Godspeed and happy sailing, old friend."

It dawned on me that she was not talking about death, but about tomorrow.

"Now let me just hold you while you try to sleep," she continued. "The way we did the other night."

"First, I'd like to talk about tomorrow."

"You'll see, it will all work out beautifully. Listen to my directions, don't run ahead of them in your mind."

"How do you mean?"

"Well, when I ask: 'What state is your ship in now?' visualize it fully. Don't answer, 'She's a mess,' and leave it at that. Take your time, look around, tell me what you see, in detail."

Two survivors, I thought, alone in a lifeboat, lost at sea. "I will," I said.

After a while, the telephone rang. I had dozed off; she took it, then handed it to me. "It's for you."

"Yes?"

"Dad?"

"Yes, honey, How are you?"

"How are *you*, Dad? Today is the day, isn't it? That's why I'm calling. I know it's early . . ."

"Never mind, love. Nice thought. I was awake anyhow."

"I've been thinking of you all the time, Dad, ever since you told me about today being the day. I *know* all will go beautifully."

"I hope so, sweet."

"Kisses, Dad, kisses and hugs. That was all I wanted to give you."

"Thank you, love."

"I have to go now. Himself is calling for his coffee."

"Don't keep him waiting, sweetheart. Thanks again."

"Sorry I'm not there, Dad, crying on the quayside, even though I know how you hated that—Coming! I'm *coming!*—Bye-bye, Dad."

"Bye, Helen, love."

I handed the receiver to Ellie, but she had dozed off. I reached over her and put it back myself. After that, I lay for a moment as I was, half across her sleeping body, and suddenly had a fleeting awareness of a life that had never been: courtship, marriage, children, joy, laughter, tenderness . . .

It was not a wish-dream, it was like the actual memory of a life that had never been. As was her wont, she picked it up. "Next time around," she said. But maybe she had not picked anything, just finished a dream, aloud. She turned her head, looked at the clock, and cried, "For Pete's sake! We're going to be late!" and swung her legs out of bed. I wanted to hang on to her, haul her back into the life we shared that had never been; but she pulled away my restraining hand and slipped away. Standing by the bedside, she reached down to help me. "Come!" she said, "we'll have to rush!" Then both the alarm and the telephone went off; the gods were throwing everything in except the kitchen sink to put a stop to this maudlin business.

She slapped the alarm to make it shut up, lifted the phone and said, "Yep?"

The phone quacked; she laughed. "You have a dirty old man's mind, Turk. As a matter of fact, pilots *do* sleep in the same bed on their launch. It's known as 'the Bedstead of Og' . . . What's that? . . . Read your Bible, friend. Yes, we're on our way, and please tell George that I'm sorry; I turned off the doorbell before going to sleep . . . No, there's a couple of kids upstairs whose idea of fun is to ring doorbells on their way down to the schoolbus . . . Okay, okay. *You* make sure there's coffee waiting when we turn up. See you."

She pulled to make me sit upright. "Time to sail, Commodore. The harbor tugs start pulling."

"Tell them *I* am sailing the ship, not they."

"That," she said, "everyone is aware of, I'm sure. Up and at 'em, love."

God, if only—

"Coming," I said, suddenly in the zone with a burst of new energy, and heaved myself out of bed. I felt the same energy each time I was about to sail: one distinct moment in which I became aware of the sirens, the call of the sea. "Okay, let's go."

"Here. Put on your blue pants." She held them out to me.

"No, I'd rather wear the gray ones."

"The gray ones look as if you'd slept in them. Here."

"Listen! Which pants I wear is *my*—"

"Aye-aye, sir. Sorry. You choose your own pants."

Feeling on top of the world and ready to sail for the stars, I put on the blue pants. Some trade unions you can't fight.

"Let's go," I said.

Her hand on the doorknob, she paused. "Godspeed and happy sailing." She gave me a fleeting kiss.

I was about to take her in my arms, embrace her, express it all without words, when there was a cough outside the door. George, told not to ring the bell, made his presence known.

I opened the door and said, "Now, listen, bubba: next time . . ."

Well, you fill in my monologue. It was all part of the joy of sailing, the start of a well-tried routine, which ended with the passing of the outer buoy, leaving behind the worries, the joys, and the love of the planet called home.

FAREWELL

5 9

Program: OOBE
Subject: Commo. M. Harinxma
FD: Col. W. Sherman, M.D.
AFD: Lt. Col. J. Henderson
PLT: Ms. Eleanor Bastiaans
RCDR: Ms. Jeanie Morris
Starting time: 1024.7 CST

PLT: All right, Harinxma, time to move. It's blue out there, the blueness before the dawn. Ready to go?

Subject: Yes.

PLT: All right, here we go. What's the situation look like from the bridge?

Subject: The ship is still full of relatives and girlfriends saying good-bye. Sobs. Hankies. Little dogs on leashes yapping, upsetting the cook because of his cats.

PLT: Time to get them off the ship.

Subject: Okay. Number One, go ahead: one long blast—*All passengers leave the ship now*.

PLT: Next move, Commodore?

Subject: I go over to the engine room telegraph and pull it to *Stand by engines*.

PLT: Next?

Subject: All right, Number One, let go aft.

PLT: The aft moorings are lifted off the bollards and hauled in.

Subject: Let go, for'ard!

PLT: The forward moorings are hauled in.

Subject: Belay the port spring on three.

PLT: The forward spring is belayed on bollard number three, port side.

Subject: Hard port.

PLT: Helmsman, hard port.

Subject: I pull engine-room telegraph to *Dead slow forward*. The stern swings out. Midships!

PLT: Helmsman, midships.

Subject: Telegraph to *Stop*. Take in the spring.

PLT: The spring is taken off the bollard ashore and hauled on board.

Subject: Telegraph to *Dead slow aft*. Ship moves away from the quayside. Tug Number One ready to take over? Pull out!

PLT: The bow is pulled out into the channel.

Subject: Tug Number Two, pull into line.

PLT: Tug Number Two pulls the ship into line.

Subject: All right, Pilot. She's all yours.

PLT: Thank you, sir. Steady as she goes.

Subject: Steady as she goes.

PLT: Slow ahead.

Subject: Slow ahead.

PLT: Tug Number One, half-speed ahead. Tug Number Two, keep on course.

Pause.

PLT: Slight port, Helmsman. Keep in line.

Subject: Keep in line, Bosun.

Pause.

PLT: Well, we're in the channel now. Follow the leader.

Subject: Follow the leader.

Pause.

PLT: Here's the first beacon. This is where I leave you, sir.

Subject: Thank you, Pilot. Drink?

PLT: No, thank you; on your return. I'm going now. Have a good trip, sir.

Subject: Thank you.

Pause.

FD: Tell us what is happening.

Subject: Pilot goes down the rope ladder. I watch over the port end of the bridge until he is on board his launch. Number One, give the three blasts. The launch answers. We wave. Number One, telephone down for the coffee.

Pause.

Subject: We are passing buoy number two now.

FD: Look ahead. What do you see?

Pause.

Subject: My God! She's huge . . . colossal . . . I've never been this close to her before . . . Telegraph on *Full speed ahead.*

Pause.

Subject: Wait a minute! Dammit, I want to zero in on the moon but can't. Let me try again. Bosun!

Pause.

Subject: I can't bring it off. We're overshooting the moon.

PLT: Harinxma, stop that! You're off course! You're headed for EVA 4—

Subject: My God, she's slipping by. Here comes cook with

the coffee. He stands still, mugs in hands, and looks at the outer buoy slipping by.

PLT: Harinxma! Don't! You're headed for EVA 4, the Rover with—

Subject: The helmsman stands still. The mate stands still. We all stand still and watch as we pass the—my God! It's the *moon*!

FD: What's going on, Harinxma?

Subject: The *moon* is the outer buoy! We're heading for the open! Number One, any signals?

FD: What the devil is going on?

PLT: Harinxma, get with it: you're shooting for EVA 4, the Lunar Rover with the crumpled fender. You must—

Subject: Where, did you say? At one o'clock? Lifeboat, or odd man?

PLT: Oh, my God! Harinxma, there *are* no lifeboats, no odd men! Head for EVA 4, the Lunar Rover—

Subject: Good heavens, no idea there were that many—

PLT: EVA 4! The Lunar Rover with the crumpled fender! Harinxma! Do you read?

Subject: Take it easy, let's sort them out first. I'll start by picking up the ones over starboard. Slow ahead, Number One.

PLT: Harinxma! Do you read? You're heading for the moon! EVA 4! The buggy with the crumpled fender!

AFD: Alert. Heart rate failing. BP?

PLT: Harinxma! Do you read me? Do you read?

Subject: Wish me godspeed, Ellie. This is it, and it is terrific.

AFD: Heart rate? BP? Subject failing.

FD: Get him out of there, fast!

AFD: Heart rate? BP? Subject expiring.

FD: Fancy! Hang in there, we're coming!

RCDR: I have LOS, sir.

PLT: What's that?

RCDR: Loss of signal, ma'am.

FD: Out! Quick! CPR!

AFD: All signals flat.

PLT: Godspeed, love, happy sailing . . .

Pause, 15.02 mins.

FD: You can wrap this up, Jeanie. He's gone.

RCDR: Yessir.

END OF RECORDING. 1055.29 CST

ABOUT THE AUTHOR

JAN DE HARTOG, born in Haarlem, Holland, the second son of a Calvinist minister and a Quaker mother, ran off to sea at the age of ten. At sixteen he entered Amsterdam Naval College, ending up as a junior mate in the Dutch oceangoing tugboat service. When war broke out in 1940, and Holland was occupied by the Nazis, de Hartog was trapped in his native country. During this time he wrote and published his first major novel, *Holland's Glory*, which became an instant and historic best-seller and a symbol of the Dutch Resistance; the German occupying forces banned the book in 1942, but it went on selling in large quantities in the underground market. When he escaped to London in 1943, he was wounded in the Pyrenees, invalided out, and appointed war correspondent for the Dutch merchant marine. There he gathered the material for his postwar novels *The Distant Shore*, *The Captain*, and *The Commodore*.

In the late sixties de Hartog, himself a Quaker, undertook the ambitious project of a multivolume novel on the history of the Religious Society of Friends. *The Peaceable Kingdom* was the first book, followed by *The Lamb's War* and *The Peculiar People*.

De Hartog has written many plays, among which the most famous is *The Fourposter*, which won a Tony in 1951 and was later turned into the musical *I Do! I Do!*, and several volumes of essays, the best known being *A Sailor's Life* (memories of life at sea before World War II) and *The Children* (a personal record for the benefit of the adoptive parents of Asian children).

In 1983, de Hartog was nominated for the Nobel Prize for Literature.